# Bad Planning
## An Asher Mystery

*Bill + Glenda,*
*Enjoy!*
*Jim*

By
## James Gaston

**Bad Planning**

Copyright © 2013 James M. Gaston

All rights reserved.

ISBN-13: 978-1495278136
ISBN-10: 1495278131

To request permission, or for other inquiries, please email James Gaston at jmgastonphd@gmail.com.

This is a work of fiction. Any resemblance to actual people, living or dead, or business establishments, is entirely coincidental. The characteristics of some actual places have been embellished or exaggerated. That is not at all usual in Texas.

# ACKNOWLEDGMENTS

I sincerely appreciate the support and patience of my partner, David Elias. He is an invaluable collaborator, proofreader, and honest critic. I'm also thankful for the many helpful comments from my friends Keith Pattillo and Billy Brookshire.

# CHAPTER ONE

Todd watched from the driver's seat while Chris removed the memory card from the camera, set it in the little plastic case, and snapped the lid firmly. Chris slipped the new disk into the camera and started formatting it. When the indicator light came on, Chris rechecked the camera and turned it off. When he leaned over and put the memory card case into his leather bag on the floor, a semi swerved from the road and slammed into the driver's side of the car.

Chris was thrown forward. His right hand jammed into the dashboard, snapping his arm below the elbow. His head, turned slightly, looking left, smashed into the windshield.

Chris couldn't understand what was happening to him. Over his left shoulder, above the steering wheel, Chris saw the silvery silhouette of a woman with long wavy hair.

*Is that an angel?* Chris wondered. *Is this what happens when you die?*

His body crumpled into the front seat.

Childhood images of angelic hosts came flooding back to him. The aspect of an angel at the car was perplexing.

A deep rumbling sound vibrated through the car seat. Then someone opened the passenger door next to him.

Chris tried to sit up. His right arm wouldn't move at all and his left arm was trapped under him. There was warm liquid in his eyes but he couldn't wipe it away. His mouth wouldn't make words. His voice was silent.

The car door slammed shut. The car moved, then rocked violently. The roaring sound faded away. Chris too faded away, in and out of darkness, in and out of disbelief.

Whenever he tried to think, Chris would go to sleep again. He could hear hissing and cracking sounds, popping noises. He tried to concentrate on some birds singing in the trees across the road. With the morning sun warming his body, Chris drifted off. He spun downward, unable to resist, sliding along the edge of consciousness.

# CHAPTER TWO

"Jesus H. Christ, I hope you're not dead. Oh shit, this is terrible," a deep voice said in a panic. "Can you hear me? I'm calling 911."

*There's someone at the car door again. Who is that?*

"I called 911. Help's on the way. "

He held two fingers to Chris' neck to find a pulse then touched Chris' head gently.

The man moved away from the car. Chris heard him say, "He's alive, all right. Looks like a head wound and his arm is broke bad. He's breathing but there's blood all over him."

*Is he talking about me?*

"No, the other one's all tore up. I can't even reach him. "

Chris strained to speak but he was mute. His lips wouldn't move. Nothing moved.

The sun was warm as Chris eased again into still-ness.

Then the man was back, leaning over him. "They asked me to see where you're bleeding from. They said not to move you."

Chris heard the man breathing rapidly, like he was frightened.

"I'm right here, buddy. I'm not going anywhere. You gotta stay with me. Medic's on the way. Won't be much longer."

Whenever Chris got still again, the man would squeeze his shoulder a little.

"Just hang in there," the man said. He put his hand on Chris' shoulder again. "Hold on, man, stay right with me."

Soon Chris heard sirens growing louder and louder. Then heavy vehicles stopped. Doors shut. Orders were shouted. Then there were people all around, talking urgently. There were strong hands touching him.

Someone said, "Get a backboard."

Hands lifted Chris' head very gently and slipped something around his neck. He could hear someone breathing hard.

A man's voice very near him in the car said, "Watch the right arm."

"Ready on three."

Then they were lifting and pulling, hurrying. He was strapped down on something hard, his legs stretched out. Then he was in motion, moving through the air, then put down on a stretcher.

Chris was glad they were helping him but he didn't like the loss of control over his own body. He was thirsty. He wanted to sit up and wipe his face.

Hands were touching him gently all along his legs and arms. Something was wrapped tightly around his right arm. Chris was beginning to feel intense pain from his arm, his head, his leg, everywhere at once. Suddenly, there was coolness on his eyes. They were washing his face. He could feel the water evaporating in the morning breeze.

There were voices talking urgently, responses on the radios. Engines idled and equipment was being moved around. Some kind of noisy machinery started up. Men were shouting over loud crumpling and metal tearing. Chris tried to focus his eyes but saw only the blurred face of a man in a light blue shirt.

The man said, "We'll be taking you in the ambulance in just a minute, sir. Can you tell us your name?"

Chris wanted to speak but his throat was too dry to make a sound. He tried to move but pain flooded over him. It was too much. He just wanted to sleep again for a while. He wanted to curl up with Kyle in clean sheets and just sleep.

# CHAPTER THREE

The weekend started off badly and deteriorated from there. Chris had spent the previous evening preparing for a weekend trip to Austin with Kyle Decker. After packing his overnight things, he rolled into bed about midnight with his big fluffy cat. As he closed his eyes, Chris startled awake.

*Damn,* he thought, *I forgot to check my calendar.*

He hadn't reviewed his calendar for Monday, a ritual he always followed on Fridays. Being punctual and prepared was more than a habit with Chris. That way everything was done on time. He got out of bed to retrieve his iPad and a red file from his leather messenger bag.

The details were all in the calendar software on his iPad. Each appointment was neatly noted beside its beginning time, along with the names of the participants and the expected topic. The menus of all three Monday meals were listed. There was a note to call a friend in Seattle and a reminder of the time difference. Monday was in order.

Chris flipped open his red file, the one where he kept his number one priority documents and any urgent reading material.

Before leaving the office, Chris had printed the City Council agenda distributed late in the afternoon and slipped it into the red file. Reviewing the agenda now, at midnight, Chris found something he hadn't anticipated.

"What the hell is this?" he muttered.

A public hearing was scheduled to rezone Tract B, an undeveloped parcel near the airport. The Director had moved up the hearing a full month ahead of schedule.

Much to his annoyance, Chris realized that his Tract B zoning exhibits were not ready as they normally would be a week before the hearing. He would have to shoot new photos of the property over the weekend. Monday morning he could organize the new photos into the presentation software and still have time for uploading the slideshow to the City Hall server.

Chris called Decker to delay their departure for Austin.

"I'm away from the phone. Please leave a message and I'll get back to you."

"It's Chris. I may be running a little late in the morning. I'll call you when I'm ready for you to come pick me up. I really need this weekend with you, big guy."

With his work completed first thing in the morning, Chris could enjoy the weekend knowing he was ready for Monday regardless of the zoning hearing being scheduled ahead of time. To shoot the exhibit photos as early as possible, Chris would pick up the camera and the Tract B file from City Hall at dawn.

Chris called Todd Watson, the department's fresh-faced, young assistant planner.

"Todd, this is Chris. Sorry if I woke you up."

"That's okay, I just fell asleep reading," Todd said. "What's up? Everything okay?"

"I was reviewing my schedule for next week and realized that Nelson added the Tract B rezoning to the council agenda. I need to run out there real early in the morning and shoot some photos. I thought you might want to do some fieldwork with me."

"Sure, Chris. What time do you want to go?"

"Can you meet me at the office at six-thirty? It shouldn't take more than an hour."

"See you then. Thanks for calling."

Todd had only been working for the City of Asher since June. A spring graduate of the University of Texas, Todd came into the department ready to learn everything about city planning. The Director originally had him updating maps and looking up property ownership. Menial assignments chaffed the new college grad. When Todd asked Chris to help him get some professional experience, Chris decided to mentor the new employee.

Todd had told Chris he was eager to learn the job as quickly as possible. If he still wanted to be a planner after getting some hands-on experience, his parents had agreed to support him through graduate school. Chris had been training Todd for the past month but they hadn't done much fieldwork.

# CHAPTER FOUR

"**I**'ll never understand what's so fucking difficult about scheduling the fucking work and then following the fucking schedule."

Chris muttered when he was under pressure and alone. He worried that he talked to himself too much and used too much profanity. But it was cathartic and no one knew he muttered except his cat.

"Everyone else is asleep or enjoying the weekend but not me. I'm unlocking the fucking office at the crack of dawn on Saturday morning to get the camera to take pictures of something that shouldn't even be on the fucking agenda."

Chris walked into the darkened Planning Department. "I should be home, sipping coffee and watering my plants, but no, not me, not good old *conscientious* Chris."

As Chris passed the Director's office, he said, "This waste of my personal time is your fault, you spineless turd."

He flipped on the hall lights.

"Holy shit. I'm cursing in mixed metaphors. I sound more like a Texan every day."

Chris had good reason to loathe his boss, Thomas R. Nelson, Director of Planning and Transportation. First, he was a traffic engineer who knew nothing about city planning, a gutless ass-kisser willing to do whatever was politically expedient. Second, Nelson was a homophobic fundamentalist. Third, he was on the take.

Nelson wore discount clothing purchased long after it went out of fashion. His cheap shirts were always a size too small and his shiny suits added a reptilian texture. The whites of the man's eyes matched the pale yellow of his teeth.

Chris went into his own office, two doors down, retrieved the city council agenda from his messenger bag, and dropped the paper in his desk tray.

Pulling the Tract B folder from the top file drawer, Chris told himself proudly, "There's the file, exactly where it belongs. When you put things away properly, you can find them again when you need them. Organization saves time."

Smugly satisfied with his obsession, Chris was flipping through the file when he heard Todd coming up the hall. Todd had one of those lanky runners' bodies. He was too lithe and too innocent for Chris' taste but Decker was really disappointed to hear that Todd was straight.

"What a waste," Kyle had said. "Women rarely appreciate such gracefulness in a man."

"Chris, are you here?" Todd said.

"In my office. Would you get the camera and one of those little memory cards from the storage closet, please? Sorry we have to do this so early but I'm leaving town for the weekend."

"It's okay, really. I'm an early riser anyway. I appreciate you thinking of me."

"I'll get the car keys from Barbara's desk," Chris said. "I'd rather not take a city car out on Saturday but I see no reason to use my own gasoline. It's bad enough we're using personal time to do this."

They turned off the lights, locked the City Hall door, and walked across the street to a row of white vehicles. It was refreshing to be back outside. Predawn coolness persisted in shaded areas, but the sun was warm where it sliced between the buildings. A beautiful early fall morning had dawned in the ten minutes Chris was in City Hall.

Chris handed Todd the keys. "Welcome to the real world of city planning. Since I outrank you, you have to drive." As they approached the car, he said, "Isn't that the ugliest logo ever plastered on a low bid car? Who comes up with this shit?"

The white Chevy sedan started on the second try and blew a gray cloud into the clear morning. Todd gunned it a little and pulled into the street.

"Do you know how to get to Tract B, Chris asked. "It's around on the north side of the airport industrial park."

"I think I can find it."

In the next block, the new sun carved shadows on the 1924 DeLeon County Courthouse, its limestone facade contrasting with dark sharp shapes. Two old men already sat on a wooden bench, talking and gesturing with hands, canes, and spit. They paused momentarily, in the practiced ease of old friends, and silently noted

Todd and Chris driving away. The gold and blue City of Asher logo on the sides of the car made the old courthouse square stewards take special note. They discussed how someone should ask the town council about people using city cars on weekends.

Driving through Asher's north side, Chris tried to recall if anyone in his six-year parade of professors at the University of Washington had mentioned planning directors who take bribes. Chris completed a degree in landscape architecture with a master's degree in urban planning at the University of Washington. He couldn't remember if they even discussed the zoning change process, except in the most general terms.

"Todd, did any of your professors at UT say anything about working for directors like Tommy Nelson?"

"Actually, I had one prof who had worked in the Dallas zoning office before getting his Ph.D. A developer was mayor at the time and the planning director was powerless. The professor warned us that local political pressure often results in bad planning."

"You know," Chris said, "it's people like Nelson who give city employees a bad reputation. The people in City Hall are wonderful except for Nelson and his nasty secretary. He's the first person I've met who is on the take."

"It's a shame the negative stereotype is so persistent," Todd said. "It's really unfair."

"I can't tell you how shocked I was when I realized Nelson was selling zoning. He's a front row deacon at the Church of Christ but he's been bought and paid for by the local developers."

"What makes you think Nelson is crooked?"

"My second week on the job I discovered a discrepancy on the zoning map. When I asked Nelson about it, he said it was correct. I tried to show Nelson the error on the map but he told me to mind my own business. And now, this whole Tract B case smells bad to me."

The big white car coughed as Todd accelerated up Hallelujah Hill. That was the neighborhood's unofficial name, derived from the rousing Sunday morning rivalry between the gospel choirs at the New Canaan Baptist Church and the AME directly across the street. Some folks called it a joyful noise, but others complained bitterly in private.

North of the Hill, Todd and Chris crossed onto the airport property, formerly an old World War II air base. A pair of small planes from the flying school were warming up at the west end of the runway. A yellow crop duster buzzed across the road ahead, touched down, and taxied toward a battered old hanger. Chris recognized it as the aerial spraying company owned by City Councilman Ben Kemble.

Chris pointed out Kemble Equipment, Inc., the largest company in the airport industrial park. Kemble's equipment was stored in an area of the old airbase littered with worn out backhoes, the cannibalized skeletons of motor graders, and a row of rusting bulldozers. His twenty-acre tract was dotted with fuel spills, leaking barrels of used oil, and piles of crushed stone. Two rows of yellow earthmoving and paving machines were parked near the runway.

"I think Kemble's operation is such an eyesore," Chris said. "I heard him bragging at the Chamber of Commerce banquet that his equipment yard wasn't bothering anyone out here except buzzards and snakes."

"That guy is so arrogant when he comes into City Hall," Todd said, "It's like he owns the place."

Chris nodded and grinned. "The only thing good about Kemble is that he is the one City Council member Tommy Nelson fears most. I love watching Nelson squirm whenever Kemble's around. Nelson turns pale and actually starts to stutter."

"I saw them talking out in the parking lot after the council work session last week," Todd said. "Kemble was yelling and Nelson looked like a whipped dog. I almost felt sorry for him. Can council members do that to staff?"

"I guess it depends on how chicken shit the staff member is. Kemble better not ever yell at me. Even if we are public employees, we're entitled to some respect."

They rounded the end of the runway and turned northeast on Old Bridge Road through a scattering of steel and tilt slab buildings. Like the remainder of the old air base land, the industrial sites were barren of trees. Johnson grass hardly even grew there after decades of herbicide spraying by the military and Ben Kemble.

A large wooden sign announced in bright red letters, *Airport industrial sites for sale, call Ted Smith Real Estate.*

"Todd, look how dramatically the landscape changes when we get past the industrial park, Chris said. "See what I mean? The road is covered in pools of shade under these big oak trees."

Chris rolled down his window and breathed in the natural beauty along with the moist early morning air. Beyond the road's narrow shoulders, thick post oak groves and yaupon undergrowth gave way to small meadows of native wildflowers.

"In late spring, the scarlet sage was blooming out here like swatches of red paint," he said. "I found it when I was taking nature photos in May. The colors were so vivid."

Actually, it was Old Fashioned Red Autumn Sage, *Labiatae salvia greggii*. Chris had looked it up in his landscape materials catalogs.

"There are three large undeveloped lots adjacent to the industrial park over here on the right. We're passing Tract A now."

Chris pointed out the window.

"Through those trees, over on the back of the property, is where I discovered some variegated blooms scattered in with the red sage. They have alternating bands of red and deep purple in the blooms that make the flowers look maroon. My friend Kyle's an Aggie. He was so thrilled when he saw the maroon blooms that he convinced me to send samples off to A&M for identification."

"I'd like to see some of them, if we have time."

"Sure, they're still blooming on Tract B. Charlie Hawkins wrote a story in the local paper asking citizens to report other locations of the maroon flowers. No one remembered it anywhere but here on Old Bridge Road. When the native plant horticulturist from A&M visited out here, he found even more of the maroon blooms on Tract B and Tract C. He nicknamed it Aggie Sage and he's filing for endangered species status for the new variety."

"It's great that you got that process started by being so observant, Chris. To think you might save a rare plant species is very cool."

"You'd think so but, within a week, Ted Smith filed to rezone Tract B from agricultural use to industrial use. The planning commission argued for weeks over the rezoning. Ted Smith brought a slick real estate attorney, named Nick Lucas, up from Houston to try to confuse them about the endangered species laws. The commissioners tabled the issue for two meetings."

"Then the Houston lawyer threatened to sue, claiming that the City was depriving the landowners from any economically viable use of their property. When the city attorney agreed with him at the last meeting, the commission folded."

Todd looked puzzled. "So, why did Nelson hurry the rezoning case onto the city council agenda? Isn't he violating the statutory notification period?"

"My guess is he was probably paid off by Ted Smith," Chris said. "It was really a stupid move on his part since the rezoning can be set aside if notification procedures are violated."

Regardless of the potential legal outcome, the Director's disregard for procedure resulted in Chris and Todd driving out on Old Bridge Road on Saturday morning to take new photos of the property.

To Chris' right, the colors on Tract C were vibrant. Patches of Old Fashioned Red Autumn Sage and Aggie Sage were blooming in the early autumn sun. Chris wished Decker was there to see this lush native Texas landscape at dawn. The oaks and yaupon clusters were thick and green, even after a hot summer.

Old Bridge Road made a curve to the right about where it passed the boundary between Tract C and Tract B. Chris anticipated taking some dazzling color photos of Tract B for the zoning hearing, maybe even a photo to enlarge for his office wall.

As they rounded the next curve, Chris yelled, "Shit! Shit! Shit!"

Todd slammed on the brakes, scattering gravel across the humpback road.

"Dammit! Those greedy motherfuckers just couldn't wait."

# CHAPTER FIVE

Todd pulled off on the right-hand shoulder of the road. Chris pounded the dashboard with his hands.

"They had no reason to do this!" he yelled. "The zoning hasn't even been changed yet. Shit! Shit! Shit!"

In that moment, staring across bare soil where trees and meadows had been, where Aggie Sage had been, Chris was devastated. Todd was speechless after Chris' outburst. He stared out the window at the cleared property.

"You know, Todd, this makes me homesick for Seattle. In King County this would never happen without a big fight. The conservationists would raise hell and get court orders to stop the developers."

Todd finally found his voice. "It's different in Texas, Chris, except for Austin maybe. Most people really don't care. Texas is so huge they figure there's always more land where that came from. They think they can do whatever they want with their land, even though that's never been true. They get away with bulldozing hundred-year old oaks to build hamburger stands that close after twelve months."

Chris sat very still in the car, leaning back against the headrest, listening to sounds from the woods remaining on the undamaged side of the road. Mockingbirds and insects called, the breeze moved through high oak branches and yaupon leaves below. The front seat filled with warming sunlight.

Chris had come a long way from Seattle and he had come on his own. He was a trained professional, a landscape architect and a senior city planner. This was his calling. Chris raised his head from the headrest, his jaw set against the frustrating scene.

"Maybe when we show these pictures at the public hearing, somebody will demand a study and we can save some Aggie Sage on the other two tracts," he said.

Chris picked up the camera, climbed out of the car, and walked out onto the dusty property to find the best angle for photo-graphing the destruction.

"Bastards," he grumbled. "This is a fucking disgrace."

Squinting through the viewfinder, he realized that it was now possible to see all the way across Tract B from Old Bridge Road to the industrial park. The nearest building was a small warehouse. A tractor-trailer rig was backed into the two-bay truck dock. A man was unloading barrels from the trailer.

When Todd walked up beside Chris and pushed the loose dirt around with his toe, Chris remembered he was supposed to be teaching Todd how to take the best pictures for the hearing. He handed Todd the camera.

"I think the warehouse provides a good background, Todd. We need something to provide scale. Since there are no trees left standing, we have to rely on the adjacent property to give the pictures some context."

Todd clicked off several pictures, turned in each direction, and took more. As Chris stood there, exasperated and beginning to squint in the morning sun, two men at the warehouse started to unhook the red truck cab from the trailer. Wheezing, rumbling, diesel noise filled the quiet morning.

Chris looked back toward the City car parked on the side of the road. He kicked at a thick, pointed root protruding from the ground like the bone of a compound fracture.

"Let's go," he said. "I thought this would be an interesting field experience for you. Instead it's just a bare lot with nothing to take pictures of anymore."

# CHAPTER SIX

The alarm startled Decker from a tantalizing dream. He resisted the snooze button only because he had to. As he showered, Decker wondered where his dream fantasies originated. He was always falling in love but it rarely got reciprocated. Until recently, that is.

While shaving, Decker's thoughts turned to the two days he planned to spend with Chris. Their reservations had been confirmed at the Four Seasons in downtown Austin. Decker had two tickets for an eight o'clock concert at the Frank Erwin Center to hear Chris' favorite vocalist, Michael Bublé. Sunday morning, they would call room service and enjoy breakfast in bed overlooking Lady Bird Lake.

Decker put on the crisp light-blue cotton shirt he'd been saving for the trip. The starched button-down fit perfectly. Decker felt sharp. He pulled on some button-fly jeans, snug from washing and pressing, and admired the way they fit. He slipped on a summer-weight sports coat.

Checking the mirror just once more, he thought, *That's it, all clean and spiffed. Not bad.*

By seven, Decker was ready to pick up Chris. While he gulped down his morning cereal and first cup of coffee, he listened to the voicemail Chris had left at 12:14 am. Half an hour and another cup later Decker picked up his cell phone and walked out on the front porch in the fresh air. He decided to call and see when Chris might be ready. He was never late for anything but this might be a first.

Kyle dialed Chris' number. His voice mail answered. Maybe he was in the shower or outside watering his garden.

"Chris, this is Kyle. Call me."

He set his coffee and cell phone on the concrete ledge by the swing. Stretching his full six foot three frame, Decker reached up to touch the brass lamp hanging from the white slat ceiling.

It was a broad concrete porch with brick columns supporting the roof. Decker had lived alone in the two-bedroom frame bungalow for three years. The older neighborhood was popular with faculty from the local college and young professionals who were buying and renovating the older homes.

Decker's former lover, a graduate student completing his thesis three years earlier had whispered one night how he'd just love to start a family in a little Texas bungalow. Decker immediately set out to buy a bungalow. He got the house at a reasonable price and started remodeling feverishly, doing most of the work by himself on a tight budget.

When the kitchen was finished, Decker asked his lover to move in with him. Decker popped the question in bright May moonlight, right there on the front steps. Unfortunately, his boyfriend wasn't ready for a long term relationship with anyone, even Decker, or in this particular bungalow in Asher, Texas. He planned to travel the world before settling down. Restoration stopped in the disappointing weeks following his graduation and had only resumed after Chris spent a wonderful spring night with Decker in the bungalow.

Decker sat down in his porch swing. The new porch swing was Chris' idea. He mentioned how perfect a wooden swing would be on the cool covered porch in early morning and talked Decker into adding one. Decker found a sturdy new swing at a little store in Fredericksburg one weekend and installed it with big bolts through a bracket in the attic framing. It was strong enough for anything Chris had in mind.

*Chris was right,* Decker thought. *It was perfect in the early morning -- and in the middle of the night.*

Decker stretched out his legs and rocked slowly. He inspected the shine on his boots and buffed one on his pant leg. He sipped coffee and looked expectantly at the phone.

The neighborhood was quiet. Decker checked the headlines on the Internet. A couple of joggers trotted by on the oak-lined street, setting off complaints from a blue jay. Next door, the Schnauzer yapped to be let out. When Decker heard a door shut, he knew the dog would begin exploring neighborhood yards and leaving evidence of its visits. Decker watched the little gray dog sniffing from lawn to lawn before it finally left the grand prize two doors down.

By seven-thirty, Decker was getting impatient. He called Chris' number but got the machine again.

At seven-forty, Decker's neighbor, Kenny Long, came out of his house across the street and sauntered over carrying a coffee mug. He was medium height, scrawny and all angles. He needed a haircut and he looked more like a cowboy than a tax appraiser in his dirty jeans, scuffed boots, and gimme cap.

"Hey, Deckerhead, how about if you drag your lazy carcass off that bench and ride down to Houston with me today?" Kenny hollered. "I got to find a part for my Goat."

Long was restoring a classic 1967 GTO in his garage. It was the car he first got laid in and he dreamed of returning it to its former glory.

"That old GTO is such a piece of shit, Kenny," Decker laughed. "You think I've got nothing better to do than dig around in grimy junkyards with you? I'm going to Austin this weekend."

"Can't keep you out of those queer bars. Well, if you need bail money, don't call old Kenny."

"You'll just have to go crawl around in rusty wrecks full of snakes and fire ants by yourself today. How about if we get some barbecue on Wednesday?"

With a wave over his shoulder, Kenny said, "All right, asshole, but save up. It's your week to buy."

Kenny walked back across the street. He climbed into his new Suburban and roared away.

Kyle's cell phone rang but it wasn't Chris.

"Sorry to bother you, Kyle, but this is Tom Luedecke," a serious voice said. "We had a traffic accident this morning out on Old Bridge Road. The vehicle had City logos on it. The driver was killed and the passenger was injured. He was taken to the emergency room. Best we can tell it was a hit-and-run."

"No shit? Who was it?"

"That's why I called you. The passenger didn't have any identification on him, no wallet or anything. Nobody at the scene recognized him, especially with his face all cut up and swollen. He's maybe five-ten, a hundred and fifty pounds, with curly blonde hair. I'm afraid he might be that friend of yours in the Planning Department."

"Oh my God. That sounds like Chris."

Decker jumped from the swing, locked the door, and bolted for his SUV. He shot past the few cars he encountered and ran three stop signs, arriving at the hospital in minutes. Skidding into the emergency driveway, he parked next to an ambulance. Decker hurried through the automatic doors.

He tried to explain at the desk that he had to see Chris Jensson. The woman looked at him blankly. When Decker barged through the green double doors, she shouted, "Wait, you can't go in there. Come back here."

Decker nearly crashed into a young man pushing an equipment cart and stopped face-to-face with Detective Ernesto Zepeda, his former partner. Zepeda grabbed Decker's left arm in a firm grip.

"You don't want to go in there all agitated," Zepeda said. "Calm down, Kyle."

"Where is he, Ernie?"

When Decker stopped resisting, Zepeda let go of him. Decker pushed Zepeda away. That was something only his former partner could get away with. As Decker walked toward the flimsy curtain surrounding an emergency room bed, his heart sank. There were no doctors crowding around, no nurses rushing in and out. The sheet was pulled all the way up.

Zepeda watched a shadow pass across Kyle's face. For a moment Decker's broad shoulders slumped.

"He can't be dead," Decker said quietly, with a catch in his voice. "He just can't be dead."

"He's not. That's the driver," Zepeda said. "Chris is over here. He's really banged up but he's alive."

Just then a nurse adjusted a flimsy curtain nearby. Another nurse in green scrubs was checking the blonde man's pulse. Zepeda and Decker moved closer to the bed.

"Can you identify him?" the stocky, middle-aged nurse asked.

"Yeah, he's Chris Jensson," Decker said anxiously. "How bad is he hurt?"

"Are you a family member?"

"No, I'm his..." Decker hesitated, "I'm a close friend. His mother is in Seattle. How serious is it?"

"Well, he has a fractured right arm, a bruised hip, shoulder, and knee, a cut over his ear requiring three stitches, and multiple lacerations. Maybe broken ribs on his right side. We're waiting on radiology and lab work to see if he has any internal injuries. He's got a concussion and hasn't been conscious much since they brought him in. When he comes around, he's irrational. Maybe he'll recognize you if you speak to him."

Zepeda noticed that the bed rail was shaking as Decker gripped it with both hands. Decker leaned over to get closer to Chris' face. There were bandages on his cheeks and forehead. He had the beginnings of two black eyes. His lip was swollen and there was a wide bandage over his right ear. Decker couldn't resist brushing the curls from Chris' forehead. He wanted to look into those intelligent blue eyes and hear Chris call his name.

Zepeda interrupted Decker's concentration. "Is that Jensson with an *e* or an *o*? Do you know if Chris is short for Christopher or something?"

"No, his name is just Chris, J-e-n-s-s-o-n. I'm gonna try to talk with him now."

Zepeda nodded.

"Chris, Chris, it's Kyle," he said softly. "Chris, can you hear me?"

Chris moved his head slightly and barely opened his eyes.

*It's him. Kyle's here.*

With all his strength, Chris concentrated on moving his lips and vocalizing. He tried to open his eyes, tried even harder to speak. A hoarse whisper came from his throat.

"I'm sorry, Kyle."

Chris opened his eyes until they were wide slits in the swelling. He managed a crooked smile.

"There was an angel," Chris said. "She pushed the car and I hit my head." His eyes closed again. "Why did she hurt me?"

Decker was confused. He looked up at Zepeda and then at the nurse, now standing near the foot of the bed.

"Have you given him pain medication?" Decker asked.

"Not yet, we only checked his vitals and dressed his wounds. They'll take him in for a CT scan in a few minutes. Do you know his local doctor's name?"

Decker bent lower toward Chris. "Can you tell me who your doctor is here in Asher?"

Chris opened his eyes again and forced another whisper, "The flowers are gone. The trees are gone."

"How did the car get wrecked, Chris?"

"The angel, Kyle, the noise and the angel."

Chris closed his eyes and his breathing became slow and rhythmical.

"That's as much as he's told us, too," the nurse said, shaking her head. "We need to get his medical records and insurance information so we can admit him. Do you know who we can call, Mr. Decker?"

"You can call Carol Bailey from the City personnel office. Carol handles their insurance claims. She can look up the doctor's name."

Decker looked back toward Chris and gently put his hand on Chris' bare shoulder. Zepeda and the nurse glanced at each other, mutually acknowledging the moment of intimacy.

Two men in blue scrubs jerked open the thin curtain. The small bedside area was instantly overcrowded. Decker stepped back as they shoved past the nurse and Zepeda. One of them, brandishing a stethoscope, told Decker and Zepeda that they would have to return to the waiting room.

Decker at first stood his ground. This rude bastard wasn't going to touch Chris. He felt a knot growing in his stomach. Zepeda took Decker's arm again and led him out of the way. The curtain pulled shut behind them.

Decker studied the tops of his boots. Zepeda nudged him toward the double doors leading back to the waiting room. Barely recovering his composure, Decker asked, "What the hell happened, Ernie?"

Zepeda consulted his notes, "A passing motorist called it in at 6:56 am. The dispatcher sent EMS and fire units. Our patrol officer responded to the scene. The city car was parked on the shoulder of the road when a large vehicle collided with it. They found Chris in the front seat, near the passenger door. The impact crushed the driver of the city car against the steering wheel."

"Who was he with? Who was the driver?"

Zepeda said, "The ID in his wallet says he was Todd Watson. He worked for the City too."

"That's the guy Chris has been training. Young kid, right out of school, maybe 22, 23."

"The other vehicle left the scene. We recovered some trim and headlamp glass from the hit and run vehicle. The ambulance messed up the only tire tracks we might have used. As far as we can tell, there were no witnesses."

Decker starred through the window in the double doors and shook his head.

"Did Chris usually have a wallet on him?"

"He has a leather messenger bag with a shoulder strap. His ID, credit cards, and cash are in it along with his keys, cell phone, and iPad. Never goes anywhere without that bag."

"There was no leather bag found at the scene. Nothing was in the car or on the ground."

"He always carries that bag, Ernie. It's his man purse. I'm sure he had it with him. Must be under the seat or something."

"Our guys looked all through the car. It wasn't there."

"Then somebody took it out of the car and then just left them there to die. What kind of sick fuck would do that?"

Decker and Zepeda walked straight through the waiting room and out through the automatic doors into the driveway area.

"Where were they? Where'd they find him?"

Zepeda flipped a couple of pages in his notebook.

"About eighteen hundred feet northeast of Industrial Drive. Their car was on the south side of the road, heading east, next to a recently cleared piece of land. Do you know what they were doing out there so early on Saturday morning in a city vehicle?"

Decker rubbed his forehead. "Near the industrial park? The only thing I can imagine is that it had to do with those wildflowers Chris found out there. But I don't know why he'd worry about that today. Doesn't make any sense. We planned to spend the weekend in Austin together."

Decker turned away from Zepeda suddenly. He put his hands in his pockets and looked at his boots again.

Zepeda stepped around in front of Decker and stared up into his eyes.

"Listen to me, Kyle. Some son-of-a-bitch ran into them and then just drove off. We're going to find the bastard and we're going to kick his ass."

Decker's expression hardened into the mask that cops use to hide their feelings. After a couple of minutes he stared away into the sky.

"Do we know what kind of truck hit them, the make, what color it was?"

Zepeda waited to see if Decker was finished.

"We have the crime scene unit out there right now. It was big, probably a semi based on where it hit the car. There's a lot of glass and red paint residue. There was also some dirt left on the road that probably came from the rig."

Zepeda paused and studied Decker's face again before he continued. Decker looked pale and he was sweating lightly.

"No witnesses so far. The industrial buildings were all closed up tight when the patrol officers went door to door. No houses nearby. We've got people interviewing some pilots over at the airport now to see if they saw anything from the air."

Decker was staring off into the clouds again and looking glassy-eyed.

"Let's sit down in your vehicle and wait for Carol Bailey."

Resigned that he would gain nothing by going back inside the hospital, Decker climbed behind the wheel of his Expedition. Zepeda got in on the passenger's side. Decker rolled down the windows.

He almost lost Chris. Decker couldn't imagine life again without Chris Jensson.

"Take a deep breath, Kyle. He's going to pull through."

"I'm sorry about that kid but, thank God, Chris wasn't driving. I'm crazy about him, Ernie. I'm planning to ask Chris to move in with me."

"You may have to wait a couple of days for that. No need to rush into it."

"I've known I wanted to be with Chris since we first met."

"You don't want to spook this guy like you did the last one, buying that house and everything."

"Thanks for bringing that up, Ernie. I appreciate your advice. Especially since your such an expert on gay relationships and all."

"Just pulling your chain, amigo. Where did you guys meet? Carol fix you up over at City Hall?"

"Up in Chicago. Do you remember that insurance investigator seminar I went to in March? Chris was up there for a city planning conference that week. We were booked on the same return flight from O'Hare but there was a snow storm. They cancelled our flight and told us to come back in the morning."

Zepeda kept an eye out for Carol Bailey as he let Decker tell him the story. Talking it out was good for him.

"Chris suggested that we check into a suites hotel by the airport. You know, they have free drinks, hot breakfast, and nice rooms. How could I argue with that logic?"

"Yeah, right, save a few bucks by sharing a room."

"So, we checked in, had a couple of drinks, and went up to the room. Before I knew it, he was stepping into the shower with me. God, he's beautiful. Blue eyes, soft blond hair all over that amazing body. He went down on me and ..."

"Whoa, partner. I don't need that visual. Too much information."

"Anyway, we completely missed break-fast and barely caught the plane. On the flight back to Austin, Chris told me how he'd spent all his savings moving to

Texas. How he can't stand his boss here but he can't afford to leave his job with the City."

Suddenly Decker sat bolt upright in his seat and turned to Zepeda.

"Shit, I just thought of something. I know someone who threatened to murder Chris."

"What the fuck are you talking about?"

"Chris told me that his boss threatened to kill him last winter. He said that ass wipe he works for, Tommy Nelson, threatened him the first month he was on the job."

Zepeda pulled his notebook out and started making notes.

"Chris had gone into Nelson's office complaining about an illegal auto salvage yard he found by the river north of downtown. There were no permits or records in the files. Nelson told Chris to forget about it. Then he told Chris to mind his own business. He said Nelson got right in his face and told him that faggots can get themselves killed around here. When Chris tried to shove past him, Nelson said he knew Chris' mother's address in Seattle and that the people with the salvage yard have friends all over. He said Chris and his mother could have a double funeral."

"Why didn't you tell me? We could've investigated it and busted his ass."

"Chris was scared shitless. I had to promise Chris I wouldn't move on Nelson."

"I'll look into it very quietly," Zepeda said, writing on a new page in his notebook.

Decker stopped talking until Zepeda looked up from his notes. "Ernie, don't write this down. This is just between you and me."

Zepeda nodded and put his pen down.

"A week later, I caught Nelson alone one night going into a convenience store. I shoved him behind the store and pinned him up against a filthy dumpster. I told him I'd cut his balls off if anything happened to Chris. He literally pissed in his pants. I just left him there whimpering."

Zepeda clicked the pen nervously.

"Did Chris tell anyone else about Tommy Nelson's threat?"

"No, that's the way things stood."

Now Todd Watson was dead and Chris was in the emergency room. Decker had been a detective too long to assume this had been an accident.

Zepeda looked up to see Carol Bailey coming across the parking lot.

"There's Carol," he said. "I'll break the bad news to her."

Zepeda intercepted Carol before she reached the emergency drive. He spoke to her briefly. Carol's hand flew to her mouth. Zepeda had to catch her as she swayed, her knees buckling in shock. Regaining her strength, Carol looked at the maroon Expedition and saw Decker watching. She patted Zepeda on the arm and walked unsteadily beside him toward the SUV. Zepeda returned to the passenger seat and got on his cell phone.

Decker climbed out of the vehicle and Carol rushed into his arms. She buried her face in his blue shirt and wept. Decker looked away into the white clouds again, swallowing his own emotions. When Carol looked up, Decker's gaze met her dark eyes, tears spilling down her brown face.

"Oh God, Kyle," she whimpered, "It's just horrible, that sweet young Todd dead and Chris in the hospital. I just can't believe it."

"I'm sorry, Carol," Kyle said. He choked up and couldn't continue.

She hugged him again, leaving wet spots on his shirtfront. Then she patted Decker on the chest and, without another word, walked to the emergency room door. Decker leaned back against the truck door and thought of poor Carol and what she must be facing inside.

Carol was a jewel. She was bright, caring, efficient, and attractive. She and her husband, Otis, were from Detroit. He was retired from the Navy. They had moved to Asher where he got a job with the Postal Service. Tongues wagged when the city manager announced that a black woman from Detroit had been appointed as the human resources director. Her outstanding performance had turned all but the most zealous bigots around.

Decker had always felt close with Carol, even closer after Kyle quit the Police Department, and it was warmly reciprocated. She was the first person Kyle had come out to at the City. She had helped him leave his Detective job with a spotless record and then gave Kyle his first contract as a private insurance investigator consulting with the City on a worker's comp fraud case. They had been good friends ever since.

Decker stood there, silently considering what he should do next. Zepeda was still on his cell phone.

Carol soon returned to Decker's side. "I gave them the information they needed. The nurse called Chris' doctor and they're sending over his records. They've called in a neurologist to assess his head injury. I'm still trying to get hold of Chris' mother in Seattle. The Fort Worth police will be contacting Todd's parents."

Carol and Decker looked into each other's eyes. Seeing the pain in his eyes, hers filled with tears. She took Decker's hand in both of hers.

"He's going to be all right, Kyle," Carol said as she patted his hand.

They stood there together, holding each other, letting the clean morning air wash over them.

Carol said, "I told the admissions clerk that Chris had to sign some papers for the City because of the accident. She said that wouldn't be possible until Chris is more coherent, maybe this afternoon sometime."

Decker climbed back into his vehicle.

"Kyle, the City Manager and Tommy Nelson are on their way to the hospital right now. I think it's a damage control thing for the press. You don't want to be here for that." Carol squeezed his hand. "Go on now. Work with Ernie on the investigation. I'll call you when Chris comes around."

Decker nodded and started his maroon Expedition.

"I'll check back after while. I need to find out what Todd and Chris were doing this morning."

# CHAPTER SEVEN

Kyle eased out of the emergency driveway and drove down the first aisle of the lot where Zepeda had parked his silver police car. Zepeda looked back over his shoulder as he opened the door to leave the truck.

"You okay, Kyle? We could leave your vehicle here and take my car downtown."

"Couple things I have to take care of first," Decker said. "I'll meet you at your office in a little while."

"Call me if you need anything."

As Zepeda unlocked the police car, it was like Decker had never really looked at Zepeda before. He'd worked with Ernie Zepeda for three years on the police force and had tremendous respect for the man but, for the first time, he noticed how short his former partner was. Zepeda could hardly see over the roof of the police car and his gray suit seemed to blend in with its faded silver paint. Decker realized how odd they must look together, Zepeda in his gray suits, Decker in his jeans and boots. Zepeda was a short, stocky Hispanic, Decker, a tall, muscular Anglo.

They made a great team but Decker had something he had to do alone now. Decker turned out of the hospital parking lot and headed south, away from downtown. In the mirror, he watched Zepeda leave in the opposite direction. Making certain Zepeda was out of sight, Decker u-turned and returned to the hospital parking area. He backed into a shady space on the back row, under some low-growing oaks, and killed the engine.

Five minutes later the City Manager's white car turned into the driveway and pulled into a handicapped space on the front row. Andy Roberts had been City Manager of Asher for four years and was respected in the community. He had survived a couple of crises and a bid-rigging scandal involving the city utilities department. Fortunately for Roberts, the fraud occurred before he became City Manager and he could blame it all on the previous administration.

Roberts' first real political problem had started over a park department worker using a city vehicle for private business. The local newspaper ran a photo of the City pickup truck in use on a weekend. Roberts didn't intend to let the press make any connection with the current situation. Roberts was a fair man and a good manager, but he was also a political animal smelling danger.

Carol waited for Roberts under the covered drive. She noticed he was still in his golf clothes.

Roberts said, "Hi, Carol, thanks again for coming over here with the paperwork. How are they doing?"

"I'm sorry, Mr. Roberts, but Todd Watson died. He didn't make it to the hospital." Tears again filled

Carol's eyes. "Chris Jensson has a broken arm, maybe some broken ribs, and a serious concussion."

Roberts stared at the ambulance still parked by the emergency room door. He was speechless as the horror of the accident flooded his thoughts. He began to pace back and forth in the driveway.

"Oh, Jesus, I didn't realize. Todd was so young. This is terrible." Roberts glanced around the parking lot. "Does the media know that Todd's dead?"

"If you didn't know, then I doubt if they do."

"I called Tommy Nelson. He's due here any minute. I'm hoping he can fill us in on what they were doing out there. I wanted him to handle this but I was afraid he'd make us all look incompetent. There's no way I'm handing it off to him now."

Tommy Nelson's dirty Chrysler turned into the drive and pulled into a parking spot marked *Doctors Only*. He got out of the car adjusting his tie, looking like he might scurry back in and flee at any moment. Finally, he walked over to the emergency room entrance where Carol and the city manager were standing.

Without any greeting, Roberts said, "Nelson, I'm sorry to have to tell you this, but Todd Watson died. Chris Jensson is in the hospital. It was a hit-and-run accident."

Nelson stiffened and stared at Roberts. His face turned paler than normal.

"I want you to fill us in on what they were working on this morning. Why were they out there in a City vehicle?"

"Well sir, I really don't know what they were thinking, taking a City car out like that on Saturday. They didn't have authorization from me."

"Do you know what they were working or not, Nelson?" Roberts asked.

"No, not really," Nelson replied, his eyes cast downward. He shifted from foot to foot. "Do you think they were, you know, having an affair?"

Roberts shot a disgusted look at Nelson.

"You're such an idiot, Nelson," Carol said.

Hoping to change the subject, Nelson asked, "What about the car, sir, was it totaled or can we get it fixed?"

Roberts stepped very close to Nelson and lowered his voice.

"Aren't you the slightest bit remorseful about Todd's death? Another one of your employees is laying in there with a head injury and you're worried about the damned car."

A television news van pulled up and parked in a tow-away zone. A man and a woman climbed out and started unloading equipment.

Roberts snarled at Nelson, "Don't screw this up. Just tell them we're still working on it."

The City Manager straightened the collar on his knit shirt and marched over to the brunette TV news reporter. Her navy suit looked too formal for a Saturday morning. She wore thick makeup to cover her bad complexion and her hair was stiff with spray.

The young woman turned quickly to face the camcorder and said, "This is Lori Latimer reporting live from Asher. Two City employees were injured this morning when a tractor trailer truck crushed the car they were sitting in and then drove away. City Manager Andrew Roberts is here at the hospital. Mr. Roberts, can you tell our Action Five viewers about events leading up to the terrifying crash out on Old Bridge Road this morning?"

She pointed the microphone at Roberts's face. Roberts looked directly into the camera.

"This is truly a tragic situation." He paused. "A valued new member of our team, Mr. Todd Watson, has died as a result of his injuries. We're all devastated by this loss. Another City employee, Mr. Chris Jensson, remains in critical condition with a head injury."

The camera swung back toward the reporter.

"I understand that they were parked in a City vehicle when the accident occurred," she said, leaning close to Roberts.

"That's correct."

The reporter paused, waiting for Roberts to elaborate, then impatiently pulled the microphone back to herself and looked at the camera.

"According to police reports, both employees work for the City's planning department. The head of that division, Mr. Thomas R. Nelson, is also here with us at the hospital. Mr. Nelson, tell us, was Todd Watson killed in the line of duty?"

She thrust the microphone toward Tommy Nelson's mouth.

All the color that had left Nelson's face came rushing back, leaving Nelson looking like an over-ripe tomato. She had asked a question Nelson couldn't possibly answer. As the camera waited, he cleared his throat and swelled his chest.

When Nelson finally spoke, his voice was an octave lower than usual.

"Our employees have wide ranging responsibilities which take them out of City Hall and into the community," he said. "You can't plan a city's future without doing field work. There is always an element of risk."

The reporter started to move the microphone away from him but, flushed by his first success, Nelson continued.

"Mr. Jensson was responsible for training Todd Watson. Of course, I have repeatedly made it clear, as a matter of policy, that the staff should not do field work without informing me or the department secretary."

Smelling blood in the water, the reporter signaled to her cameraman to keep rolling and moved in closer to Nelson.

"Are you saying that Chris Jensson violated departmental policy and it led to the other man's tragic death this morning?"

When Roberts stepped forward to sidetrack the conversation, Nelson realized his mistake. Nelson leaned away quickly, as if the microphone had suddenly become a poisonous snake. The reporter again turned her microphone toward Roberts.

Looking directly into the camera, Roberts said, "We haven't had time to determine precisely what Mr. Jensson was working on this morning but he is a dedicated professional who often puts in extra hours to get the job done. I'm sure that he, in no way, contributed to this tragedy."

Realizing that the line of questioning had played out, Latimer asked, "Can you tell us what's being done to catch the driver of the hit-and-run vehicle?"

Relying on his experience working with the Chief of Police, Roberts lapsed into law enforcement jargon.

"Of course local law enforcement is pursuing every lead. The Asher Police Department is examining evidence recovered from the scene. We are asking anyone who might have witnessed the incident to contact Detective Zepeda at the Asher Police Department."

"Can you tell us the make and model of the vehicle police are on the lookout for?"

Since Roberts didn't have a clue what the truck looked like, he responded, "The investigation is underway at this point in time but we are confident that the perpetrator will be apprehended quickly."

The cameraman signaled to Latimer to wrap it up. His camera followed Latimer as she stepped away from the City officials. She put on her somber face and looked directly into the lens.

"That's the story from Asher where City officials tell us a City planner lost his life when a truck crashes into a City car this morning. Action Five News will bring you the latest information when it becomes available. This is Lori Latimer reporting live from Asher Regional Medical Center."

As soon as the camera stopped, Latimer started helping the cameraman pack up the equipment. A large man in a worn checked sport coat, who had been leaning patiently against the news van, approached Roberts. They obviously knew each other.

Roberts looked at Carol and Nelson.

"Of course you both know Charlie Hawkins, city editor of the Asher Citizen Daily," Roberts said.

It was clearly more of a warning than an introduction. They nodded.

"Can you get us bios on Todd Watson and Chris Jensson for our lead article?" Hawkins asked. "You know, family, where they're from, how long they've worked here, human interest stuff. We'd also like to know what all they did for the City, what they were working on currently, and so on."

"Mrs. Bailey can help you with some information about Mr. Watson and Mr. Jensson, Charlie. As you know, some personnel records are confidential."

When Hawkins glanced at Carol, his features softened. A barely perceptible smile flickered across his face as he nodded toward her. Then his eyes locked on Roberts's face.

"When will you be able to tell us exactly what they were doing this morning?" Hawkins asked.

"I'll have to refer you to the Police Department," Roberts replied. "I'm certain they will be handling this as a felony hit-and-run."

Roberts glared at Nelson again to make sure he would keep his mouth shut this time. Studying his fingernails, Nelson shuffled from foot to foot.

As Roberts had anticipated, Hawkins turned to Nelson and asked, "You're their supervisor, aren't you? What were they working on way out there this morning?" He stood poised with his pen and pad ready.

Nelson looked nervously at Roberts. "I have nothing to add at this time."

Hawkins looked at the two neutral faces and decided he had come to a temporary impasse. As he shuffled toward the hospital door, he said politely, "I'll talk with you later, Ms. Bailey."

Roberts turned to Carol.

"Has anyone called Todd's family yet?"

Carol nodded. "The police are notifying Todd's parents. I also called Chris' mother and left her an urgent message."

"Thanks again, Carol. I owe you one," Roberts said.

He walked toward the parking lot and drove away without a word to Nelson.

Nelson looked blankly at Carol, turned, and walked away, unconsciously mimicking his boss's departure.

When Carol returned to the emergency room, Hawkins was in the hallway making notes on a little pad as he cradled his cell phone with his shoulder. Hawkins nodded, gesturing to Carol that he would be through with his call soon.

Carol got a drink from a nearby water fountain while Hawkins finished his call. He leaned over as he approached her, to speak with her confidentially.

"Your boss is a prick and Nelson is like dog shit stuck on the bottom of Roberts' shoe. Can't the City Council find someone better than that?"

"Oh, Roberts isn't so bad."

"What the hell happened out there this morning, Carol?"

"The boys must have been catching up on some field work. Evidently, a semi ran into them while they were parked on the side of Old Bridge Road. Todd died instantly. Chris has a bad concussion and a broken arm. I hope they catch the bastard."

"They will, Carol. They never get away clean from a hit-and-run."

While Hawkins and Carol talked in the hospital hallway, the scene had turned violent out in the parking lot.

When Tommy Nelson got into his car, Decker's vehicle roared up behind him, blocking Nelson in the parking space. Decker jumped out, stormed up to the van, opened the door, and jerked Nelson out of the car.

Nelson stammered, "What are you doing?"

Decker slammed Nelson against the side of the van. Nelson vainly tried to pry Decker's hands from his shirtfront.

"You ass wipe," Decker said. "I told you if anything happened to Chris, I'd be coming for you. Tell me what you know about this or I'll start knocking your teeth out."

Nelson held his hands up in surrender. He found enough voice to squeak out, "Wait, wait."

A silver Chevy skidded into the curb only feet in front of the minivan. Zepeda hurried to where Decker had Nelson pinned against the driver's door.

"Kyle, what are you doing?" Zepeda asked.

"Leave me alone, Ernie."

"Not a chance. This is no time for you to interrogate anyone. What's the problem here?"

Decker stepped back and Nelson sagged against his car. Zepeda moved between the two men.

Nelson looked to Zepeda for help.

"He's insane, stop him before he kills me."

Zepeda kept his eyes on Nelson and spoke over his shoulder to Decker.

"You got some reason to be assaulting this guy?"

"I told you he threatened to kill Chris," Decker said. "I warned him. Now get out of the way, Ernie."

Zepeda took Decker's arm and pulled him toward the police car.

"Shouldn't we do some investigating first? Maybe see if there's any evidence that this particular fuck up is even involved? I know you're upset but you can't beat him up right here in public. You don't need him filing assault charges on you."

"Somebody killed Todd and hurt Chris. Nelson here is at the top of my list until we find somebody else."

"Use your head. If you think he did it, let's get some evidence. I'll get a warrant and throw his ass in jail. But for now, tell Mr. Nelson you're sorry you frightened him."

Decker walked back over to Nelson, still leaning on his car door. Nelson recoiled and held his hands up in defense.

"Sorry I startled you Mr. Nelson. Mistaken identity. I thought you were the bastard who murdered that kid and nearly killed Chris this morning. Of course, if you were that guy, you'd be turning yourself in to Detective Zepeda here. I'm sure you'd rather go to jail than wait for me to catch up with you on the street somewhere."

Decker straightened up Nelson's rumpled clothes and opened the car door for him.

"Have a nice day," Decker said with a fake smile. "I'll move my vehicle out of your way in just a minute."

Zepeda walked to Decker's Expedition with him.

"That was real good, partner. Now how about if we go get some coffee and figure out how we're going to find the truck driver?"

"I'll meet you at Janek's cafe," Decker said, getting into his Expedition. Then he looked out the open window directly at his former partner.

"Thanks, Ernie. I nearly made a stupid mistake. I'd never forgive myself if he got off because of me."

# CHAPTER EIGHT

Coffee was always fresh at the Commerce Street Cafe. The Saturday breakfast crowd was much the same as weekdays, except a couple of lawyers were in golf clothes. A big round table in the corner was the domain of County Judge Claude Faber and his courthouse cronies. A couple of four-tops next to the judge's table were informally reserved for City Hall types.

When the little bell on the cafe door announced Decker's entrance about nine-thirty, the City Hall table was up to six, three men in jeans and Saturday clothes, two in firefighter uniforms, and Ernie Zepeda. Decker waved at Gus Janek, the restaurant owner, as he made his way to the table.

After the city group acknowledged Decker's arrival with nods, handshakes, and shoulder punches, conversation picked up where it had left off. The older of the two firemen, Captain Ballerstedt, said, "I'll tell you what, he was really pinned in there. We had to fold back the roof and cut through the dashboard with the Hurst tool to pry the steering wheel off of him."

One of the younger men in jeans asked, "Hey, ecker, don't you know the guy injured in that wreck this morning?"

The waitress said, "Oh my word, are you boys still talking about that terrible business this morning. That poor boy!" She shook her head. "Just let Kyle drink his coffee before it gets cold."

Ballerstedt laughed. "Judy, honey," he said, "that coffee's so hot, Kyle's friend could heal up and be sitting here in person before it cools off. Why don't you run get Kyle some food now and let us talk?"

Taking his coffee from the waitress, Decker thanked her and looked down the table toward the other men.

"The man who was injured is Chris Jensson. He has a concussion and he's still pretty much out of it. The driver's name was Todd Watson."

Ballerstedt said, "Tell him we're real sorry we couldn't do anything to help the other guy. Killed on impact."

Judy arrived with Decker's plate, providing a gap in conversation just long enough for talk to return to fishing. Decker was thankful for breakfast and glad to hear the fishing stories spreading from the other end of the table. He ate his biscuits and gravy in silence, listening to lies compounding like interest on a new loan.

During breakfast, Zepeda kept an eye on Decker. After the reaction Decker had to Tommy Nelson at the hospital, he wanted to make sure Decker didn't fly off the handle at somebody else.

After they finished breakfast, Decker and Zepeda stepped out into the fall sunshine.

"Ernie, while you check in over at your office, I think I'll go over to City Hall and see if I can get some idea about what they were working on this morning. Maybe Chris left something on his desk that will help out."

"It's Saturday. How do you plan to get into the building?"

"When I drove by there, the parking lot was half full. I guess there's some kind of meeting in the council chamber this morning."

"How about if we both go to City Hall? I could stand some exercise after that big breakfast."

While they walked the two blocks to City Hall, Zepeda called the dispatcher for any update on the hit-and-run case. At the sheriff's office behind the court-house, reserve deputies were checking in to search for the hit-and-run truck.

The sun and walk did Decker some good, settling his breakfast and filling his lungs with fresh air. When he saw an empty space in the line of white city cars in the lot, he wondered again what Chris and Todd were doing out by the airport. Chris hadn't mentioned anything to him about going out there. They'd spoken Friday afternoon, but only to confirm that Decker would wait for Chris' call to come pick him up this morning.

The door to City Hall was unlocked for a United Way campaign planning committee meeting in the council room. About twenty people were watching a slick video produced to excite them about coercing donations from their coworkers. Decker grinned when Zepeda put his hand over his wallet. They had the same conversation each year when the City Manager's designee sent out the letter telling them what their voluntary donation was expected to be. A cop with two kids and one paycheck didn't make enough to give it to United Way.

When the Transportation and Planning Department door closed behind them, Decker felt an intense emptiness in the suite of offices. He had been in the place a couple times but never on weekends. This time, it felt strange and painful. He walked directly to Chris' office and switched on the light.

His desk was clean, no notes, no papers, only his in-box, name plate, phone, and computer. The in-box held a copy of the upcoming city council agenda that was always distributed on Friday afternoons. The only other paper in the tray was a flyer selling new planning law books. Decker looked around the office. Chris' credenza and shelves were neat and dusted.

Decker sat down in Chris' chair and slid open the desk drawer. Its contents were meticulously arranged.

Zepeda looked over his shoulder.

"I like this guy. Everything's in its place. Even the paper clips are sorted by size in the tray. He could do a lot for your life style, Kyle, keep you organized."

"You should see his pantry. Every can and package is in its place, labels toward the front, sorted by food type."

Other drawers held legal pads, a stapler and tape dispenser, a box of tissues, and some small bottles of juice and mineral water. Decker read a thank you card from somebody in Seattle for a birthday gift Chris had sent and a note from a city planner in El Paso inviting Chris to come visit him for a weekend. No way Decker would let Chris fly off to El Paso without him now.

Decker leaned back in Chris' chair, thinking out loud.

"Something caused Chris to hurry out to Old Bridge Road this morning before he was supposed to leave with me for Austin. It was work related or he wouldn't have taken the City car."

Zepeda nodded. "That doesn't help much."

"Since Chris and I weren't planning to come back to Asher until late Sunday night, something must have required his attention before leaving town.

The only other place to look was Chris' file cabinet. As Zepeda thumbed through the orderly files, he realized each one was tabbed and that they were organized behind task-oriented categories. In the front of the drawer, Chris kept a list of the categories and, under each category, a penciled list of files.

There was a file missing. It was not where it belonged in the drawer and it wouldn't dare be misfiled.

"A file for a zoning case on a Tract B is gone. What do you know about this Tract B?"

Chris had taken Decker out there to see the Aggie sage. He tried to envision Tract B. From the road it was just trees and undergrowth with some low grasses where the flowers bloomed.

"It's partly wooded, mostly oaks and yaupon. That's where some of those rare flowers are that Chris discovered. Didn't you say that the wreck was near some recently cleared property?"

Zepeda pulled out his notebook and found the page he needed.

"That's what the patrol sergeant who worked the incident told me over the phone."

"You know, Chris mumbled something about flowers being gone when I was trying to talk with him in the ER. It didn't make any sense at the time."

"We need to drive out there after while."

"When Chris did field work, he always took the file and a camera."

Zepeda held up three fingers and ticked them off.

"The bag wasn't in the car. The file isn't here in the drawer. That leaves the camera."

"I saw him get it out of the supply closet once," Decker said. He got up and walked down the hall to check the supply closet, Zepeda following close behind. They weren't surprised to find it missing.

"What kind of camera is it?" Zepeda asked.

"Chris was bitching about how big and clunky it is. Great resolution though. I think it's a Canon. He said it has a big dent in the top."

"A Canon camera with a dented top and, by now, with the serial numbers sanded off the bottom. Should be a snap to identify, if we ever see it again. Worth checking the local pawn shops."

Decker leaned against the wall.

"So, they were out on Old Bridge Road taking photos of something, probably this Tract B. Chris usually did that the week before public hearings to use the photos in the exhibits."

Zepeda went back to Chris' office and scanned the City Council meeting agenda in the desk tray. There it was.

"There's a public hearing on the council agenda about rezoning Tract B for industrial use."

"That's it," Decker said. "They were out there shooting pictures of Tract B.

# CHAPTER NINE

Decker called the hospital. He got transferred around until he was connected with the nurse who told him that Mr. Jensson's condition remained unchanged. He was still listed as critical due to a severe concussion. She said he had been moved to a private room and no visitors were allowed due to security.

Decker and Zepeda left City Hall and looked around for Chris' new Prius hybrid. Decker explained that Chris was always careful to park it in the shade, spending an inordinate amount of time analyzing where shade would be as the day wore on.

"I always figure my vehicle will just be damned hot, or hotter than hell, take your pick," Decker said.

"The heat just doesn't bother me unless I focus on it. I learned that in the army," Zepeda replied.

"Chris says parking in the shade saves on fuel because it takes less energy to cool down the car in the summer. The shade also preserves the *sea glass pearl* paint job, whatever the hell that means."

"I guess you notice the sun more when you come from a place where it rains all the time."

They looked in areas shaded from morning sun and found Chris' sea green Prius on the west side of the old three-story DeLeon National Bank. Chris religiously locked the car with the alarm set even though, in Asher, auto thieves were statistically less likely to strike than lightning.

They circled the car, looking in each window for the bag, camera, or file. Decker didn't have a key and didn't want to set off the noisy alarm. He was certain that nothing would be in the car. Chris' car was immaculate, not even a crumpled napkin or coffee cup littered the floor.

As they stood by the car, Zepeda said, "We should check his apartment next to be sure Chris didn't leave his bag and the camera at home."

"Chris would never leave his bag and the city camera at his place."

"Assuming they were really doing field work."

"What are you implying, Ernie, that they were running off at dawn in a City car to grab a quickie? You can forget that. If Chris wanted to seduce Todd, he'd just take him home to bed. He wouldn't risk being caught having sex in a car."

"Really? He's not the adventurous type?"

"Not yet, but I'm hopeful."

They retrieved the detective's car from Commerce Street and drove over to check Chris' apartment. Decker had a key.

He'd never been in the apartment when Chris wasn't there. It felt familiar but uncomfortable, like taking care of a friend's place during their vacation.

Chris' huge brown-striped cat walked to the bedroom door, stopped to stretch, then sat motionless, staring at them. That was the first time Decker had even thought about Sasquatch. He would need to take care of the cat while Chris was hospitalized. The cat was fine for now but Decker would have to remember to feed Sas every morning and clean out his stinky cat pan.

"Well, old boy, where would Chris leave something important?" Decker glanced around the silent apartment then addressed the cat again. "I wish you could tell us what the hell's going on."

The cat did not respond. He just looked bored and slightly annoyed that his nap had been disturbed by anyone other than Chris.

Decker began tentatively looking around on the antique wooden library table Chris used as a desk. Chris had found it at a used furniture sale in Round Top one weekend. Decker had hell loading it into his Expedition. Then they had to carry it into Chris' apartment in the middle of the night. He recalled it was like moving a grand piano in the dark. Decker smiled remembering how they had christened it that night. It made the furniture delivery worth the effort.

Decker looked in the two drawers. "God, he's organized. I've never seen anyone who filed their bills *before* they paid them. Look at this, Ernie, he keeps his charge card receipts in chronological order, waiting for the statement to come in."

He found the duplicate key to Chris' car so he could store it in his garage until Chris could drive again. Then Decker looked around the living room.

"I'm telling you, Kyle," Zepeda said, "this guy is so neat, he could be a good influence on you. I'll look in the kitchen while you check the bedroom."

Zepeda found that everything in the kitchen was put away, even the breakfast dishes. The cat yawned and padded across to the kitchen to see if Zepeda had made himself even remotely useful. Sas looked at Zepeda, then looked at the refrigerator, then back to Zepeda.

"No luck, fur ball. You'll have to wait a while."

While Zepeda searched the kitchen, Decker went into the bedroom, the inner sanctum of their relationship. He held Chris' pillow to his face and deeply inhaled his fragrance.

Sasquatch entered the bedroom and eyed him suspiciously. The cat never approved of Decker's intrusion in this room. Decker put the pillow down.

"He'll be home soon," Decker said, more to himself than to the cat. "He's going to be okay."

Decker sat down on the bed. A photo of the two of them was on the dresser. They were outside a small pottery and woven goods shop in San Antonio's La Villita area. It had been their second weekend outing. Chris had reserved a room at the historic Emily Morgan Hotel on the northeast corner of Alamo Plaza.

The famous Alamo mission, reconstructed because of its historical significance in the Texas Revolution, always seems so out of context among the skyscrapers and downtown traffic. While they were in San Antonio, Chris and Decker had visited four of the missions located along the San Antonio River. The Mission San Jose was his favorite.

Chris looked so happy in the photo that Decker got a lump in his throat.

When he got up from the bed, he saw Chris' rolling overnight bag by the closet door where his matching garment bag was hanging. Chris was packed for the weekend. He lifted the overnight bag onto the foot of the bed and zipped it open. Chris had packed his favorite blue T-shirt, the one that matched his eyes so well. Decker was holding the soft shirt, standing with his back to the bedroom door, when Zepeda came in.

"Find something interesting?"

The bag was still on the bed, standing open. Decker looked at it, then at Sas, who glared from under the dust ruffle. Decker tried to collect his thoughts. He'd been trying not to think about Chris in pain or the injuries to that beautiful young body. The reality of it suddenly rattled him. Decker sat down on the bed, the T-shirt still in his hands.

Zepeda said, "Maybe you should head back to the hospital, Kyle. Just let me work on this today."

Decker stood and dropped the shirt back in the overnight bag. He looked around the small bedroom and in the closet.

"Forget it, Ernie. Let's get back to work. The way I figure it, Chris must have decided to shoot the pictures early this morning because we were leaving later this morning for the weekend."

"Well," Zepeda said, "we've looked at his office, in his car, and here. There's no sign of any of his stuff."

"I still don't understand why Chris' things and the camera weren't in the car. Most hit-and-run drivers don't rifle through the other vehicle, especially when there's an injured person in it who might identify them later. Maybe someone assumed Chris was dead too since he was bloody and unconscious."

"Or maybe somebody followed them out to Old Bridge Road. Do we know where Nelson was early this morning?"

"I was just about to ask Nelson that when you interrupted my interrogation."

Zepeda walked to the apartment door and grinned.

"You're not supposed to beat up suspects without me," he said. "Besides, he might have whipped your ass without my backup."

Decker rolled his eyes.

"Be careful not to let Chris' cat out. He never goes outside since Chris had him declawed and neutered."

"I don't blame him," Zepeda smiled. "I wouldn't either."

# CHAPTER TEN

While Decker and Zepeda were walking to the car, Zepeda said, "Let's head back to my office so I can get your statement."

"What the fuck are you talking about?"

"First, you're romantically involved with one of the victims. That automatically puts you under suspicion. Second, Chris works for Tommy Nelson and you've assaulted Nelson twice. Nelson's attorney could argue that you're irrationally jealous and violent. Let's just get your statement taken down so your ass is covered."

Decker studied Zepeda. The look on the detective's face was impossible to read. Zepeda waited patiently until Decker's moment of hesitation passed. As Zepeda unlocked the car, Decker's eyes never left his face. Decker got in on the passenger's side, Zepeda started the car. Then Zepeda waited with his hand on the gearshift.

"Yeah, you're right," Decker said. "I'm damned sure involved. Let's get something on the record documenting that Nelson threatened Chris at work."

As they pulled out onto the street and accelerated well beyond the speed limit, Decker thought about the morning, about how he needed an alibi. He remembered his neighbor was down in Houston prowling filthy junkyards.

"There's someone who can verify that I was at home this morning at the time of the collision. Kenny Long talked with me while I was waiting for Chris to call."

Zepeda glanced at Decker, then back to the street.

"Kenny wanted me to ride to Houston with him today to look for parts for that old GTO he's restoring. I was out on my porch and we talked for maybe five minutes."

"If you know how can we reach him, I'll get Luedecke to contact him."

"I've got his number but he'll be gone all day. He won't leave Houston until it gets too dark to see what he's doing. My guess is he'll get home around nine or ten tonight."

Zepeda steered the silver car into a reserved parking place behind the police building and turned off the ignition. He turned in the driver's seat to face Decker. Zepeda took his pad and pen out and started making notes.

"Isn't that the Kenny Long who buys a lot of weapons?"

"Yeah, that's the one. Do you know him?"

"He's a strange one," Zepeda said as he slid out of the car. "Doesn't like us minorities one bit."

"That could describe lots of people."

"You're right about that. There are way too many bigots in Texas carrying loaded firearms."

"No kidding. There's a whole bunch who don't like gay people too. You aren't the only kind of minority, you know."

Zepeda held the door for Decker to enter the station and the desk officer buzzed them through the security door. They made a couple of turns down a hallway lined with small nondescript offices.

Zepeda sat down behind his gray metal desk. The detective's chair and matching gray metal file cabinet completed the furnishings on his side of the office. Even his stapler and hole punch were gray. A gray and white nameplate on the desk read *Detective Ernesto Zepeda*. When Zepeda was behind the desk, his gray suit matched the furniture. The effect was so monochromatic that the black desk phone and a stack of manila folders seemed colorful.

Zepeda pulled his note pad out of his pocket and put it in front of him on the desk. He opened his note pad and clicked his ballpoint.

"Before we go into the interview room to tape your statement," Zepeda said, "maybe you should tell me more about your relationship with Chris Jensson."

"My relationship with Chris Jensson is that we're lovers. I don't know what else you want me to say, Ernie. He's in the hospital and the bastard who put him there is getting away while we're sitting here covering my ass with a statement."

Zepeda rolled his chair back from the desk and stood up. He wasn't a whole lot taller standing than Decker was sitting down.

"You know the drill," he said. "Humor me."

Decker gave him a brief explanation of his relationship with Chris. He was straight-forward, sticking to facts and omitting any details that could be sensationalized in court.

Five minutes later, Zepeda and Decker went down the hallway to a small room with four chairs around a conference table. Zepeda turned on the video recording system. The interview progressed quickly, sticking to the details Zepeda already knew regarding Decker's involvement with Chris and his alibi for early that morning.

Zepeda asked Decker about his relationship with the victims of the hit and run. Then he asked if Decker knew of any reason why someone might want to harm Todd Watson or Chris Jensson. Decker related the story of Nelson's suspected bribery and the death threat made against Chris and his mother in Seattle. Zepeda clarified the timeframe and, for the record, that Decker had not witnessed the exchange personally but that Mr. Jensson had told him about it previously. Decker also stated that Nelson had intimidated Chris to the extent that he was afraid he would be fired or harmed physically.

Luedecke was waiting when they completed the interview.

"Mr. Jensson's been stirring some, Kyle," he said. "The nurse told me on the phone that he's been asking for you whenever he comes around. They have him medicated for the pain."

Luedecke looked at Zepeda and then back to Decker.

"Are you and Jensson, you know, a couple or something?" Luedecke asked.

Decker said, "No, not officially anyway. But we're in a relationship."

"That's cool. I'm glad you have someone in your life again, Kyle. I hope he gets better soon."

Zepeda and Decker walked out into the sunlight again.

"You know, Ernie, I think I'll scoot on over to the hospital now and spend some time with Chris. I'm ready for a break after that grilling you gave me in there."

"I've grilled burgers longer that that. You just got off easy. While you go see Chris, I'll go interview Tommy Nelson and then start checking the pawn shops. Maybe someone was stupid enough to sell that camera right here in Asher."

# CHAPTER ELEVEN

Nanci yelled across to the next trailer, "Turn down that noise or I'm going to call the cops again."

"Shut up, you whore," her neighbor yelled back. "If you didn't spend all night wiggling your ass, you'd be awake all day like decent people."

Returning to her phone call, Nanci said, "I'm sorry, Reverend. I can hardly hear you. My neighbors watch those awful TV shows all day with people hollering at each other. Daytime TV is getting downright obscene."

They both laughed.

The caller said, "Nanci, why don't you leave that undeserving husband of yours and move in with me in Waco? You know I'd treat you right, and you could stop dancing for a living."

"You better quit asking me, sweetie. I just might take you up on it someday. Will you be at the club tonight?"

"I'll be there, if you are. You know I can't stay away when you're working.

"You're always so horny, baby, I hate to see you all frustrated like that."

Nanci lit a cigarette, took a deep drag, and exhaled.

"Are you tense right now, Reverend?" she purred.

"You know it Nanci. I'm harder than a Baylor boy watching porn."

"I'll help you with that tonight, Reverend," Nanci said. "Bye, for now."

Nanci hung up and went to the door of her mobile home.

"You assholes must be deaf," she yelled. "Why don't you get hearing aides before we all need them?"

She rattled the door. The effort didn't provide much emphasis, though, since she didn't want the little window to fall out of its aluminum frame again.

Nanci grumbled to herself, "How am I supposed to sleep with all their racket, not to mention the damned artillery going off and the helicopters flying over?"

A dozen Abrams tanks were on the firing range over at Fort Hood. Even though it was miles away, the intermittent pounding of heavy shells always set her nerves on edge. Pairs of Apache attack helicopters thumped over her trailer park almost every day.

Since she was awake anyway, Nanci thought she might pick up a few bucks modeling before going to the club. Working an afternoon at Mama Delight's lingerie boutique was sometimes good for an easy $100 and didn't tire her out before her late night job.

Nanci gulped down the remainder of her coffee and started the shower in her tiny closet of a bathroom.

Unlike her lanky husband, she could get a nice bath in the tiny prefab shower. She was invigorated.

Nanci stepped out and wrapped a towel around her body and used a second towel to dry her short dark hair. Even strippers can be modest when they're at home, especially in a trailer park full of soldiers and perverted old Army retirees.

When Nanci first moved to Harker Heights, she had a retired sergeant next door who thought she was one of the public attractions. He would sit up and spy on her when she came in at three in the morning. The sergeant's wife finally caught him and brained him with his night scope. Besides, there was a big difference between exotic dancing and simply walking around naked. Dancing paid better.

Nanci pulled on a red tube top and cut-offs. The picture of her husband on the dresser reminded her again of her mission.

"Ronnie boy," she said to the photo, "when I have enough money for a better car, I'm out of here. I'm going to dance in one of those expensive Dallas gentlemen's club. You'll never see me again unless you have a twenty-dollar bill to fold under my G-string. I should have left when they bounced your sorry ass out of the Army for being so stupid."

After a quick salad and some yogurt, Nanci grabbed her cigarettes and purse, found some big round sunglasses, and traded a few more insults with her neighbors. She coaxed her old Escort into starting and drove the two blocks to Veteran's Memorial Highway.

Ten miles to the west, the highway runs directly into the gate of Fort Hood, the largest Army base in the known universe, according to the regional boosters. Between Harker Heights and the Army post is the city of Killeen, where guys can buy guns but they can't spend Saturday night in a titty bar. Harker Heights is the nearest destination for soldiers looking for sexual adventure.

Some folks consider adult entertainment a step up from the town's origin as a pig farm. Before Harker Heights became a thriving red light district, permanent residents raised pork for the Army mess halls. Eventually, the rich pig farmers moved to the highest hills, probably to escape the odor, and everyone else lived beneath them. Gradually, retired Army officers settled on the hills with the wealthier local folks. Everyone else, Nanci included, continued to live at lower elevations in cheap frame houses or in acres and acres of rundown trailer parks.

Nanci, and other women who were married to soldiers or left behind by them, found work in the strip joints. There were a dozen Harker Heights bars and whorehouses catering to an endless supply of lonely men.

Nanci entertained several steady customers who craved sexual excitement, like her preacher friend from Waco. Unlike most of the other strippers at Cowgirls Roundup, Nanci almost never turned tricks and didn't do drugs or drink much. Dancing naked was her job.

Nanci didn't mind that the Reverend bribed a bartender for her phone number. During the previous December, he couldn't get away from Christmas duties at the Living Word Family Church in Waco. So he deposited $200 directly into Nanci's checking account for a month of good phone sex. He always paid her $20 for lap dancing and $50 for a hand job in the dark corner.

Nanci parked at Mama Delight's and exchanged greetings with the proprietor at the door. The shop was small, but always clean and it smelled of incense. Mama Dee was a tiny woman, not five feet tall, with delicate Southeast Asian features and streaks of gray in her jet-black hair. Rumor had it that she was a Saigon whorehouse madam some Army general flew to the states as a favor. Nanci never asked.

Because of her own size, Mama Dee wouldn't hire tall, beefy girls, only small women not much taller than herself. Some places preferred big busty blondes, but Mama Dee specialized in intimate wear for petite women. Many of her models were pretty Asians or Hispanics with small, firm breasts.

Mama Dee's pieces were sewn in a sweatshop right in Harker Heights using imported fabrics, lace, thread and elastic. It was also rumored that her materials entered the country in military aircraft without customs inspection. She paid almost nothing for the products, displayed them for a fee, and sold them for outrageous prices to men who didn't dare take the lingerie home.

Nanci didn't really care as long as she could get work and the conditions were good. "Mama Dee, are you expecting much business today?" Nanci asked.

"Saturday after lunch always steady, baby. You want to model today?"

"If you can use me today, I would be grateful."

"Grateful enough to fuck with customer today, Nanci?" Mama Dee giggled.

Nanci smiled demurely.

"Mama Dee, you know I am not that kind of girl. I only model the underwear."

"You so pretty. You make lot of money anyway without fucking customer. Please wear the red panties and white silk robe today."

"Thank you, Mama Dee. I won't dis-appoint you."

Nanci slipped into the dressing room. The clothes were immaculately laundered and wrapped in tissue. Mama Dee's concern for hygiene was always a comfort to Nanci. She found the red and white outfit neatly folded on a shelf.

As Nanci peeled off her top and shorts, She stood up straight and studied herself in the full-length mirror, checking for imperfections. There weren't many. She brushed her short hair straight down, like all Mama Dee's models did, and put her things in a little woven basket that locked in a shelf. Nanci unwrapped her costume and slipped on the red thong panties. She put on the silk robe, tied it loosely, and adjusted it to drape artfully over her bare breasts.

Nanci smiled at herself in the mirror and said, "Ready for work."

She went out into the showroom with Mama Dee to wait for her first customer. Nanci could hear another model talking to a customer in a viewing room in the back of the shop.

"Looking good, baby," Mama Dee said. "You're so pretty, customer will buy panties every time. You'll see."

"Yes, they fit very nicely. Thank you again for letting me work today."

One of the other models, a young Asian woman, came out of the small hallway leading to the viewing rooms followed by a middle-aged man.

"Mama Dee," she said, "Mr. Jones would like to buy this green negligee, these sexy panties, and this lace bra."

It was uncanny how most of Mama Dee's customers were named Smith or Jones. The model turned to the customer and flashed him an adoring smile.

"Next time you're in the mood for shopping, Mr. Jones, remember where you saw this delicate piece."

She opened the front of her robe revealing that she had nothing else on, and then gave him a little bow. Mama Dee intercepted his hand as he reached toward the model, expertly leading him to the counter.

"That will be $92.50, Mr. Jones," she said.

Reaching for his wallet, the man said, "By the way, how much is the white robe on that other girl?"

"You want her to model that lingerie? You can rent a viewing room again, Mr. Jones."

"I don't really have time, but I might like to buy that robe now, right off her rack."

He chuckled at his own pun and smiled at Nanci. She returned his smiled and turned a full circle, careful to add enough bounce to make the robe even more alluring.

"That robe sells for $49.95 plus tax," Mama Dee said. "Would you like to see how well it was made?"

Mr. Jones was positively in a sweat after Nanci swung around slowly and sensuously a couple more times. She untied the robe, letting it fall open seductively as she faced the customer. He finished pulling out his wallet and sat down in a chair next to the counter. Nanci stroked his neck with the white silk. Her exposed nipples were level with his face.

Mr. Jones fumbled with his money, never taking his eyes from Nanci's nipples. He told Mama Dee that he would take it.

Nanci let the robe slip off slowly, one shoulder at a time. As she stood before him wearing only the red panties, she reached over his head to hand the robe to the proprietor, allowing her breast to brush his face. Nanci flashed a teasing smile at Mr. Jones, and then walked quickly to the dressing room for another robe.

When she returned with an identical robe on, the customer was gone and Mama Dee was paying Su Lin, the other model, with a ten and a five from the till. She also handed Nanci a five.

Mama Dee smiled.

"Good work, Nanci. You help the next customer."

"If I'd known he had that much money," Su Lin said, "I would have invited you in for a duo, Nan. No telling how much we could have sold him together."

Nanci laughed and put her five in a small envelope with her name on it by the cash drawer. The other model did the same with her cash then they sat down together on a love seat near the dressing room door to wait for more business.

The two dancers had known each other for six months. Su Lin's husband had been in Iraq for two tours but he wouldn't send her any money. She was afraid to ask the Army for help, so she started working the clubs and modeling shops.

"Nanci, I thought you moved to Dallas to seek your fortune and dance for rich Texas oil men," she said. "What are you doing back here?"

"I don't know where you got that. I've been in town the whole time. I started dancing at Cowgirls. I guess that's why we don't run into each other much any more. You still dancing at Sonny's Cabaret?"

"Whenever I can. I like it because Sonny leaves me alone when I'm in the dressing room. He won't touch me because he thinks I look like a boy. Sonny mostly hires big bleach blondes with huge tits.

"Mama Dee's is better, so clean. It always smells nice here."

"I guess I  thought you had left town because that string bean husband of yours came in here last week. He rented a room  and Toni modeled for him."

"Ronnie was in here? You sure?"

"He only bought one little thong but he had a lot of cash. I'm sure it was him. Your picture was in his wallet, right next to his license."

"I should've left him already."

Nanci got up and paced around the shop.

"As soon as I get my hands on that money, I'm leaving his worthless ass forever."

# CHAPTER TWELVE

Lori Latimer and her cameraman were shooting video when Hawkins pulled over to the side of Old Bridge Road. He parked off the pavement across from the Channel Five news van. Hawkins lifted himself out of the tattered front seat of his old station wagon and ambled toward the television news crew.

"Start over, Ed," Lori said to the cameraman. "That noisy car distracted me. It interrupted my train of thought."

"No problem,"

Ed knew full well that Lori Latimer couldn't make a train with her thoughts if they were covered with Velcro. Being the station owner's niece qualified her as a television journalist even though she was dumb as dryer lint. Ed was assigned as Lori's crew because the station security guard caught him smoking grass in the parking lot. The news director decided that working with Lori for a few weeks would be far worse punishment than being fired.

Ed lowered the camcorder from his shoulder and lit a cigarette while the disheveled man sluggishly crossed the road. Hawkins stopped to examine the dashed orange lines the accident investigators had spray-painted on the pavement. Lori stood with a hand on each hip, the cordless microphone clutched like a weapon in her tiny fist. She was wearing her impatient expression as the stranger approached.

"Didn't we see you at the hospital earlier?" Lori asked inquisitively. "You can't keep following us around, you know. We have a story to cover here."

"What story might that be?"

"There was a hit-and-run right here this morning with a fatality. Another man is seriously injured in the hospital."

"Looks as though it happened over there, where all the debris is." Hawkins pointed to the area where the roadside was rutted and littered with shattered glass.

Ed looked away and coughed to keep from laughing.

Looking at the videographer, Hawkins said, "Not many visuals. I guess you could show that somebody bulldozed all the vegetation off this tract. It used to look like the land over there." Hawkins pointed at Tract C. "There were some rare wildflowers out here. Don't you wonder who scraped it off?"

"We're trying to report on a car wreck," Lori snapped. "If you don't mind, we have work to do. You can watch but you must stand behind the cameraman and stay very, very quiet."

"How generous of you, Miss Latimer." Hawkins took his ragged note pad from an inside coat pocket and started clicking a ballpoint pen. With a straight face, he said, "Even though I was reporting news stories when you were still pooping your diapers, I'm always willing to learn from a colleague in the broadcast media."

Ed laughed out loud this time as Hawkins shuffled over to the crash site.

"Dammit, Ed. Why didn't you tell me he was a reporter?"

"They pay me to take the video, Lori, not to ask the questions. Do you reckon we can get this piece done soon? I'm meeting someone for lunch back at the motel."

Ed lifted the camcorder to his shoulder and adjusted his focus to catch Hawkins in the background. Anything would be better than Lori by herself.

Hawkins squatted down about where the emergency crew removed Chris from the wrecked City car. He scanned the roadway in both directions.

It would require gross negligence for a semi to hit a car sitting on the shoulder. The view was clear and the road was plenty wide for passing a parked car unless the truck was meeting another vehicle head-on. Contrary to the Asher Industrial Park advertising, there was not much traffic around, especially on Saturday morning at dawn.

He studied the tire marks, dirt, and debris. There were lots of footprints in the glass and loose soil. Two sets of tracks lead way out into the property.

Hawkins followed the footprints to their destination in the middle of the empty lot. One man had stood with his feet apart, planted firmly in the soil, facing away from the road. The other man seemed to follow him. Then the first man walked to a torn tree root, did something with it, and then returned to the car. Again, the second man seemed to follow the first man. Hawkins studied the spot where Chris had stood.

He drew a little map of Tract B on his notepad and carefully noted all the details. Then Hawkins stood with his feet apart, looking away from the road. There wasn't much to see, just the barren property and the industrial tracts beyond. There was a warehouse with a transport trailer parked at the dock. He noted it on his diagram. A small airplane was droning up into the midday sky from the airport. There wasn't much else to see.

Hawkins walked straight ahead toward the warehouse. The soil was uneven and soft underfoot. He stopped to review his notes from interviewing the responding police and fire-fighters. He could find only one commonality in his scribbled notes.

A semi cab without a trailer had hit the parked city car earlier that day on the road behind him. Also, at some point, a semi had delivered the trailer to the dock now in front of him. Although maybe it wasn't the same truck in both instances, it sure might have been. He wondered if the police had drawn the same conclusion.

Hawkins pulled a dirty handkerchief from his coat pocket and wiped the dust from his forehead. He watched the television news crew trying to get a decent piece of video for their noon show. Hawkins couldn't hear what Lori was saying but he knew how badly she was mutilating the language. Viewers must not realize they are listening to the editorial opinions of a high school cheerleader who flunked out of college and was hired by her mother's brother under extreme duress.

People who watch the local television news fluff aren't learning what's going on in the world. They are simply filling another half-hour of their lives with slick commercials and meaningless copy, badly read, over colorful visuals.

Seeing Lori Latimer in person proved the wonder of modern cosmetics but makeup, lights, and camera angles failed to disguise her stupidity. Microphones exposed the fraud each time her mouth opened. Her video pieces contained misinformation, fabrication, exaggeration, and exploitation, none of which Lori Latimer could spell. It was sensationalist soft news presented in perpetually present tense.

Hawkins rarely thought of his stories as being entertaining. They were informative. Some were exceptionally well written, even clever. Thinking about television news made Hawkins more dedicated to finding the truth and writing it down.

His jaw set and his head down, Hawkins walked the hundred yards over to the warehouse. The trailer was unpainted and lacked any company logos or identification numbers on the sides. The warehouse was unidentified too, providing no hint of the occupancy.

Hawkins remembered the difficulties Ted Smith had with the warehouse construction. Smith's contractor didn't want to do anything according to the city building code so Smith appealed. The City gave him several waivers and exceptions, supposedly because the Economic Development Commission endorsed the project. Hawkins had investigated that story for the newspaper, hoping to scratch up some information about Smith's influence at City Hall. He came up dry, but the situation had piqued his curiosity about Ted Smith.

Hawkins tried to open the trailer doors but everything was locked up tight. He stood in the shadow of the trailer, looking back across Tract B at the news crew packing up their equipment. Squinting, Hawkins spotted the torn tree root sticking up in the middle of Tract B, close to where someone had stood looking toward the warehouse. From that vantage point the man had a clear view of the loading dock. If a truck had been attached to the trailer that morning, he would have seen the rig, maybe even the driver.

The Channel Five vehicle rumbled to a start. It was an extended van with a dish folded down on the roof among several spring-mounted antennae. The sides, front, and rear were painted with garish red, blue, and yellow station logos.

"Of course," Hawkins muttered, "it's right under my big nose.

He thought, *There are only a couple of reasons not to paint a company logo or advertising on a trailer, to prevent people from knowing who owned it or from guessing what might be inside. Big rigs are rolling billboards. Why would anyone pass up the opportunity for cheap, highly mobile advertising? Because whoever owned this trailer wanted to remain anonymous. That's an unusual strategy for a legitimate business to take.*

Hawkins' curiosity turned to the warehouse. With Ted Smith's penchant for high profile marketing, it was uncharacteristic of him to miss a chance to hang a self-promoting sign somewhere on so large a building. Blank walls were usually display space for Ted Smith's smiling photo. There were no signs on this building at all, not even a phone number for police to call in an emergency.

The less information Hawkins was able to find, the more curious he grew. He had learned over the years that people with nothing to hide leave information everywhere. Others are so careful about leaving nothing that the lack of information makes them stand out.

He sat down on the loading dock steps in the shade to make more notes. As he studied the building and the trailer, looking back across the barren Tract B, Hawkins wrote down all of his impressions. Careful observations guided by intuition and healthy skepticism more often than not provided insights that would break a story. He just had to concentrate.

*Something always gets overlooked,* Hawkins thought. He slid off the dock and crawled under the trailer. On hands and knees, Hawkins inspected the rear dual wheels and axles. Moving forward, he noticed a small red tag near the middle of the front axle. It couldn't be seen except from directly under the trailer. Carefully untwisting the wire securing it to the brace, Hawkins held the tag by the edges and rolled over on his back to study it.

"Well, well, look what we have here," Hawkins mumbled.

He fished around in his pocket and pulled out his notepad. He slipped the tag in between two clean pages and returned the notepad to his pocket.

Hawkins rolled back over on his hands and knees and crawled out from under the trailer. Standing with a grunt, he dusted off his sleeves and looked around to see if he had been observed.

Satisfied that nobody else was around, he hustled across Tract B to his car. It whined, wheezed, and sputtered to a start. Hawkins cranked the power steering until it squealed and then sped off the way he came.

# CHAPTER THIRTEEN

Chris had been in the hospital only a few hours but it seemed much longer to Decker. He checked with two blue-haired volunteers at the hospital reception desk to get the room number. When Decker turned around toward the lobby, a familiar face was looking up at him. Carol Bailey's broad smile was a heart-warming surprise.

"How's it going, big guy?" Carol asked, touching Decker's arm.

"We have a couple of leads. Zepeda is following up on them now." Decker said. "Have you seen Chris yet?"

Carol's nodded. Her smile disappeared.

"I just came from his room. He's pretty banged-up, Kyle. The nurse said he's stable but still not out of the woods yet. His face is bruised and his knee is swollen. They put a cast on his right arm."

"I'll go sit with him for a while."

"Chris is really upset about Todd. He's blaming himself."

"Maybe he'll feel better if I'm there."

Carol's smile returned.

"I think this guy's got his hooks deep into you, Kyle Decker."

Carol gave Decker a quick hug and a kiss on the cheek and hurried out the door with a wave.

Decker stood there a moment, savoring Carol's affection. When he realized that the reception desk volunteers were watching him, he quickly took the stairs to the second floor.

A uniformed officer was sitting in a metal folding chair at Chris' door reading a novel. She was a large, athletic woman in her thirties who was all business when Decker approached. She checked Decker's identification. Decker was on a very short list of people cleared to enter. Decker welcomed the security.

Decker hesitated, preparing himself to be the stoic Texas boy he was raised to be instead of a worried gay lover. He knocked quietly on the door. When there was no response, he pushed the door open a little and peeked in.

The spotless room was quiet and still. Only the sounds from the hallway disturbed the silence. Sunlight spilling through the blinds filled the space between the window and Chris' bed. A television was mounted high on the wall at the foot of the bed and a roll-around service table already held two flower arrangements.

He slipped inside and closed the door softly. Decker forced himself to look at the person in the hospital bed. Except for his head, shoulders, and arms, Chris was covered with a light blanket tucked neatly under both sides of the mattress. He wore one of those thin blue hospital gowns. An IV tube led down to his left hand from a bag hanging by the bed. His right arm, in a white cast beginning above his elbow and ending at his knuckles, was supported by a pillow.

There was a big bandage over Chris' right ear and a smaller bandage on his lower lip where a bruise spread down to his chin. Carol was right about the bruises. Both of Chris' eyes were puffy. Both had dark reddish-purple crescents under them and there was a purple knot on his forehead.

Decker's heart pounded in his ears as he walked around to the side of the bed by the window. He watched Chris breathing, his chest rising and falling under the covers. Chris was a miracle in his life.

He wondered if this extraordinary man had grown to love him too.

Decker reached over the bed rail and stroked Chris' left arm. He savored the texture of the soft blond hair on his forearm. Decker was amazed by his perfect, masculine body and by the sweet, intelligent man within.

He moved the curls on Chris' forehead and put his hand against his cheek.

"Wake up, Chris," he whispered.

Chris turned his head slightly toward him. Decker leaned over the rail and kissed him lightly on the mouth.

With a catch in his breath, Decker said, "I love you, Chris Jensson."

Chris' eyelids moved and opened slowly. A weak smile wrinkled his swollen lips.

"I'm glad you're here, Kyle. I was hoping you'd still want to kiss me. I must look like shit."

Chris started crying quietly.

"Do you need something for the pain, baby?"

"No, I'm already so doped-up I can hardly stay awake. I just can't believe this happened. Carol said we were hit by a truck. Todd didn't have a chance."

"I'm so sorry about Todd. I've been worried about you."

"His parents will be devastated. I wish I'd never called him this morning. He'd still be alive."

"It isn't your fault, Chris." Decker smoothed Chris' hair and kissed him again. "We're going to catch the bastard who did this. You just concentrate on getting well."

"I'll be alright. The doctor said I'll probably be okay once this headache goes away." He touched his forehead with his left hand and then pointed to the cast. "The fracture was a clean break and should mend all right. Otherwise, it's mostly cuts and bruises."

Decker carefully lowered the bed rail and gently hugged Chris. He felt Chris' warm breath on his neck.

Chris sighed deeply and said, "You're such a sweet guy. I love you, Kyle."

Chris nuzzled Decker's neck and ear.

"Excuse me," a man's deep voice interrupted, "I didn't know you were having a moment."

Decker stood up quickly and raised the bed rail with a snap.

"Sorry I startled you," the young man said. He was dressed in a white medical coat and he carried a metal clipboard. "The guard said you were Chris's friend so I guess you must be Kyle. The nurse said he's been asking for you all morning."

Decker looked at the doctor as he approached Chris' bed.

"Right, I'm Kyle Decker, I'm his..., I mean, Chris and I are..."

Decker trailed off, looking at the bed rail, searching for a good word to use in the situation.

The doctor smiled at Chris and Decker.

"It's all right, really, hugs are nice" he said. "I'm Doctor Murphy, by the way, your neurologist. I just stopped by to check that knot on your noggin."

Decker folded into the sunlit guest chair as the doctor scanned the chart he had carried into the room. His pen scratched the paper and clicked loudly in route to his pocket.

"You needed a couple of stitches over your right ear." The doctor rubbed his chin. "I've studied your MRI. That bump on your forehead is over a small intracranial hematoma. That means you have a serious concussion but I think you'll be fine as long as there isn't more swelling."

"And if there is?" Chris asked.

"Well, we might have to drain it using a little surgical procedure I know. No big deal, really. We just get out the old drill and, you know, make another hole in your head."

"Oh, shit. That doesn't sound good," Chris muttered.

Chris and Decker looked at each other as the doctor studied his bruised face.

"I really don't think surgery will be necessary," Dr. Murphy said. "I'll be finished here in a minute and you guys can get on with what you were doing, within reason."

The doctor clicked on a penlight and shined the beam into each eye as he lifted Chris' eyelids with his thumb. The chart and the pen came out again, and the doctor scribbled more notes.

A nurse opened the door and looked in.

"It's almost time for your meal to come up from the kitchen, Mr. Jensson. I can get it for you pretty soon," she said.

The nurse turned to Decker and continued. "Would you like to run to the cafeteria before it gets crowded?"

"No thanks. I had lunch."

Decker remained firmly planted in the guest chair, making it clear that he had no intention of budging.

"No problem, you can stay as long as you like," the nurse said over her shoulder. "I really think our patient is out of the woods now, don't you Dr. Murphy?"

Dr. Murphy laughed.

"Thanks for assisting me with the diagnosis, Eloise."

"Anytime," Eloise said. "It comes with the room service."

She left again in a blur of stretched white polyester, her shoes squeaking on the waxed floor.

The doctor lifted the sheet from Chris' feet and ran an instrument along each sole. Chris jumped appropriately, twice.

"Are you actually a doctor or is this a comedy routine?"

"Oh, don't let my age and quick wit fool you, Chris. I graduated in the top three-fourths of my class. That qualifies me to count the bumps on your head and to tickle the soles of your feet."

As Dr. Murphy opened the door and hallway noises filtered into the room, he stopped and said, "I'll be around in a couple of hours to see you again. Don't get too carried away in here. There's no lock on the door."

As soon as the doctor was gone, Chris said, "Kyle, come over here and hug me again. I know I look like hell but you look great. I need for you to touch me."

They hugged again and caressed. Chris showed Decker some of the other damage done to his body. To speed his recovery, Chris asked him to kiss all of the bruises. Kyle kissed a few uninjured spots too, just for good measure. Chris started to get an erection.

"We better stop before I get in that bed with you," Decker said.

He stood up and adjusted himself. Then Decker walked over to the window and leaned on the windowsill.

"If I'd known you needed to do some field work. I would've gone out there with you," Decker said.

"I'm glad you weren't with me. You might have been hurt too. If Nelson would do his job, this wouldn't have happened at all. He moved the Tract B hearing ahead of schedule."

"I hate to think this is all because of a damned zoning hearing."

Chris frowned.

"To top it all off," Chris said, "those greedy bastards have already bulldozed Tract B. The trees and the flowers were all destroyed. The whole property has been scraped down to loose soil."

"Do you think your wreck had something to do with Tract B?"

"I can't see how. They're going to get it rezoned anyway. I was hoping my photos might at least save Tract C."

"The camera is gone. So is your leather bag."

"Can you believe that? Somebody ripped off my bag."

"When we catch the asshole that rifled through the City car, we're nailing him for theft and failure to render aid. I don't know how anyone could steal your things and just leave, knowing you needed help."

"Carol is calling all my credit card companies this afternoon to report my cards as stolen. They got the keys to my car, my apartment, your house, even City Hall. I couldn't care less about the City camera, but I really need my iPad and phone. "

"I picked up your spare car key so I can store your car in my garage until you can drive again. I'm taking care of Sas too."

"Thanks for watching him, Kyle. You're such a sweetheart."

Chris's began rubbing his forehead with his right hand.

"God, my head is pounding."

Decker held Chris' hand. In the brief silence, Decker's thoughts turned to what he should be doing besides standing there feeling useless.

"You know how much I rely on that iPad," Chris said. "I keep all my important information in there. It isn't just work stuff, I won't even know when to go to the dentist or change the oil in my car without my calendar. I hope you can get it back for me somehow."

"When I get my hands on the guy who rammed his truck into you, he's going to pay, big time. We'll also find whoever took your things. When I catch him, the iPad will be the least of his problems."

"You don't think the truck driver took my bag?"

"I think the thief probably came along after the truck left. Why would the truck driver take time to steal your things instead of leaving right away?"

Chris shook his head.

"There was no traffic out there. How could someone not see that butt-ugly white car sitting on the side of the road?"

"It doesn't make sense."

"You know, I kind of remember the passenger door opening before the paramedics got there."

"That was probably the guy who called 911," Decker said. "He was just a good Samaritan. He didn't steal your things."

"I'd like to thank him when I can."

"We hope maybe who ever took your stuff will try to hock it. We're checking the pawn shops."

Decker leaned over the bed rail and nuzzled Chris' hair. He kissed his bruised cheek, then kissed him lightly on the mouth.

"I don't want to frighten you but, until we know more about what happened, there'll be a patrol officer outside your door. We also have a unit checking on your apartment in case someone tries to use your keys. Luedecke talked to your apartment manager about changing the lock."

Decker pulled a small canister out of his pocket and showed it to Chris.

"This is pepper spray. If someone gets past the guard, spray it toward his face and make as much noise as possible. Try not to get it in your own face. It burns like hell."

"I'm sure I'll be fine."

"Keep this stuff handy, anyway. Just in case."

Decker tucked the pepper spray next to the cast. When he looked up, there was a sparkle in Chris' blue eyes that pain and bruises couldn't obscure.

"I really love you, Kyle Decker. I think I want to move in with you when I get out of here."

"I'd like that very much. My place has plenty of room. There's even a porch swing."

# CHAPTER FOURTEEN

**W**hen Decker came out of the hospital, Zepeda was waiting by the entrance in his silver police car. Decker climbed in and turned to Zepeda.

"Well, what did that turd Nelson have to say for himself?"

"He started out threatening to file assault charges on you for dragging his sorry ass out of his van this morning." Zepeda grinned. "After I explained that we needed to establish where he was this morning, he decided to let that drop."

"What did he have to say for himself? Where was he?"

"In bed with his ugly wife. She verified that he was right there with her until the City Manager called."

"Did you believe her?"

"Absolutely. They verified it."

Zepeda made a face like he'd smelled bad leftovers.

"They're into making home movies. Trust me, you don't want to hear the details."

Zepeda started the car and eased down the driveway. Decker was deep in thought as they turned toward downtown. After a couple of blocks, Zepeda broke the silence.

"How's Chris?"

"Much better. They're keeping him overnight to monitor the swelling."

Zepeda patted Decker on the shoulder.

"That's good news, my friend. Now, let's get down to some serious police work. I think we should go out by the airport and see where this all happened. I need to put things into perspective."

Decker nodded.

Ten minutes later they rounded the curve on Old Bridge Road next to Tract C. As Tract B came into view, Decker whistled.

"Shit, Ernie, I can see why Chris was so pissed-off. They scraped this lot right back to the bare soil."

Zepeda pulled over to the side of the road and turned on the emergency lights and directional amber light bar in the rear window. They walked up to the scene of the crash.

"No skid marks on the road. Either the driver didn't see the City car or swerved into it at the last minute." Zepeda made notes in his pocket notebook as he spoke.

"It must have been a swerve. Otherwise he would have hit the front of the city car, not behind the front left quarter panel at the door."

Zepeda pointed to the spray-painted orange lines on pavement and soft dirt on the roadside.

"Here are the four tire marks from the car. The impact moved the car diagonally a couple of feet from where it was parked."

Pushing pieces of debris around with the toe of his boot, Decker said, "We've got three types of glass: headlamp glass, turn signal glass from the truck, and window glass from the car. Looks like the rest of this stuff is from the paramedics and the extrication work the fire department did."

Zepeda wrote down everything Decker said, a practice they had adopted when they first began to work together. When Zepeda caught up, he looked around the road area.

"The truck driver must have seen that car parked here. The weather was clear. There wasn't any traffic. Unless he fell asleep or was drunk, he had to see that white car sitting here."

Zepeda studied Decker's reaction.

"Or ... it was intentional," Decker said.

They looked out across the barren property. Three sets of footprints led away in the dirt, two left by medium-sized men, and one by a larger man with a tendency to shuffle.

"Ernie, are you thinking what I'm thinking? If there were only two of them, why's there a third set of prints?"

"I saw on the noon news that the Channel 5 news crew was here earlier. Charlie Hawkins was out here looking around. He was in the background of their video. Hawkins must have walked over to that warehouse and then back across the property to his car."

Zepeda brushed the dust off his shiny black shoes with his handkerchief.

Decker picked up a piece of broken headlamp from the roadway and tossed it into the dusty lot.

"Nothing else to do here," he said. "Let's go to the impound lot and see what the City car looks like."

They headed east and turned right just before the old river bridge. The narrow road meandered along the west bank of the DeLeon River back into the downtown area, passing the abandoned brick buildings of the old meat packing plant.

Stories were told of times before the lake was built when the DeLeon River took on a red sheen downstream from Asher slaughterhouses. The railroad brought cattle up from the Texas coast and took fresh meat north to Austin, Waco, and Dallas. Fort Worth, of course, had its own famous stockyards. The Asher packing plant and tannery shut down in the late forties after the war economy cooled and before the fifties boomed.

The city impound lot was just across the river from downtown. The East Side, as it was called, was the wrong side of town. Decades before Asher annexed territory east of the river, the area just across the bridge had grown into a strip of taverns for the meat packers and tannery workers. It had been a rough place, festering with vices prohibited inside the city limits. The East Side was preached about from some Asher pulpit every Sunday morning for eighty years until a brave City Council annexed the whole nine yards and City police began enforcing vice laws across the river.

As the undeveloped land along the highway became more viable for development, car dealers, mobile home sales lots, and discount furniture stores flourished. The local Chevrolet dealer stored impounded and wrecked cars for the police in the back of his used car lot on the East Side. Since the dealer's wrecker service had an exclusive contract with the city, someone was always on duty.

Zepeda parked near the locked gate and he and Decker walked into the office of the paint and body shop. They got the gate key from an attendant and easily found the demolished city car. It looked like it had struck a telephone pole in front of the driver's door. That's where the car was crushed. The steering wheel and shattered windshield had been thrown in the back seat when the car was towed from the scene.

While Zepeda was studying the red paint on the crumpled white car, Decker searched under the seat for Chris' things. Decker was careful to avoid the blood but, when he looked under the seat, the smell from the driver's side got to him. Decker threw up in the weeds by a chain link fence.

Zepeda looked up into Decker's pallid face.

"Kyle, why don't we go get Chris' car and take it over to your house."

"Sounds good to me," Decker said. "I want to check on Chris again."

"I'll drop you off at the hospital later. Then I'll go by two of the pawn shops but you have to go over to Reliable. I can't stand the old queen that owns the place."

# CHAPTER FIFTEEN

Zepeda went to talk with two of Asher's three pawn-brokers, an unremarkable pair of entrepreneurs. One was nothing more than a loan shark with a few dusty guitars in the window. The other, Pete's Pawn-A-Rama, was a junk dealer who also made loans on jewelry and guns. Neither of them had seen the City's camera or Chris Jensson's things. It was nearly four in the afternoon when Decker stopped at the third pawn shop.

It was in a small strip center on the state highway near its intersection with I-45W. A new blue awning with Reliable Pawn in large white letters was visible from the Interstate exit ramp. Unlike Pete's, where the windows were painted over with red and yellow signs, the windows at Reliable Pawn were hung with merchandise and tasteful banners declaring sales on everything from shotguns to kitchen appliances. The owner, Robert Flynn, also had a back room where he sold gay fetish videos, leather gear, BDSM toys, and a variety of specialty erotic wear.

Known as *Fleur* in his youth, Rob was one of the flashier drag queens in Austin and New Orleans. He also had a reputation for being an insatiable submissive, the centerpiece of countless group events.

He was able to operate a successful pawn shop only because his leather play buddies protected him. Nobody who robbed Rob had ever lived to spend the money. And, as flamboyant as he was, no one ever harassed him. Gay men could tease him but only if they smiled first.

"Kyle Decker!" Rob hollered. "Come on in here, gorgeous. God, don't you look hot in those tight jeans? Just what can I do for you on this fine afternoon?"

Decker smiled.

"Just keep your panties on, Rob. I'm in sort of a hurry right now."

"Oh, you'd be surprised how fast this big girl can move for a stud like you. I remember watching you skinny dipping with the boys over at that pool party two summers ago. Very impressive package."

"We were just having a good time."

"So was I, honey, and I don't even swim. Why don't we step into the back room for a few minutes and let me fit you with a new thong or something?"

"Thanks for the offer, Rob, but I really need to find a camera right quick."

"Well, absolutely. They're right over here. We can take a camera in back and try it out in private."

Decker bent down to look through the case where pawned cameras were piled three deep. There were several Canons, including one with a dented viewfinder.

Rob moved a couple of cardboard boxes of country music CDs from the glass counter top.

"We don't sell many cameras, but this shit goes like hot cakes."

"I just need to look at that Canon right there. The one on top. Did someone bring that one in today?"

"Oh, I get it. You're here on an insurance investigation, aren't you?" Rob bent down to get the camera out of the showcase. "As a matter of fact, this one was pawned an hour ago."

He handed the camera to Decker like it smelled bad.

Decker held it up to the light and turned it over so he could see the bottom. The City inventory number had been scratched off, leaving fresh silver hatch marks on the camera body.

"What're you looking at the bottom for? You know I don't take stolen goods in here."

"Well, you did this time. This camera belongs to the City of Asher."

Rob grew more serious and put on his little red-framed half glasses to look at the camera in Decker's hands.

"You sure? I didn't see any ID numbers on it."

Decker pointed to the dented view finder.

"See this eye piece? It was damaged at last year's Christmas party. People will testify to that."

Rob looked disgusted, standing with his hands on his hips.

Decker said, "There's also a missing iPad and iPhone. They were in a leather bag. Do you have those too?"

"No, she just brought in the camera."

"Who brought in the camera, Rob? I need a name."

"It was that little slut, Tanya Crutchfield. She's always pawning radios and other worthless shit in here. Since the camera was scratched, I only gave her thirty bucks for it. I don't know if it even works."

Then he made a pudgy fist and shook it in the air. His heavy gold bracelets rattled.

"I'm going to pinch her tits off. Bringing me a hot camera!"

"Save the false indignation, Rob, and tell me where can I find this Tanya Crutchfield."

"Oh," he said with a sigh, "she works at the Highway Inn on the service road. She's a scrawny little bitch with dirty brown hair. Wears a cheap maid's uniform. Has a couple of those rings pierced in her eyebrow. Thinks she's hot shit."

"I'm taking the camera with me, Rob."

"Whoa, big fella, you're not a cop anymore. You have to pay me $30 for it."

"It's up to you but I'll have to call Detective Zepeda for authorization first. We're working together on the case. He'll be right over with a warrant and some uniforms to go through everything in the store looking for more stolen items."

"For thirty bucks? Fuck that shit."

Decker was walking toward the door with the camera in hand when he stopped.

"This Tanya Crutchfield, did she mention where she got the camera?"

"You know, she came in here with some song and dance about her boyfriend's this or that. She probably took it from some john."

**James Gaston**

As Decker opened the door to leave, Rob shouted, "You tell that cunt she owes me thirty bucks and the interest starts now."

# CHAPTER SIXTEEN

The large man shifted his weight nervously in the seat and stared out the windshield. He was maybe six foot three, two hundred and fifty pounds, wearing an expensive western shirt and brown slacks. His sharp-pointed lizard cowboy boots were scuffed and worn. Acne had left deep scars on his face. He had short, graying hair that was thinning on top. His menacing pale blue eyes scanned the road. A heavy gold ring scraped the steering wheel whenever he moved his thick right hand.

He held a cell phone in his left hand, waiting for it to ring. He shifted in the seat and nervously tapped his ring on the steering wheel. When the call came through, a loud voice with a Texas accent growled in his ear.

"What the fuck were you thinking?"

"The stupid shit was going to turn himself in, Mr. Lucas," the big man said quietly, "We'd all be in jail if I hadn't stopped him right then."

Lucas hissed through his teeth.

"That's bullshit!" Lucas said. "You should have let me handle it. We could have flown him out over the Gulf and gotten rid of the body. No questions asked."

"Our problem died with him. Only three people know what really happened, counting you."

"Aren't you forgetting that one of those fucking city bureaucrats didn't die. You don't know what he saw. Do you?"

The big man shifted in the seat again.

"He wasn't even looking. He didn't know what hit him. Besides, his head was split open. He was out of it."

"You better hope he didn't see you. You're staking your fucking life on it."

There was a pause filled with tension.

Then Lucas asked, "Does anyone else know about the shipments?"

"No sir, the driver and the two boys burying the load don't even know what it is. Just barrels. We couldn't empty the warehouse yesterday because the cops and news people were around. The boys cleaned it out tonight."

Lucas said nothing. The big man looked at his gaudy Rolex.

"By now there's no trace of anything in the warehouse, Mr. Lucas."

"I'm suspending our Asher operation until further notice. We're going to store the shipments further north for a while. We'll use the Mexia location."

The large man was visibly relieved.

"Yes, sir. I understand."

"I'll see you at the zoning hearing," Lucas said. "We've got to get a building permit this month and be operational in sixty days."

"I told you, I'm taking care of it," the large man said confidently. "The property's been cleared off. Besides, I made sure that the council vote's already wired."

"I've heard that shit before. Make it happen this time."

Lucas disconnected the call and speed-dialed another number. It went to voice mail. He pushed another button to enter his return number, then set the cell phone on the dash of his Mercedes. By the time he had changed the CD, the phone rang quietly.

"Who's calling?"

"It's me, Mr. Lucas. I'm in Harker Heights," the caller said. "I'm hauling a couple of cars into Houston from Waco tomorrow afternoon. I'll be staying in a motel on I-10, near the terminal."

"Can you pick up a truck load Monday morning?"

"Yes, sir," came the reply, "I'll be all fueled and ready."

"Good, be at the terminal at seven and pick up the load. Haul it up to the Mexia. You've been there before. Then return the empty trailer to Houston Monday afternoon."

"When do you want me to pick up that empty trailer we left in Asher?"

"Just leave it there for now. We're going to use the Mexia warehouse for a while."

"Yes, sir. Got it."

"Be careful. The police will be looking for your truck."

"A buddy of mine is replacing the fender and lights tonight. The paint won't quite match but it'll be street legal again."

"Good thinking."

"I swear to God, Mr. Lucas, it really wasn't my fault. This big guy was in the truck with me, said he worked for you. Your guy jerked the wheel right when I was passing the car."

"What do you mean *my* guy?"

"Well, that big guy, the one who wrecked my truck. He ..."

"Wait," Lucas interrupted the truck driver. "We shouldn't discuss it on the cell phone. "

"I feel really bad about the two men in the car."

"That's enough! When you get to the terminal Monday morning, there will be a nice cash bonus to cover your repairs and reward you for being loyal."

"Thanks, Mr. Lucas. I'd never be disloyal, sir. Even when Ted Smith wanted me to go to the cops with him, I said I wouldn't do it."

"Good for you. I know you and Smith go back a long way. No telling what can happen to a guy who's disloyal. Shit happens. You know what I mean?"

"I'm not sure."

"Staying loyal to me is the best way to stay healthy."

"Yes, sir. I get your meaning."

"Good. You just drive your loads and let me take care of everything else. I'll call you Monday night."

Lucas dropped his cell phone on the seat and turned up the car stereo. He was almost home, his sprawling house and stables on two hundred quiet acres of southeast Texas countryside.

About the time Lucas poured a drink for himself and stretched out on his ten-foot leather sectional to watch the preseason football scores, the big man Lucas had talked to first had turned into the industrial park in Asher.

His large pickup roared down an old gravel road to the back end of the old airport property. The dual rear wheels scattered gravel and briefly sent a plume of dust into the clear night air as he came to a sudden stop.

The headlights of the pickup went black and the big diesel sat there rumbling in the dark. After a couple of minutes, the headlights flashed twice and went dark again. Two hundred yards away, near the edge of the taxiway, a flashlight signaled once from the blackness. The truck lurched forward with the headlights dark and sped across the concrete runway.

As he approached the far side of the taxiway, the large man could make out the shape of a flatbed truck parked with a ramp extended to the ground. He pulled up next to the flatbed and turned off his motor.

The only sound remaining was two men arguing in the darkness fifty feet away. The large man walked around the flatbed and lit a cigarette. The voices went silent and two young men, Rusty and Lee, quickly approached the truck.

"I thought you said you'd help us bury this shit," Rusty complained. "I had other plans tonight."

"Yeah," Lee said, "those goddamned barrels are heavy and we need a backhoe to fill that bunker. Fuck this hand shoveling bullshit."

The large man moved quickly for his size. The force of his backhand caught Lee full in the face and knocked him off his feet. He bounced off the truck tire on his way down.

Rusty stepped back out of reach, making sure he had room to move if the large man turned toward him.

The large man growled at Rusty.

"Put the dollies and ramp back on the truck," he said. "Then drive it to the shop, with the lights off, and you can go on to your date.

He nudged Lee with his boot.

"You and I will finish up here with the shovels."

The large man stomped away, leaving Rusty to help Lee to his feet again. Within five minutes, Rusty was gone with the flatbed. Lee was shoveling dirt into the entrance of an old underground ammo bunker. The large man stood by smoking, watching as Lee wheezed and grunted in the dark.

An hour deeper into the cooling night, Lee stabbed his shovel into the loose dirt and sprawled on the damp ground.

"I've got to stop for a few minutes. My jaw is killing me."

"You pussy. You're lucky I didn't hurt you worse."

The large man took Lee's place by the hole and dirt flew at twice the previous rate. He worked silently except for the steady rhythm as the shovel bit into soil and it slid off into the hole. Ten minutes passed before Lee picked up the other shovel. Finally, they smoothed the surface and closed the metal hatch.

"When I saw these old bunkers," Lee said, "I had no idea we'd have to fill them up by hand in the middle of the fucking night."

"Piss and moan," the big man said, "that's all you boys do. I swear to God. I raised you kids, put a roof over your heads, and all I hear is pissing and moaning."

They put the shovels into the bed of the black pickup.

"What's this all about anyway?" Lee asked. "Why do we have to bury these barrels at night and be so quiet about it?"

"The less you know, the better. Don't ask any more stupid questions."

"Yes, sir," Lee said, looking at his watch. "Would you tell Mom I'll be really late getting home? I got a date too."

# CHAPTER SEVENTEEN

"Ernesto, Ernesto, wake up sweetheart," Maria said softly. "There is a phone call for you."

Zepeda grumbled.

"It's Sunday morning. I have to sleep."

Maria handed him the cell phone and left the room. After sixteen years of marriage to a cop, she understood that his calls required privacy. Zepeda propped up against the headboard and put the phone to his ear.

Without any greeting, he said, "I'm not taking any calls until after lunch."

When the caller replied, Zepeda sat upright and opened his eyes, wide.

"Sorry, Chief, I didn't know it was you. Yes, sir, I'm listening."

Zepeda ran his hand through his hair and stood up by the bed.

Police Chief Jack Dixon continued, "We've got a dead body at a farmhouse on 2410. Our patrol unit is on the scene. Looks like a homicide so I want you out there right away."

"Yes, sir. Any identification?"

"It's Ted Smith, the real estate agent. Smith has a lot of influence with the city council. Roberts will have his tail in a ringer over this."

"The other City staff won't miss him."

"He's made a lot of enemies," Dixon said. "By the way, Ernie, how is Decker's boyfriend doing?"

"Sounds like he'll be okay."

"Carol Bailey called me yesterday. Decker's still on retainer for the city's insurance carrier. There will be a big claim because of the fatality. Give Decker anything he needs but stick close. He's too personally involved."

"Maybe I should take him out to the scene with me this morning, keep him busy."

"Good idea. This case might encourage him to come back on the job. Decker's a damned good detective. Do this by the book, Ernie, and watch the chain of custody on the evidence since Decker's a civilian."

"Right, Chief. I'll call you as soon as we determine what's going on out there."

Zepeda called to tell Decker about the homicide and his orders from the chief. They had to secure the murder scene and examine Ted Smith's body.

"So what? The Chief called you directly. I'm really fucking impressed."

"Come on, Kyle, Dixon wants us to investigate a high-profile murder together. It's going to be a big case."

"Why does he want me involved? We have our hands full with the hit-and-run manslaughter already."

"Think about it. A City employee killed yesterday and a prominent businessman found dead today. This is a bad weekend to be Police Chief. He knows we're his best team."

"Look, Ernie, I'll help you out but I'm not on Dixon's team anymore."

"I know, you're batting for the other team ... or maybe you're the catcher."

"Very clever."

"Little play on words. Thought you'd like that."

"I'm over at the hospital. Pick me up out in front. I'll watch for your car."

A few minutes later Zepeda was dressed in his gray suit. He swallowed some juice, kissed his kids and Maria good-bye, and went to work.

Decker was quiet while he and Zepeda drove across town with a fresh morning breeze blowing through the car windows.

Finally, Zepeda asked, "How's Chris this morning?"

"Kind of depressed about Todd. Chris blames himself for Todd being out there."

"He might need some counseling later. What about the head injury?"

"Doing better. He's in a lot of pain but the MRI and brain scan were okay. They're probably going to release him tomorrow."

"That's a relief. Did he remember anything else about the truck or the stuff taken from the car?"

"Not really. He was putting something in his bag when it happened. He remembers a lot of noise and he's still convinced that he saw a silver angel hovering above the steering wheel."

Zepeda looked at Decker while they waited at a red light.

"People imagine all kinds of shit during physical trauma, life flashing before your eyes, everything shifting into slow motion or time standing still, going toward a bright light."

"Chris thinks maybe it was his guardian angel."

"Who's to say? It could have been a lot worse."

Decker looked out the side window and was quiet again for a couple of minutes.

"That stupid Lori Latimer went up to the hospital room yesterday. The guard kept her from getting to Chris," Decker said.

"What a complete idiot. I hope the media doesn't hear about this murder until the scene is secured."

"You know about how long that'll last. The news vans will probably meet us there. Who found the body?"

"One of our patrol units. They were out that way in their district and drove by because of them is looking for a house. They're sitting on things until we get there."

"Man, I hate being around dead people," Decker said.

"Me too. I saw way too many homicides working the west side of San Antonio for six years. Some nights we'd respond to two or three bodies when the gangs were going at it. You almost get used to it."

"I hope I never get used to it."

# CHAPTER EIGHTEEN

The farm on FM 2410 had been vacant for quite a while. The weeds were tall around the small brick house and out buildings. Zepeda parked in the gravel driveway next to an Asher patrol car. There were two officers at the scene, one sat in the cruiser looking pale and the other one got out to brief Zepeda and Decker.

"We were real careful not to disturb anything except his wallet, Detective," the officer said, handing the billfold to Zepeda. "We called in on my cell phone. Didn't want a bunch of TV cameras up our ass."

"Looks like you built a little tent over him or something," Zepeda said. "What the hell is that for?"

The officer looked at his shoes, shaking his head, and put his hands on his hips.

"We threw a blanket over him," the officer said. "You know, to keep the flies off until you got here. He's already stinking bad. Besides, we just couldn't stand to look at it any more."

Then the officer pointed toward the body without looking up at it.

"This thing is really sick. That's not a tent pole, Detective, it's the murder weapon."

Decker pulled on new latex gloves as they walked over to the body. He lifted one side of the blanket.

"Mary, Mother of Jesus." Zepeda crossed himself, instinctively. "What will they think of next?"

Ted Smith was laying face down, spread eagle, his arms and legs outstretched. Someone had impaled him with a Ted Smith Real Estate yard sign. The bright red sign was sticking up out of his back. He looked like an insect in a high school bug collection, mounted on a straight pin, complete with an accurate specimen label.

Decker turned to the officer, "Did you guys touch the sign?"

The officer shook his head, unable to speak.

Zepeda looked at him empathetically.

"Why don't you go back to the car and wait for the crime scene van?" he said. "Don't let anyone else come around here."

The patrolman took the blanket and walked back to his car, careful not to look back at the body. After putting the blanket and his gloves in a plastic trash bag in the trunk, he conferred with the other officer. They both walked out toward the road to control access to the property.

Decker began his narrative as Zepeda took notes.

"The body's been here overnight. Some animal has chewed on the right hand in a couple of places."

Flies were soon swarming around the body, bothering Zepeda while he made notes.

"Smith is wearing tan slacks and a green sport coat over a white knit shirt. Looks like he belongs at the county club bar. A fancy watch and two gold rings with diamonds are still on the body."

Zepeda opened the wallet the officer had given him.

"Wallet still contains ninety-two dollars and several credit cards. This was no robbery."

Zepeda looked carefully at the real estate sign.

"Kyle, there was no way to hold this thing and stick it that far into the body without leaving fingerprints on the top of the sign unless you're wearing gloves."

Decker moved around to get the angle right for reflection.

"I see some prints along the edges of the metal surface. There's soil on the crossbar where the killer's foot pushed down on the sign and soil on the back of Smith's blazer near the wound. There's some blood staining on the jacket around the wound."

Zepeda pointed his pen at Smith.

"His shoes aren't scuffed like he'd struggled or like the body was moved," Zepeda said. "No drag marks on the ground."

Decker squatted down beside the body, brushing flies from his own face. "Smith's hands are partly open, nothing in them. His nails are clean. He didn't struggle with the killer and he didn't dig them into the soil when he was stabbed in the back. He must have been unconscious already."

Decker was checking for scalp wounds when a man walked up, blocking his light. Decker turned to see a man in his early sixties, medium height, with a pronounced potbelly. He wore expensive western boots, a dark suit, a silk tie with a Sheriff's badge tiepin, and a Stetson.

"Hey, Zepeda. I understand you got a murder here."

Zepeda shook hands with the DeLeon County Sheriff, Bob McAdams.

"No shit, unless he fell backwards onto this sign and then rolled over facedown."

"What are you doing here, Decker? I thought you were a private investigator now."

"Chief Dixon asked me to consult on this one. Why are you here, Sheriff?"

"One of our units saw your cars. Thought I'd check it out, see if you boys needed any help."

"We got it handled," Zepeda replied. "Watch where you step there, Sheriff."

Adams stepped back a little.

"Who is this poor bastard?" he asked.

Zepeda said, "Name's Smith. He's a local real estate agent handling this little farm."

"Really? I met him once at some damned meeting or other. Looks like somebody killed him last night."

McAdams rubbed his chin authoritatively and said, "Probably a drug deal gone south. These sadistic bastards just like to kill people. If they took his car, we need to get the make and model on the air."

"As far as we know, this has nothing to do with drugs or auto theft," Zepeda said. "If you don't mind, Sheriff, we have a lot of work to do here and this body's getting really ripe."

"I'll just get on out of your way now," McAdams said.

The Sheriff strode away, displaying the practiced confident walk expected of men of power and position. Then he stopped and made a call on his cell phone.

"Shit. He's calling the TV people, Ernie."

"You can count on that. It's an election year. There's nothing more dangerous than getting between the Sheriff and a news camera."

Zepeda motioned to the patrolman in the car. He estimated that they had about ten minutes before the murder scene became a three-ring circus.

When the officer approached, Zepeda said, "Radio the dispatcher and tell them we need Chief Dixon out here right away. The Sheriff's probably called the media. Park your car blocking the driveway. In fact, get the tape out and block off the whole area from beyond the barn over there, to the house, and out along the road. Don't let anyone but our people inside the crime scene until the Chief gets here."

As the officer trotted away, Decker returned to his investigation of the body.

"Smith's pants pockets contain the usual loose change, breath mints, a hanky. The sports coat has a small cell phone, some of Smith's business cards, and a leather case containing keys to a Cadillac, a Suburban, an office, and probably a house."

"If they stole his car, Sheriff McAsshole," Zepeda said quietly, "they forgot to steal the key first."

He placed Smith's business cards and the keys in an evidence bag and dropped them into his own coat pocket. Decker held Smith's cell phone and hit redial and showed it to Zepeda. Zepeda noted the phone number of Smith's last call and Decker dropped the phone into another evidence bag.

By the time Zepeda and Decker finished examining the body and the real estate sign, activity was increasing out at the roadside. Fortunately, two more Asher PD units had arrived with the crime scene van.

Zepeda briefed Lieutenant Gene Stratton, head of the crime scene unit, and made sure he started getting prints from the real estate sign first. Decker directed two officers to start searching the area between the house and the barn.

Chief Dixon arrived in a suit and tie straight from church and pulled his car in next to the patrol unit. He spoke with the patrol officers while Zepeda walked over to greet him.

Chief Dixon said. "What have we got out here?"

"I've never seen anything quite like this, Chief," Zepeda said.

Zepeda led the Chief over to Smith's body.

"Holy shit," Dixon said. "What a way to go. Did you confirm the identification, Ernie?"

"Yes, sir. The body matches his driver's license photo."

The Chief squatted down and looked at Smith's face.

"That's Smith, all right. I met him at a Chamber of Commerce banquet last spring," Dixon said. "Did you see any wounds besides the stab wound in his back?"

"I didn't find any. We don't think he was conscious when they jabbed the sign in him. He didn't curl up or scratch any soil under his nails. This isn't as simple as it looks, Chief."

The patrol officers at the driveway began arguing with the first news crew to show up. They were waving their arms and pointing toward the body.

"I better get over there before Mc-Adams," Dixon said. "No telling what he'll say to the media."

Zepeda could see other vehicles coming down the road including two television trucks. A helicopter was approaching from the north.

"Hurry up," Decker shouted to the officers scouring the area. "We're about to be overrun with idiots. Make sure you don't overlook anything laying around."

The teams were looking into clumps of weeds and around out buildings when the news chopper came in low for video.

"Somebody call Channel Five and tell them to get that damned helicopter away from here," Zepeda yelled.

The rotor wash was beginning to swirl dust into everyone's eyes. Zepeda and Decker took refuge in the barn. It was stuffy and smelled like cow manure, but at least they could see in there. The barn was empty except for some moldy hay and a few worn out yard tools. As Zepeda stood there thinking about the bizarre scene outside, he realized that there was something peculiar about the odor he was inhaling. It was more than the fetidness of hay and animals. It only took him a minute to pinpoint the odor.

"This barn smells like diesel fumes," Zepeda said.

"Yeah, the owner probably worked on tractors or something in here."

Decker was looking around the barn. In the center of the barn, near the large sliding door, he could clearly make out wide tire tracks.

"We got some fresh tire tracks embedded in the hay over here. Must have been a large vehicle." He followed them to the center of the barn. "Here's a small puddle of oil." Decker checked it with his finger. "It's fresh. There's been a large diesel vehicle in the barn recently. We need Stratton to get some pictures of the tire tracks and an oil sample."

Zepeda worked away in his notepad. When the helicopter finally thumped off into the distance, Zepeda put away his notebook. He and Decker went back outside.

Chief Dixon walked back from the road where he and Sheriff McAdams had been telling the media that it was too soon to say anything.

"Zepeda, Decker, you help Stratton and his crew get this crime scene taken care of. Get this body out of here as soon as possible," he ordered. "By the way, McAdams over there has decided drug dealers stabbed Smith and stole his car, simple as that."

"Open and shut, Chief. That's the way the Sheriff likes them," Decker said. "Shit for brains."

Dixon nodded. "Well, I'm out of here," he said. "We're having a thing at the church this afternoon and I've got to be there. Good job, guys."

"See you later, Chief," Zepeda said.

The coroner's van pulled up near the body.

Stratton and the crime scene unit still had to finish up but they no longer needed Zepeda and Decker. Stratton logged the evidence bag with Smith's keys in it and gave it back to Zepeda.

As they were leaving, Sheriff McAdams followed Zepeda and Decker to their car. The news cameras tracked his movement.

"Hey, Zepeda," he said, "what in hell were you doing in that barn?"

"Just doing my job, Sheriff. Looking for evidence."

McAdams smiled.

"You guys let us know as soon as you have the information on Smith's car," McAdams said. "My deputies will help you look for it along with that truck from yesterday morning."

Zepeda started the car and turned around to enter the two-lane road. When Lori Latimer saw Decker and Zepeda leaving, she rushed to Zepeda's open window with her microphone and cameraman.

"Detective, can you describe the murder victim for our Action Five viewers? Who was killed?" she asked breathlessly.

"We're not releasing that until the family has been notified," Zepeda answered. "Sheriff McAdams over there may be able to provide more details."

The road cleared instantly as Latimer and the other reporters focused on Sheriff McAdams. Three video cameras zoomed-in on McAdams before he even realized what was happening. He was picking his nose.

Zepeda and Decker laughed out loud as they turned onto the road to town.

While they were waiting at a red light, Decker studied the business card he took from Smith's pocket. The address was in an aging retail area near downtown, close to the Chamber of Commerce building.

Zepeda dialed Chief Dixon and told him he needed a warrant for Smith's office and residence. The Chief called Zepeda back in five minutes to say they had warrants for the two premises and Smith's car, if they found it.

When he hung up, Decker said, "You know, Ernie, I think I'll let you drop me back at the hospital so I can get my vehicle. While you check out Smith's office, I'll see if I can find Tanya Crutchfield."

"That should make a good joke. A gay guy goes into a motel looking for a hooker ..."

# CHAPTER NINETEEN

Fifteen minutes later, Zepeda pulled up to the address on the card. Ted Smith's bright red sign dominated the one-story strip center. The only car in the lot was a shiny red, gold-trimmed, new Cadillac parked in front of Smith's agency. Zepeda parked and went to the real estate agency door. The lights were out and the office looked deserted. Zepeda tried the door. It was locked.

He decided to check out the car before the office. The detective looked in the car windows. Slipping Smith's keys out of the evidence bag in his pocket, Zepeda inserted the one with the Cadillac symbol into the front passenger door. It was the missing car, the one supposedly stolen by drug dealers. The door opened with the ease expected of a luxury car. New car smell greeted him at the door and soft leather seats invited him inside.

Zepeda searched around the front seat. He discovered two country music CDs and learned that Smith habitually tossed gum wrappers and empty beer cans under the seat. Multiple listing printouts littered the back floorboard, along with fast food wrappers and real estate flyers.

Zepeda closed the door with a soft thump and moved around to the back of the car. He unlocked the trunk carefully. When there was one homicide, sometimes another dead body turned up by coincidence. Anticipating the worst, Zepeda stepped back and raised the lid slowly with his fingertips. To his relief, the trunk contained only a pile of metal yard signs. A mental image of Smith's body skewered with an identical red sign flashed through Zepeda's thoughts. He shuddered and was about to close the lid when a dark green file folder caught his attention.

He retrieved the file and eased the trunk lid down until it closed automatically. The file was filled with maps and legal papers, most marked with the familiar City of Asher logo. On the folder tab was a neatly typed label just like the files in Chris Jensson's office. It said, *Petition to Rezone Tract B, Airport Industrial Expansion.*"

Zepeda locked the file folder inside his police car then unlocked the office door. Smith's small outer office was messier than his car. There were two red waiting chairs. The green carpeting was worn and dirty. The corner coffee table held a big red ashtray and was littered with brochures and advertising flyers. The wall behind the white laminated reception desk displayed a huge photo of Ted Smith in a red sport coat, smiling with contrived sincerity.

Zepeda looked into Smith's private office where the atmosphere shifted to garish executive decor. A massive oak desk littered with papers and mementos filled the center of the room facing the door. To Zepeda's left was a built-in electronic entertainment wall. The wall to his right held a well-stocked wet bar and a seven-foot blue leather sofa. It matched the two blue leather guest chairs and a tall executive desk chair. Photos, plaques, and trophy bass were scattered around the walls.

Zepeda didn't know exactly what he was looking for. He poked around the papers on Smith's desk. Most of it made little sense, contracts written in legalese and deeds written in metes and bounds. There was a bundle of several copies of the public hearing notice sent out by the City about Tract B when it went to the Planning Commission. The same notice was in the file folder he had found in Smith's trunk. Zepeda counted eight notices in the bundle, each addressed to a different owner but mailed to the same post office box. He put them in his coat pocket.

While Zepeda looked through the deceased man's mail, the front door opened and he heard someone enter. Zepeda walked back into the outer office.

"Oh, hi there, Ernie," Charlie Hawkins said. "I saw your car out front. I heard Smith was dead so I thought I'd see who's here."

"Well, Smith's not here, Charlie. You might try the morgue."

"That's his red Cadillac out front."

"I guess he got out to the crime scene some other way."

"I'm sure you are busy but I'm a little curious. Exactly what happened to him?"

"No comment. You'll have to leave now. I'm involved in an ongoing investigation here."

"I heard that he was killed by drug dealers somewhere out on FM 2410."

"Where did you hear that?"

"I was having some coffee over at the Commerce Street Cafe a few minutes ago when a couple of County deputies came in. I heard them talking about how Smith had been stabbed in the back with one of those damned real estate signs he puts out all over town. They also said drug dealers killed him and stole his car."

Zepeda did no reply.

"Don't you think that's strange since his car's here at his office."

"Look, Charlie," Zepeda said with an edge to his voice, "I don't need you in my way right now. Why don't you come by the station in the morning?"

Hawkins settled into one of the chairs and pulled a little digital recorder out of his pocket. He sat it on a side table, pointed at the glowing red light, and smiled at Zepeda.

"How was Ted Smith murdered, Detective Zepeda?"

Zepeda shook his head back and forth, staring at the recorder. Hawkins turned it off and returned it to his pocket.

"Ted Smith's body was found early this morning," Zepeda said. "He had apparently been dead for several hours. But, you can't print that until we notify the next of kin. I don't know if that's been done yet."

"You know, Detective, I think we might be able to help each other here."

"You need to leave now."

"Just hear me out a minute, Ernie." Hawkins stood up again. "I've been investigating Smith for a feature story. I know quite a bit about Ted Smith's background, which doesn't add up, by the way, and you know a lot about his death. I need details for the paper."

Although he was uncomfortable even speaking with a newspaper reporter, Zepeda could see the advantages of making a deal to hear Hawkins' research on Smith.

"Tell me what you know about Smith's background,then I'll decide what I can tell you about his murder. But let's go to my office."

Hawkins shook his head. "What I'm offering to share with you has to be handled carefully. I don't think the police station is the place to discuss information that I received from what we call undisclosed sources."

"All right, let's just talk right here."

"Sounds okay by me," Hawkins said, sitting down again. "I've been working on this piece about Ted Smith ever since he was appointed to the Asher Economic Development Commission. I thought it was odd that this guy came out of nowhere, set up shop, and immediately got himself put on every committee at the Chamber. He was moving into the elite circles of this little metropolis but nobody knew, or cared, much about who he was or where he came from."

"So what?"

"Last month, the City Council appointed Smith to the commission without any discussion at all, just out of the fucking blue. He took poor old Luther Johnson's spot after Luther got drunk and fell out of his boat into Richards Reservoir. Smith was a rising star but I just couldn't buy the whole thing. I figured there had to be someone powerful pulling strings for Smith so I started looking into who he was."

"So far, Charlie," Zepeda frowned, "you've told me nothing I couldn't read in your own newspaper."

"That's just the starting point, Ernie, don't be so impatient. This Ted Smith guy was not on the level."

"Ever met a real estate broker who was?"

"This Smith guy was a total fraud. First of all, he claimed to come from Mississippi, said he was in retail sales there before coming to Texas."

"I don't care about his resume," Zepeda said, "I want to know what he was doing that you thought was so suspicious."

"I'll get to that in a minute. He never went to school at Southern Miss and nobody ever heard of the guy in the towns he listed. He's actually from Tennessee. He got an associate degree in auto mechanics from a junior college before he joined the Army in 1991. He skipped out on a Memphis girl who happened to be growing more pregnant at the time. She swore Smith was the father."

"Good reason to lie about his back-ground. Get to the point, Charlie."

"Smith's career in the Army was less than distinguished. He was assigned to an outfit that repaired tanks and personnel carriers and heavy equipment like that. They sent him to Germany for four years, during which time he was investigated for black-marketing tools and parts. After Europe, he was stationed up at Fort Hood until he was discharged three years ago."

"How did you tap into his service record? That stuff is confidential."

Hawkins' only reply was a smile.

Zepeda made a mental note to revisit the question.

"If he came out of the Army three years ago, how did he become a successful real estate salesman so fast?"

"I wondered about that myself. When the Army canned him, Smith got a government retraining grant through the Private Industry Council to go to real estate school in Killeen." Hawkins looked around as if he might be overheard. "He also did some hauling for various companies around the state on a cash basis on weekends, you know auto transports, midnight towing services, dropping off vehicles at the docks in Houston. Much of this is unsubstantiated, of course."

"Let me get this right. While the feds paid for his retraining, Smith was hauling hot cars to Houston for export?"

"According to his landlord. I couldn't get any confirmation on that from anyone else."

"How did he end up in Asher?"

"He came here straight from Killeen. Somehow he managed to get a broker's license, which is better than the salesman license. It allows people to open their own agency. I haven't gotten access to his Real Estate Commission file in Austin yet, but I'm working on it. I bet he lied on the application."

"Maybe so," Zepeda said. "That explains how he started selling real estate in Asher."

"Actually, he started *buying* real estate in Asher. I can't find where he's sold much yet, just a couple of houses. Most of Smith's closings have been land out by the airport."

"Do you have a list of the property?"

"I got it from the tax office. Everything has Smith's local post office box as the address of record."

"How do you know it's Smith's post office box?"

"Because I hung around the post office a couple of days and he cleaned it out at the same time both days," Hawkins grinned. "We journalists know how to do leg work too, Detective."

"Tell me more about why Smith left the military."

"Well, best I can reconstruct things, Smith was the sergeant over a small unit that did towing and field repairs on tanks and vehicles at Fort Hood. During a National Guard field exercise, four of Smith's soldiers were out fixing a broken down tank. They didn't know it, but the MPs had been watching one of them. The MPs caught two soldiers sitting in the tank doing coke and busted all four of them. Smith was held partially responsible and the Army discharged him soon after that."

"How did you come by that confidential Army personnel information?"

"I told you. Sometimes I have to use unnamed sources. Now, how about if you tell me how he died."

"Look, Charlie, somebody killed Smith late yesterday. We have to wait on the autopsy but it looked like he was stabbed with one of his signs. Drug dealers didn't do it. They would have robbed him but he still had his jewelry and wallet. We don't know yet what he was doing out there or who he was with. That's all I have right now."

Hawkins struggled to get up out of the low chair. Zepeda waited until Hawkins had stood and straightened his coat.

"There is one more thing," Zepeda said. "What were you doing out on Old Bridge Road yesterday?"

"I was looking for information about the hit-and-run. There wasn't much to see."

"You didn't turn up anything unusual over at the warehouse?"

Zepeda studied Hawkins' closely, weigh-ing the truthfulness of his response. Hawkins looked him straight in the eyes, without a flinch or blink.

"Like I said, there wasn't much to see."

# CHAPTER TWENTY

Decker checked on Chris and then went by to feed the cat. It was nearly eleven when Decker drove to the access road to the Interstate and made a loop around to the Highway Inn. The motel was built according to the stock floor plan used for cheap motels. Registration was in the front and guest rooms line both sides opening onto the parking lots. A maid's cart was sitting outside one of the doors on the second floor balcony.

He took the stairs to the second floor at the back of the motel. Approaching the cart, Decker heard country music coming from the room, a nasal voice yowling something about a good man. Moving cautiously, he looked into the open motel room door.

A woman fitting Tanya Crutchfield's description was sitting with her feet propped up on the stripped bed, smoking and singing along with the radio. Decker's shadow at the doorway startled her. She jumped to her feet, spilling a soft drink on the cheap round table. She picked up the can and dropped her cigarette in it before tossing it in the waste basket.

"Be through in a minute," she yelled before she switched off the radio. She hurriedly wiped up the spill with a dirty sheet and started stretching clean sheets onto the bed.

Decker stood in the doorway until the maid gathered all the dirty sheets and towels. Pushing past Decker in the doorway, she put the dirty laundry in a laundry bag hanging from the cart. She grabbed a stack of clean towels and took them into the bathroom.

She came back through the room door.

"There you go. All done."

"You did a fine job."

She seemed embarrassed that she was caught singing along.

"Please don't turn me in. I was just taking a little break."

"Are you Tanya Crutchfield?"

"What the fuck is going on here?"

"I need to ask you some questions." Decker handed her a business card. "I'm working with the Asher Police Department on an investigation."

"I've got work to do."

"If you cooperate, I'll be out of here in a few minutes. If you don't, I'll report you for possession of stolen property."

"I don't know what you're talking about."

"I just want to find out where this camera came from."

The woman looked at Decker, first with confusion, then with confidence. She looked at the camera in Decker's hand and shook her head back and forth.

"Never seen it before. Now fuck off. "

Decker knew she had recognized it. He pulled his cell phone out of his pocket and held his finger over the speed dial.

"Guess I better call Detective Zepeda."

She glared at him and held up her hands.

"All right, all right." She stomped her foot. "Shit!"

"Is your name Tanya Crutchfield?"

"Yes, that's my goddamned name. Now put the phone away. I'll tell you about the fucking camera."

Decker pocketed his phone.

"Yesterday morning I came to work about eleven to clean rooms. About noon, this guy I knew checked in while I was getting coffee in the lobby. We met before once when he was staying here overnight."

Tanya dug a lighter and cigarette packet from her uniform pocket and lit one. She blew the smoke out of the corner of her mouth, away from Decker.

"Like I said, I knew this guy. He asked me to spend some time with him. He gave me the camera, as a gift."

"So then you pawned it?"

"Yeah, nothing wrong with that. I didn't want it so I thought I could get some cash for it."

"I don't suppose your john had a name."

She smiled at him and took a long drag on the cigarette.

"Well, what was the man driving? What did he look like?"

"Like I said, I was up in the lobby when he came in. Somebody in a red car dropped him off. Last time the guy was here, he drove a rig and parked out in the back lot."

"So, what did this guy look like?"

"Tall skinny guy, kind of homely, you know." She pointed at her head. "Not too bright."

"Any tattoos, birthmarks, that sort of thing?"

Tanya shook her head, then smiled.

"He's hung like a horse, in case you're interested."

Decker looked directly into Tanya's eyes. "I need a name on this guy, Tanya. Do you know how to get in touch with him?"

"Yeah, sure, he invited me to come by and meet the wife and kids."

"If you think of anything else that might help us locate this man, call me. You don't want me to come back here with Detective Zepeda."

"That's all I know. Now let me get back to work."

Decker stopped at the front desk on the way out. The clerk remembered the tall guy got out of a red Cadillac. The physical description matched what Tanya gave Decker, except the clerk didn't comment on the size of the man's genitals. The man registered as John Buck and paid cash in advance for one night. The clerk said a black pickup truck picked him up about six and the clerk didn't see him return.

When Decker pressed the clerk about Tanya spending time with the same man on a previous occasion, the clerk said the maids never have anything to do with the guests. He referred Decker to the housekeeping manager who, conveniently, didn't work Sundays. Decker left a business card so the housekeeping manager could call him on Monday, like that would happen.

# CHAPTER TWENTY-ONE

Decker met Zepeda at Tim's BBQ, DeLeon County's famous barbecue place, where they'd been cooking great briskets overnight, seven nights a week, for over forty years. The smell of mesquite smoke greeted them like an old friend.

"You know, Ernie, that aroma is sweet enough to convert a vegetarian."

They got in line to order at the counter and watched the church crowd file past the salad bar. Conversations nearby focused on Ted Smith's gruesome demise at the hands of a Mexican drug gang. Asher citizens were simultaneously shocked and thrilled over the weekend's happenings.

"No self-respecting Texan would fill up on lettuce when there's Czech sausage and great brisket to eat," Decker said.

"Barbecue ought to be named one of the basic food groups," Zepeda said. "How's Chris doing?"

"I only got to see him for a minute. They were taking him in for another brain scan. The neurologist is still concerned about the swelling."

"That doesn't sound good."

"I've got my fingers crossed that they don't have to operate. I could tell Chris is pretty worried too."

They carried their trays to a quiet table in the back and settled where they could see the diners and the front door.

"I found the hooker who pawned the camera," Decker said. "She gave me some information on a truck driver who spent the afternoon screwing her at the Highway Inn yesterday."

"Way to go, bubba. Let's go pick him up."

"That'll be difficult without a name, address, or license number. At least I have his description."

"Did the hooker have Chris's other stuff?"

"No, just the camera."

"Well, while you were consorting with a prostitute, I found Chris' Tract B file in Smith's car. There was also a stack of legal notices on Smith's desk about the zoning hearing."

"I'll take the file and notices over to the hospital after lunch and show them to Chris."

"Chief Dixon gave me a call. He wants me working on the Smith homicide as my top priority."

"I don't plan to back off on the hit-and-run just to look for some shit bag's killer."

"Don't worry, Kyle, we can handle both cases. Now, tell me more about your hooker."

"She's really not my type."

Decker retold the story, ending with the description of the man who was dropped off and picked up again by someone in a black pickup.

"This john must be the truck driver who hit Chris," Zepeda said. "If he was dropped off, maybe he was having his rig repaired. Not many places in Asher you can get that done."

After dripping more sauce on his brisket, Decker said, "I've been thinking, Ernie. What if these two murders are related? Maybe something to do with the property up for rezoning?"

"Why would anyone kill two people over a vacant piece of land?"

"Somebody might have big money riding on the council's zoning decision?"

Zepeda took a long sip of iced tea.

"I guess it's possible. People have been murdered over real estate before," he said. "Was Chris trying to prevent the zoning?"

"He was doing everything he could. He hoped the wildflowers could be listed as an endangered species and that would stop the development. I guess that's why Smith went ahead and scraped off the lot."

"There might be some connection since the City file was in Smith's possession."

Decker was quiet while he drank some iced tea. Zepeda knew Decker was mentally arranging and rearranging the evidence, sorting events into their logical sequence. He wanted to let Decker's mind work in silence, so he excused himself and went to wash the barbecue sauce off his hands. When Zepeda returned, the table had been cleared and the tea refilled.

"Ernie, someone removed the file from the City vehicle after the wreck. You found it in Smith's trunk. He must have been involved somehow."

Decker wiped the condensation from his tea glass. Then he nodded.

It was Zepeda's turn to think out loud.

"The truck driver gave the hooker the camera taken from the City car. The file from the City car ended up in Smith's Caddy. Maybe the truck driver gave it to him."

Zepeda made some notes.

"Maybe Smith knew who committed the vehicular homicide."

"And they knew the zoning file might be of interest to Smith," Decker said. "I don't know squat about zoning so I don't know why the stolen file would interest Smith or why he'd take a chance of being caught with it."

"There's something else too, that stack of public hearing notices I found on Smith's desk. The City mailed them all to Ted Smith's post office box but they were addressed to different people. Any idea what that would mean?"

"Beats the hell out of me, partner. I'll ask Chris."

Zepeda answered a call from Luedecke on his cell phone.

"Thanks, Tom," he said. "Tell Stratton I'll come in and review the forensics from the crime scene after I search Smith's apartment."

He took out his note pad again and jotted down a name and address. Then he looked up at Decker and smiled.

"Killeen PD just called us," he said. "They picked up a housewife trying to use Chris' credit card at a store up there. She claimed it was all a misunderstanding. She thought it was her husband's Credit card."

"She in the Killeen lockup?"

"No, she must have sounded convincing. Her pastor vouched for her so they cut her loose on personal recognizance. They haven't located the husband yet."

"Got a name and address on her?"

"Nanci Evans. She lives in Harker Heights."

"Let's drive up there after lunch."

"All hell's breaking loose on the Smith case. Dixon wants me to brief him at four this afternoon."

"Dammit, Ernie, when are we going to Harker Heights?" An edge crept into Decker's voice.

"The City Council's whipping up a shit storm about the Smith murder, Kyle. The City Manager's already riding the Chief's ass. We've got to figure out who killed Smith, and fast."

"Fucking politicians! What about Todd Watson? Did they just forget about a City employee who was murdered yesterday?"

There was a long, uncomfortable, silence.

"You could go to Harker Heights without me."

"You're right, Ernie. I could."

First, Decker wanted to see Chris again.

# CHAPTER TWENTY-TWO

Decker spoke briefly to the reserve officer guarding Chris. He told Decker that Carol Bailey had been by to visit earlier. Decker tapped on the door and opened it enough to look in.

Chris was alone, sitting up in bed reading a paperback. A broad smile lit up his face when Chris realized who was at the door.

"Hi there, big guy. I was hoping you'd come by soon."

Chris put his book down and held his arms up for a hug. The IV tube was gone, as were a couple of the bandages.

Decker wrapped his arms around Chris and nearly lifted him from the bed. Chris grimaced and his body stiffened.

"Sorry Chris, didn't mean to hurt you. I forgot about your sore ribs."

"I'm sore all over. The nurse said that's what happens when you're hit by a truck."

Decker kissed him gently on the mouth and both cheeks. The bruises on Chris' face were turning purple and expanding. He had a shiner under each eye.

"You certainly look colorful. How's your head doing?"

"A lot better than it looks. Dr. Murphy said the brain scan looked fine this morning. I can go home tomorrow."

Decker sat down on the bed and draped his arm across Chris' legs. Chris flinched.

"My right knee is sore too."

"Sorry. Where can I touch you that doesn't hurt, baby."

Chris smiled and put Decker's hand on his crotch.

"That feels really good."

"Mmmm." Decker snickered. "You have been missing me."

"Better stop, Kyle. Eloise might walk in and we do *not* want to piss that lady off."

"I have so much to tell you," Decker said. "I recovered the City camera at a pawn shop."

"Did you find my messenger bag and my iPad?"

"Not yet. Just the camera."

Then he described the series of events beginning with the pawn shop and camera.

"Also, early this morning," Decker said. "Ted Smith was found murdered at a farm out on 2410. Ernie and I went out there."

"I'm sorry the man's dead," Chris said, "but he was a real pain in the ass to City staff."

"Not any more."

Chris pointed at the evidence bag Decker had with him.

"What's that?"

Decker pulled out the file and bundle of notices and handed them to Chris.

"Ernie found your Tract B file in the trunk of Smith's Caddy. He found these on Smith's desk."

"Wait, I don't understand. How did Ted Smith get this? I had it in the car when we were hit."

"There must a connection between the wreck and Smith. Whoever took your things knew that Smith would be interested in the Tract B file. Why would Smith want this file?"

"I don't know, really. We let anyone view these files on request. Maybe Smith wanted to see the staff report or if there were any adjacent property owners objecting to the rezoning."

"Is that what those notices are about?" Decker asked.

Chris thumbed through the bundle of notices. Then he went back through the pile and studied the mailing labels.

"That's interesting," Chris said. "These notices were for the earlier hearing, last spring. They were sent to the owners of property around Tract B but they were all mailed to the same post office box. They would go to different addresses unless all of the adjacent property is owned by the same person or company."

"It was Ted Smith's post office box. What the hell does that mean, Chris?"

"Well, state law requires the City to mail a notice of the public hearing to the owners of all land within 200 feet of the property in question. We get the names and addresses from the DeLeon County Central Appraisal District."

"But these aren't made out to the same person or company."

"All I can figure is that Smith's real estate company had arranged to pay the taxes for all of these owners. The area across Old Bridge Road is an old undeveloped subdivision. The lots were sold back before the airbase was closed but the houses were never built. Tracts A, B, and C are owned by a Houston group headed by a lawyer named Nick Lucas."

Decker put the file and notices back in the evidence bag.

"If I understand this right," he said, "the other land owners never saw these notices because Smith received them all."

"Could be. Smith probably has contracts pending to purchase the adjacent properties and he paid their taxes as compensation."

"So, if the other property owners probably don't know about the hearing, won't they miss the opportunity to object to the rezoning."

"For all we know, they support Smith's plan. The rezoning could raise their property values."

"Smith won't be around to cash in on it."

"He was just the broker. Someone else was financing the deal and stands to make all the money."

"It strikes me that this zoning must be extremely important to someone."

"There's something rotten about all this or Nelson wouldn't have moved up the hearing and the developer wouldn't have cleared the property already. Those fuckers got Todd killed."

"Take it easy," Decker said, stroking Chris' hair. "Take it easy, baby. Don't get your blood pressure up."

"Shit, Kyle." Chris muttered. "Fucking greedy bastards."

Decker wrapped his arms around Chris again and held him quietly for a minute.

"I have some other news for you," Decker said. "Your credit card turned up in Killeen this morning. "

"Really? Did they catch the person using it?"

"Killeen PD picked her up. It was a woman from Harker Heights."

"My credit card was in my bag. She must have it too."

"I don't know yet. I'm driving up there this afternoon to find out."

"Please, be careful and watch your back. I couldn't stand it if anything happened to you."

"Piece of cake. I'm just going to question a housewife."

"Oh, I almost forgot to tell you that my Mom called. She's flying into Houston in the morning. She'll drive to Asher straight from the airport."

"That's great. I'm looking forward to meeting her. What have you told her about us?"

"Everything." Chris smiled. "Well, the censored version, anyway."

"Then she must know how much I love you."

"And how much I love you too, Kyle."

Decker leaned over and kissed Chris carefully on the mouth.

"I better be heading out," he said. "I'll be back really late tonight so I'll call you first thing in the morning. You get some rest."

"I'll be right here waiting for you."

# CHAPTER TWENTY-THREE

Decker headed to his own neighborhood but he pulled into Kenny Long's driveway. Long's head and shoulders were hidden under the hood of the old GTO. The lower half of a skinny human was still visible but his upper half was inside the jaws of the old black car. Country music filled the garage, punctuated with a wrench ratcheting.

"Way to go, you tough old bitch," Long shouted to the engine block, "take that big, thick bolt. Squeeze it tight."

Kenny grunted as his torso twisted with effort.

"Tighter, tighter, just the right torque. Oh yeah, baby, it feels *soooo* good."

Long was so absorbed in labor that he didn't notice Decker approaching.

Decker squealed in falsetto, "Oh Kenny, it's too big, your bolt's too thick for me. That bolt belongs in a Ford."

Decker drummed his hands on the fender. Long bumped his head as he backed out of the GTO's gaping mouth. He shook a torque wrench at Decker.

"You asshole. What the fuck are you doing sneaking around here this afternoon?"

Long wiped his hands on a red rag and shook hands with Decker.

"I need a cold beer. Figured you were good for one."

"Come on over here and sit down while I get a couple out of the fridge."

Like many Texas men, Kenny Long had a special beer refrigerator right in the garage and two lawn chairs within reaching distance of the fridge. Decker sat in one chair and Long plopped into the other as he handed over a cold bottle. They both tossed the caps in a fifty-gallon drum Long used for trash.

"You owe me a whole case of beer for talking to that greaser Zepeda." Long laughed. "Your old buddy Kenny stuck up for you."

"You know I'm really hard up when they have to call you for my alibi. I appreciate you helping out."

"They told me your new boyfriend was in that hit-and-run," Long said, growing uncharacteristically serious. "When you catch the fucker driving the truck, we'll cut his balls off with a rusty fishing knife."

Decker took a long drink from the cold bottle and shook off the condensation. Long opened a cabinet door and pulled out a bag of pretzel sticks. He rattled it at Decker.

"Had lunch yet, Deckerhead?"

"Shit, man, you've had that stale bag of pretzels for two years. They don't even sell that brand any more."

Long threw the bag back into the cabinet.

"Can't say I didn't offer."

They sat silently, listening to inane country radio and drinking beer out of the bottle.

Decker said, "Don't let this go to your head, jerk-off, but I need to ask you for a favor."

"I figured that out already or you wouldn't come sneaking into my garage. If you need lawyer money, you'll just have to go to jail. They'll just love your ass in the shower."

"I'm not going to jail. I'm going to Harker Heights."

Long studied the grease under his nails.

"Tough choice, jail or Harker Heights. I bet jail is safer and cleaner."

"I want you to go up there with me this afternoon. I may need a witness."

"You serious? What's going on?"

"Killeen PD picked up a woman for using Chris' credit card. The woman lives in Harker Heights. Zepeda is tied up on a homicide today. Some real estate agent got killed and Chief Dixon thinks that takes a higher priority."

"Whoa, back the truck up there, son. Explain what the hell you're talking about and why I should give a shit."

As Decker launched into the whole story of Chris, the wreck, the Asher police, the stolen items, and the Smith murder, Long retrieved more beer from the fridge and listened without much interruption.

"The credit card was in Chris' bag that was stolen from the City car after the wreck," Decker said. "I have to find out how the woman in Harker Heights got that credit card."

Two bottles later, Decker ran out of story and Long stood staring out into the yard. Decker remained in the lawn chair, sipping his beer and waiting for Long to say he'd ride with him to Harker Heights.

"Well, what the fuck," Long said. "I got nothing better to do. My wife's at her mother's so I'm off my leash tonight. When do we leave?"

"How about right now?"

"You better remember this next time I want you to go get parts with me." Long pointed his finger at Kyle. "You're crawling under there with the fucking fire ants next time."

"Harker Heights will be a step up after Houston."

"If you want me there to watch your back, seems like you're expecting trouble. You owe me too much barbecue and beer for me to let anything happen to you now."

# CHAPTER TWENTY-FOUR

"Shit, Kenny," Decker said, "I've been waiting half a damned hour. Are you finally ready to go?"

Long jumped into the front seat of Decker's maroon Expedition and slammed the door. He turned to Decker.

"Are you going to start this piece of shit Ford or not, Deckerhead? I'd like to be home before next week."

Their friendly argument continued, as usual, while Decker drove out to Interstate-45W and turned north. After half an hour, Decker cut off onto a state highway to head northwest over to meet I-35 at Salado. They crossed rolling fields in the center of Texas as the weather darkened, turning grayer and gustier by the hour. Decker had to pass more than one farmer carrying huge round hay bales down the road. The weatherman had forecast a weak cold front and it was blowing across Texas with typical fall suddenness.

As they approached the exit for Killeen and Fort Hood, they turned westward and descended through a deep highway cut. Beneath swirling gray clouds, the twenty-mile vista presented an odd topography of steep rounded hills rising from flat arid valleys. The freeway extended to the west, sweeping away in long parallel curves. North of the freeway, a railroad track angled off toward distant communities and Fort Hood.

Long turned on the GPS on the dash-board as Decker drove down toward the valley floor.

"Looks like Harker Heights is the first decent-sized place we'll come to. This freeway goes on through Killeen before it peters out at Fort Hood. I guess they built it just to get the US Army to Interstate 35."

Decker explained, "Military transportation was the justification for spending zillions of taxpayer dollars on interstate highways. Now we just subsidize highway contractors and the motor freight industry. Highways are major opportunity for congressional pork."

"Shit, Kyle," Long said, shaking his head, "You could intellectualize a hard-on. The highways are about the only thing Congress has done right. I'd like to see you try to get around Texas without interstate highways. You'd be shit out of luck"

"My point exactly," replied Decker. "There used to be trains and intercity bus lines everywhere. After WWI, General Motors bought most of the streetcar lines and bus lines and closed them all down. Everybody had to buy a car and the taxpayers built the highways."

Long moaned.

"I knew you'd get around to some conspiracy theory about it," Long said. "Public transportation just carries people into your neighborhood you don't want there."

"If you can't afford a car or you don't drive, you're just screwed," Decker said.

"Right. Welcome to Texas!" Long said. "If you can't drive yourself, then go fuck yourself."

Decker shook his head. After a few minutes he pointed out the window to his left.

"Look at all those new houses on the side of that hill."

"Yeah," Long said. "Look at all the mobile homes over on this side. Why would anyone build a big house in a hill overlooking a bunch of shitty trailer parks? Not hardly the view I'd want from my front window."

"Well, we're in Harker Heights," Decker asked. "Would you look up the address now? It's 1600 Delta Avenue."

Long typed the address into the GPS.

"It's not far. Just over on the north side of Veterans Memorial Highway. Take the next exit and cut across town."

A few blocks north, Decker stopped at a traffic light at Veterans Memorial Highway. Decker and Long were both astonished as they surveyed the scene up and down both sides of the highway.

"Jesus, look at all the titty bars!" Long shouted. "My opinion of this town has just improved."

"We found the commercial district and the red light district at the same time."

"Look at that sign! Nude mud wrestling. We gotta check that out."

"Only if they're naked guys doing the mud wrestling."

"You're messing up my wet dream here, Decker. Don't tell me you pansy-asses have a problem with strippers."

"Just the wrong gender for me," Decker said. "These women really know how to tease money out of horny straight guys. Twenty bucks for a five-minute lap dance and you can't even touch her tits. That's pathetic, Kenny."

"If you're through pissing in my soup, Decker-head, turn right up here. I think that's Delta Avenue."

"What a beautiful neighborhood."

"Only if you like old cars up on blocks and trailers with rusting paint. Slow down, I think this trailer park is 1600 Delta Avenue."

A hand-painted sign, black stenciled on white-washed plywood, read, *Delta Place Mobile Home Park, lots available.*

"I'm not surprised there are lots avail-able," Decker said. "This is a flood area and you can see the sewer plant right through there, between those trailers."

"I bet it's really fragrant around here on a winter morning," Long said, wrinkling his nose. "I'm kind of glad the wind is kicking up this afternoon."

"When it floods, I bet they get polluted water backing up in here from Fort Hood and from Killeen's sewer plant. All these towns just flush their toilets and it goes on downstream."

"God, Decker, now you're getting intellectual over shit itself."

"It happens."

Decker turned into the gravel street looping through the trailer park. The road had once been as-phalt but had mostly reverted to chalky bare soil. There were little nameplates on some of the trailers, military style, noting whose quarters they were. Other units, evidently including Nanci Evans' trailer, had no identification at all. Decker completed the loop and stopped at a small concrete block building serving as a laundry and office.

An aging man with a belly bulging over the waist of his fatigue pants was near the door of the laundry room pouring soapy water out of a mop bucket.

Decker and Long parked nearby and walked over to him. He looked up at Decker and motioned them over to the building.

"Come in out of the wind, boys," he said. "It's starting to get downright chilly out and my arthritis acts up in cool weather. Can you believe it? I retired here so I could stay warm."

The old man wheezed at his own humor. He dropped the bucket noisily on the concrete floor and wiped both hands on his grimy camouflage pants. He fished a bent cigar out of his shirt pocket and lit it with a worn Zippo adorned with Army insignia.

"What can I do for you? Need a place to live?"

"Actually, I'm looking for one of your tenants, Nanci Evans," Decker said.

The man's attitude changed immediately. He crossed his arms and stuck out his chin, holding the cigar between his teeth and blowing smoke in two plumes from his mouth.

"What the hell you want with Nanci?" he grumbled.

"I was just driving through town and wanted to stop and visit. I didn't have a number to call and get directions."

The man stood as erect as his posture allowed, planted his gnarled fists on his hips, and glared up at Decker like a career sergeant.

"Son, I can spot a bullshitter a mile off. Unless you got some official reason for being here, get back in your vehicle and move out."

Decker studied the man for a minute. He had obviously spent years in the Army facing down younger, bigger men, but he would also yield to authority. Decker stepped in closer to the man and switched on his cop demeanor.

"Police business. We're investigating a felony offense that may involve Mrs. Evans. It would be easier for all of us if we could just talk with her quietly."

The man scowled fiercely.

"What do you want Nanci for?" he snapped. He jammed the cigar back in his mouth and puffed until it glowed, enveloping Decker in a pungent cloud of smoke.

"Just save the taxpayers a lot of money and tell us which trailer it is," Decker said, in a stern tone of voice. "If you don't, we'll call in some back-up, seal off your whole damned trailer park, and search door-to-door until we find her. "

"Think you're a real hard-ass, don't you?" the man said.

Decker pulled out his phone.

"It's your decision," Decker said. "We'll be sure to tell all your tenants that the search was all your fault."

The man puffed a couple more times and, reluctantly, pointed his bent cigar toward a faded green trailer not far down the road.

"Number eight, but she's not there right now. I saw her leave earlier. Nanci and my old lady have a pissing match going but I kind of like the girl. She dances at a place called Cowgirls, over on the highway."

"What kind of car does she drive?" Decker asked.

"A beat up old Escort, kind of faded brown color. Her worthless husband shows up sometimes in his damned semi and parks it in a vacant lot. I heard him leave this morning and I haven't seen him since. Killeen cops were here looking for him about noon."

"We're going to watch their place for a while. We'd appreciate it if you didn't tell anyone we're here."

"Yeah, sure, just stay out of my way. I have a lot of work to do around here today and I don't need any trouble," the man said. "Sorry about giving you a hard time but we get bill collectors and lowlifes asking questions sometimes."

"Well, just keep this to yourself," Decker replied.

They walked back to Decker's SUV and parked it where they could see the Evans' trailer.

After nearly two hours of swapping lies, taking naps, listening to country music, and watching light rain occasionally splatter on the windshield, Decker and Long were getting discouraged. Nanci Evans was a no show and Long had to go to the bathroom.

"Let's go see if this chick's at work," Long suggested.

"Let's get supper first. I'm getting hungry," Decker said. "There's a good place to eat in Belton."

The place Decker had heard of was called the Pecan Tree Restaurant. Typical of Texas cafes at dinner, the place was packed with regulars looking to fill up on home cooking. Decker and Long blended right in.

They knew what they would order before they were even seated. A waitress was serving four customers near the door. She unloaded her tray of steaming plates of chicken fried steak, mashed potatoes, and cream gravy, dropping one in front of each hungry diner. Long and Decker simply nodded to each other.

Their instincts were correct. The chicken fried steak was above average, the cream gravy was outstanding, and the pecan pie lived up to their expectations. The cafe's iced tea glasses were huge and never empty for long. Since this trip was on Decker, he picked up the tab and left a polite tip.

"I'd give that place an eight point five," Long said as they left.

"I've never heard you give a restaurant, or a woman, a ten on your scale, Kenny. I sure want to be there when it happens."

They headed back west to Harker Heights and drove the length of Veterans Memorial Highway from the east city limits to the Killeen Airport on the west city limits. Near the west edge of town, by the city water tower, they found a bar with a large neon woman displayed on the roof that read *Cowgirls Roundup*. But it was more than a sign.

It was a work of neon erotic art. A giant cowgirl stood out against the dark gray sky. Her white boots and cowboy hat were outlined in twinkling lights. Her body was painted a slightly pink flesh tone. Layers of blonde hair, outlined in flashing yellow neon, flowed from under her hat. Her waist was tiny, unlike her breasts, which were exaggerated beyond reason and defined underneath with white neon crescents. Two star-shaped pasties seemed to spin as their red neon shapes flashed in sequence. Finally, each slender hand pointed a six-shooter skyward, firing off intermittent blasts in white strobe lights.

"Jesus Christ," Decker said, "she looks like Darryl Hannah in that fifty-foot woman flick, only bustier and in a G-string."

"Every man's dream," Long said, "a giant naked blonde with big guns."

Decker pointed to the sign over the door advertising *Live Nude Dancers*.

"At least the strippers are all alive."

At seven o'clock on Sunday night, the parking area in front was already filling. Decker pulled into the gravel parking lot lined with vehicles. A black Hummer, aging pick-ups and SUVs, and several motorcycles crowded near the building. Decker turned off the radio, switched off the engine, and looked at Long. They could hear music thumping from inside the bar.

Long said, "Are you ready to get on with this or are we just going to sit here picking our teeth and farting all night?"

Decker responded by singing along with the country tune from inside. "I got the money, honey, if you got the *tiiiiime*."

As Long climbed out of the SUV, he grumbled, "It's bad enough that I'm traveling out of town with a known homosexual. Now you start singing to me in the parking lot of a titty bar full of soldiers. That, Kyle frickin' Decker, is not a healthy thing to do."

"I'm here strictly on business," Decker said. "I certainly have no sexual interest in you, or the working girls inside. Remember, we're searching for this woman because she had Chris' credit card. I'm doing this for

**James Gaston**

Chris. That's the only reason I'd go into a sleazy titty bar."

"While you try not to look at the naked women," Long laughed, "I plan to enjoy it enough for the both of us."

He grabbed the battered door handle and yanked it open.

# CHAPTER TWENTY-FIVE

Ernie and Maria Zepeda were in the kitchen cleaning up the dinner dishes.

"I'm going to run over to the hospital and see Chris Jensson for a few minutes, honey," he said.

"You've been working so much this weekend, Ernesto. Can't you just spend Sunday evening with your family?"

"I won't be gone long, just an hour or so. There are some things I really need to ask Chris and I want to see how he's doing."

"Well, try to get home before the kids go to bed."

When Zepeda arrived at the hospital, Chris had just finished his dinner and nurse Eloise was helping him get settled in the bed.

"Hey, Chris," Zepeda said. "How are you doing?"

"Not bad, Ernie," Chris said, adjusting the pillow under his cast. "I'm sore all over but it could have been a lot worse. This is my nurse, Eloise."

Zepeda introduced himself to Eloise and asked her to stay in the room for a minute.

"Chris, if you're up to talking with me about the wreck, I need to videotape your statement."

"Sure, I'm up to it. I just have a little headache."

Eloise looked skeptical.

"Couldn't this wait until tomorrow, Detective?" she asked.

"I might not have time tomorrow. There's another case I'm working on. This won't take long."

"It's okay, Eloise," Chris said. "Let's do this while it's quiet around here."

"Only if you stay calm. You know what Dr. Murphy said about your blood pressure."

"Would you mind staying here with us, Eloise?" Zepeda said. "You can keep an eye on your patient."

"Only for a few minutes," she said. "He needs his rest."

Zepeda set up the small video camera on a tripod. He started the recording by stating the time, where the interview was being conducted, and who was in the room. Eloise stood behind the camera.

Then Zepeda asked Chris to tell him what happened on Saturday morning. Chris explained why he and Todd were out doing fieldwork and about the the situation with Tract B. When Chris described the wreck, he started to get very emotional.

Eloise got Chris some water and checked his monitors.

"Are you about done, Detective?" she asked. "We really don't want his blood pressure to get too elevated."

"Just a couple more questions," Zepeda said. "Chris, did you notice any other vehicles on the road or in the area?"

"Not really, just some guys unloading a trailer at a warehouse over behind Tract B. I saw them when we were taking the photos."

"Was there a truck at the warehouse?"

"Yes, I guess there was. It wasn't attached to the trailer. I kind of remember it starting up when we were walking back to the car."

"Can you describe it? Maybe the model or color?"

Chris closed his eyes and thought about it. His head was pounding.

"Not really, Ernie. I was so pissed off about the property being bulldozed that I wasn't paying much attention. The truck might be in the photos if we had the memory card I took out of the camera. It's in my bag, the one that's still missing."

Chris started rubbing his forehead.

"That's enough," Eloise said. "You'll have to finish this some other time, Detective Zepeda."

Zepeda stopped the recording and unscrewed the camera from the tripod. He looked at the nurse but her expression was unyielding this time. She wasn't intimidated in the least.

Zepeda was.

"Okay," he said. "Thanks for your help, Eloise. Mind if Chris and I visit in private for a while, just as friends?"

"Five minutes, that's it," she said. "But the police interview is over."

Eloise tucked the camera under her arm.

"You can pick your camera up at the nurse's station," she said. Her shoes squeaked on the waxed floor as she left the room.

"Sorry about that, Ernie. She's just worried about me."

"That's a good thing. Now, let's talk about you and Kyle."

# CHAPTER TWENTY-SIX

When Decker and Long stepped through the door, cigarette smoke and loud music washed over them like a tidal wave. The small entry area was dark except for a light over the middle-aged cashier who wore a decidedly unfriendly expression around the cigarette hanging from her mouth. A single bulb overhead distorted her long nose and pointed chin.

Without ever making eye contact, she yelled, "That'll be ten bucks each cover charge. Two drink minimum."

Decker dropped a twenty into the tray.

"Through the door on your left. Don't touch the dancers."

"She reminds me of my mother-in-law," Long said, "I sure hope the strippers are friendlier."

The smoky haze in the room was illuminated by spotlights directed at three stages. The sound system pounded as young women in various degrees of undress danced for the patrons.

Long and Decker stopped to get their bearings. A bar ran across the left side of the room, tended by two muscular young men in *Cowgirls Roundup* logo T-shirts. A central runway extended halfway across the room from a mirrored stage on the right. A brass pole anchored each end of the runway, giving the dancers something to swing around. Small round stages flanked the runway on each side, each with a brass pole in the center. The runway and both round stages were lined with chairs where men stared up at the live sexual fantasy.

When Long and Decker took chairs beside the runway, a topless dancer moved toward them with a broad smile and a practiced bounce of her breasts. She was a tall woman with thin legs and red spike heels. She took a swing around the pole, stopping in front of Long and Decker. Gyrating to the music, she squatted down in front of Long. Her hands circled each artificially enlarged breast, rubbing and tugging on her big nipples.

Long pulled a wad of bills out of his pocket and peeled a five off the top. He folded it in half lengthwise. She spun around to face him, sat down on the stage, and spread her legs wide apart. Slowly, she lifted the side of her G-string until the tiny garment failed altogether to protect her modesty. Then, smiling, she stretched the G-string out at her hip where several other bills were held in place. Long slipped his gratuity under the strap.

The stripper spiraled again to standing and slapped herself on the behind. She smiled again and danced away.

Decker was teasing him when a waitress walked up with a tray. She wore a pair of white boots, tight blue shorts, and a fringed, transparent vest.

While they ordered, she leaned over to place napkins in front of each of each of them, bringing her natural young body in for closer inspection. Decker took only a second to order but Long couldn't help staring at her breasts. With a smile and a pat on Long's arm, she was off to fetch the drinks.

"You know," Long said, "my wife has a vest just like that. She wears it when she waits on me at home. I make her get dressed so I can enjoy my beer."

"Maybe she'll let you wear it sometime. You'd look real cute in that."

Long shot him the finger.

News of tippers spread fast among the dancers. The next dancer had been scouting the patrons near the runway and spied Long. Unfortunately, her exotic dancing was less than alluring. The rapid pelvic thrusts she substituted for interpretive dancing took on a violent appearance the harder she worked. In desperation, she pulled off her G-string and swung it in large arcs over her head like a lasso.

Long tossed a couple of ones onto the stage. Three soldiers started hooting and whistling for her to come to their side of the runway. She snatched up the money at her feet and strutted toward the soldiers.

As her number ended, the announcer said, "The devil made Tammy do it guys, not the management. Put your hands together for her special effort."

The waitress returned with two cold beers. Decker wiggled his finger for her to lean closer so she could hear him. She put an arm around his shoulders and her ear near his mouth. He could smell her subtle perfume and feel her hair sweep against his face.

"Can you tell me if Nanci Evans is going to dance soon?" Decker asked.

"I think she's up next. Are you a fan of Nanci's?"

"A buddy of mine told me her act was worth catching."

"That's right," she said. "She's a great dancer. The customers just love her. I'll tell her to watch for you over here and show you her best moves."

"That would be wonderful. By the way, you have a beautiful body."

"Thank you so much," the waitress said.  She stood up and held open her vest, proudly displaying her soft, natural breasts. "Now, if you boys need anything else, just give me a wave."

Long was discussing what he would like to have the waitress do for him when the man seated next to Decker suddenly stood and turned toward Decker. Decker and Long stopped talking and both looked at the guy, wondering what was up.

He looked down at Decker and said, "Were you asking about Nanci."

"Yeah, what about it?" Decker asked.

"Well, she's a friend of mine. She didn't mention expecting anyone here tonight. You mind telling me what business you have with Nanci?"

Long stood up and moved around behind Decker.

"Mind telling us who the fuck you are?" Long asked.

The man stepped toward Long in a threatening way.

Decker jumped to his feet and stepped between Long and the man. Seeing Decker at full height, the man decided not to escalate the situation and backed away a couple of feet.

One of the brawny bartenders came around the end of the bar and hurried toward them. When the man saw the bartender coming, he grabbed his drink and moved down the runway toward the stage.

"What do you suppose that was about?" Long said.

"I don't know, but I'm glad he backed down so easily."

The bartender approached Decker and Long, who were still standing.

"Everything okay over here?" he asked.

"No problem," Long said, "but thanks for asking."

Decker was checking out the hunky bartender. He was late-twenties, almost Decker's height, may be six foot even, with thick shoulders, a flat stomach, and a small waist. He spent serious time in the gym. His tight slacks displayed another well-developed attribute.

He caught Decker cruising him and smiled.

Their eyes met. Then he gave Decker a long look up and down.

"You guys been in here before?" he asked.

"First time," Decker said. "Not usually my kind of bar."

He nodded at Decker, knowingly, and held out his hand to shake.

"I'm Joey. I work security here and help out behind the bar."

"Nice to meet you Joey. I'm Kyle and this is Kenny."

Joey's grip was firm but friendly. He put his other hand on Decker's forearm. Their eyes met and lingered.

Joey nodded. Then he shook Long's hand, but only briefly.

"I'm real sorry if that guy was bothering you. He's a regular customer. Big tipper. The girl's call him the Reverend. If he comes back over this way, I'll handle it. We don't need any fights in here, especially with all these high-strung soldiers around."

"Thanks, Joey," Decker said. He put his hand on Joey's massive bicep "We appreciate your attention."

Long finally realized that something was going on between Decker and Joey.

"We'll be fine," Long said. "How about another beer?"

"Next round's on the house. I'll tell your waitress."

When he left, they sat back down.

Long said, "I wouldn't want to mess with Joey. How about you, Kyle?"

"I'd love to mess with him."

"Bet he'd come out on top."

"That could be fun," Decker said, smiling.

Long winced and shook his head.

"Our next dancer is always a favorite," the announcer said. "Let's hear it for our own little cowgirl, Naaaanciii."

The crowd, which had grown since Decker and Long had entered the bar, started cheering and clapping. The huge speaker system began thumping Robert Palmer's version of *I Didn't Mean to Turn You On.* Strobe lights flashed on the center stage. The petite figure of Nanci Evans strutted out in a cropped white T-shirt, tight blue jeans, and snakeskin cowboy boots with tall heels. The cowboy hat she wore was soft white with a snakeskin band and a blue jay feather.

She made a couple of turns around the pole and took off her hat, careful not to crimp the brim. As she stretched her arms to lift the hat off her head, the short T-shirt revealed both pink nipples. Whistles came from the bar area. Swinging around with her cowboy hat in one hand, she gently placed it on the Reverend's head and blew him a kiss. Then Nanci retrieved her hat and carefully put it near the curtain. As soon as she spun away, the Reverend looked at Decker maliciously.

Decker did not respond to the provocation.

Nanci strutted to the end of the runway, near Decker and Long. As she swirled and danced, she grabbed the sides of her jeans and they tore away completely, unsnapping down each side, to reveal a sequined G-string in metallic green.

Long couldn't restrain himself. Sweat was already beading on his forehead. He was taking in the perfect pair of legs dancing almost within reach. Her calves emerged from the expensive boots and ended at the most perfect firm behind he'd seen since college.

A couple of steps and twirls later, Nanci stood right in front of Decker. She spun around, facing away, and bent over double at the waist less than a foot from Decker's face. Decker viewed her from her boots up.

"Having fun yet, handsome?" she asked. Then she licked the inside of her left knee.

Decker grinned. Long looked on, enviously.

Nanci spun around the pole and then gripped it and lifted both legs off the stage. She pulled herself up the pole, hand over hand, until she was about five feet above the floor. The soldiers went wild as she slid slowly back down to the stage into the splits.

Nanci returned to the Reverend. She stood straddling his drink glass, slowly crossed her arms, and pulled her T-shirt off over her head. She flung it back by the stage curtain. A cheer went up as she danced and caressed her own slender body.

Dressed only in her boots and G-string, Nanci started working the stage for tips. She strutted, swirled, and squatted near each customer along the runway, giving each man a close-up view of her perky breasts and firm behind. By the time she returned to Long and Decker, bills were spouting from both sides of her G-string. The thumping music segued into another of Nanci's favorites, *Addicted to Love.*

Nanci turned her full attention to Long. She slid his beer out of the way as she danced closer to him. Long folded another five dollar bill.

Nanci squatted down and placed her hands gently on Long's head. Her hands slid down across his ears onto his shoulders and she pulled him forward, brushing her nipples against his cheeks and lips. Long's eyes closed in pleasure, savoring the sensation. He slipped the five under her G-string.

"Thank you, honey," she said.

Then she danced away in a gyrating turn back to the Reverend again. When the number ended, Long sat dazed, staring blankly at the curtain closing behind Nanci Evans. Then he realized the Reverend was glaring at him with the hateful look of a man who could do something stupid.

The announcer's voice boomed. Long tugged on Decker's sleeve and motioned that they should move to a table away from the runway.

When they were reseated, he said, "Damn, that's one amazingly sexy woman."

"Don't forget what we're here for, Kenny. That's the *housewife* who had my boyfriend's credit card. We have to get her alone and look her in the eye for a change."

"When she rubbed those beautiful perky nipples on my face I got a major bone," Long said with a smile.

"I'd rather have Joey rub something on my face."

"You are one sick bastard, Decker."

The waitress arrived with two fresh beers.

"I figured you guys could use a cold one after Nanci's performance. Isn't she fantastic?"

"I'll say," Long replied, not faking his enthusiasm. "She's one of the best dancers I've ever seen."

"Could you ask Nanci to join us over here when she finishes dressing?" Decker said.

"She can join you, dressed or not, it's up to you."

"As much as we enjoyed her act, my friend here might not be able to handle it if Nanci came over naked. He can hardly walk as it is."

Long squirmed in his chair.

The waitress gave Decker a wink. Then she reached into Long's lap and gave his crotch a squeeze.

"Oh, my! That's a big gun, cowboy."

"Careful there," Long said. "It's loaded."

"I'll get Nanci for you, honey."

Long and Decker watched as the waitress went through a door next to the stage. She returned in a couple of minutes with Nanci in tow and pointed to them.

Even though a busty blond was wiggling her cleavage right in his face, the Reverend was watching Nanci.

Nanci was dressed as before in her cropped T-shirt, jeans, and boots, but without the hat. She made her way toward them with a bottle of water in hand.

Decker pulled out a chair for her. She glanced at Joey before she sat down.

"Hi y'all, I'm Nanci," she said with a big smile. "Liz said y'all wanted me to join you but, before you say anything, I have to tell you right off that I am not a prostitute. If that's what you're after, I'm not your girl. I'm a dancer, not a hooker."

Decker was surprised by her bold introduction. He stared at her for a moment.

"I'm Kyle Decker, and this is Kenny Long. I assure you we aren't going to proposition you, Nanci."

"Well, how did you like my act?" she asked.

"You were wonderful," Long sighed. "I mean, you're a really talented dancer."

"Nanci," Decker asked, "is that your jealous husband over by the stage?"

"God, no," she laughed, "That's one of my regular customers. He's more jealous than my husband."

Decker and Long exchanged glances. The silence made her a little nervous.

"Why are you asking about my husband, anyway?"

Nanci took a long drink of bottled water and looked at Decker and Long expectantly.

Finally, Decker said, "Nanci, I hate to bring this up, but we have to ask you about the credit card you used this morning."

"Shit, you guys are cops!" Nanci looked toward Joey at the bar but then thought better of it. "I thought that cleared up. It was just a misunderstanding."

She tugged nervously on her little T-shirt.

"You were using someone else's credit card," Decker said,.

"Not really," Nanci explained, "I thought it was my husband's credit card. It was all just a mistake."

"The credit card were stolen yesterday morning," Decker said.

"I found the credit card in Ronnie's pants pocket. I didn't even look at the name on it. I thought it was his, which meant I could use it too, being his wife and all. I swear, I didn't know it was stolen."

Decker and Long looked at Nanci and then at each other. Neither was sure if she was lying or just naive. There was an awkward silence as the music thumped and a short Latina performed in the background.

"Look, Officer," she said. "I have the paper y'all gave me this morning. It shows I was released to my minister for counseling. The form's in my purse if you'll just give me a minute, I'll get it from my locker."

She bolted from the table nearly in tears and hurried back to the stage door.

Joey watched her. So did the Reverend. The waitress saw her too and looked over at the table where Decker and Long sat sipping their beers. Decker motioned for her and she came right over. She stood with a hand firmly on one hip.

"Is Nanci all right?" the waitress asked. "Joey won't like it if you guys made Nanci cry."

Joey watched them from the bar, ready for her signal.

"It's a private matter," Decker said. "She just went to get some papers from her purse to show to us."

"You guys just better be careful with Nanci. Joey's keeping an eye on you over here."

Fortunately, Nanci returned to the table. The two exchanged a little hug and Nanci told her she was fine. Nanci sat down and opened a small purse. She took out a green paper, unfolded it, and spread it out on the table.

"See, this is the form they gave me. It says that I was detained but not charged. It says right here that I was unaware the credit card was stolen."

They all stared at the green form from Killeen PD.

Decker said, "It looks like you're in the clear, all right."

"But I don't understand," Long said. "Why did your husband have a stolen credit card? Do you know where he got it?"

"I don't know. You'll have to ask him."

"Where can we find your husband, Mrs. Evans?" Decker asked.

"Ronnie, my husband, he's a truck driver. I never know where he's going or when he'll be back. I can show you his picture, if that would help you find him."

Nanci pulled a small wallet from her purse and fumbled with the plastic snapshot sleeves. She retrieved a photo and dropped it on the table. It showed a tall, thin man standing in front of a large red semi. The front license number was clearly visible.

Decker was thinking about the motel maid's description of the man who gave her the city's camera. It had to be Ronnie Evans.

"Mind if we hang on to this photo?"

"Sure, I never want to see him again. When you catch that stupid bastard, tell him not to come home."

While the announcer introduced the next performer, Nanci stood and gathered her purse and water bottle.

"I've really got to get back to work now."

They stood up and thanked her for her help. Decker handed Nanci two twenties. She waved goodbye and returned to the dressing room.

The waitress rushed over.

"You guys might want to leave pretty soon," she said. "Maybe you can come back sometime when you're not causing a problem."

While Decker settled the bill, Long excused himself to visit the men's room. Decker pressed another twenty into her hand. She gave Decker a hug and a kiss on the cheek as she left the table.

Decker put his wallet away and waited for Long. That was when he noticed the Reverend was no longer sitting by the runway. Decker suddenly had a bad feeling and headed toward the men's room.

When Decker tried to push open the restroom door, it was locked. He kicked the door as hard as he could, planting his size twelve right by the door handle. The door flew open.

Decker charged through just in time to see Kenny Long bash the Reverend over the head with a metal paper towel dispenser. He hit the guy again as he fell. A small handgun clattered on the tile floor and slid into a puddle under the urinal. Long dropped the towel dispenser. It was splattered with blood.

"This crazy fucker threatened to killed me while I was pissing! He had a gun on me when you came busting through the door."

"For Christ sake, Kenny, put your dick away, will you?"

Long looked down and zipped up.

"You better pick up that weapon before he comes to," Decker said.

Long looked at the pistol lying under the filthy urinal.

"No way, I'm not touching that piece," he said. "You want it, you pick it up."

"What's going on in here?" Joey said as he crowded into the small restroom.

The three men looked at each other, then at the Reverend, who was groaning and bleeding on the floor between them.

"He must have slipped and hit his head on the towel holder, Long said. "I was just coming to get you."

Joey obviously didn't believe the story. He crossed his arms, flexing his enormous biceps. Decker was impressed.

"We better call the paramedics," he said. "Where'd the firearm come from?"

"Must have fallen out of his pocket," Long said.

"Sure it did," Joey said, with a grin.

Long and Decker glanced at each other. They had what they came for, the photo in Decker's pocket. Some lunatic they didn't even know was on the floor, semi-conscious. The bartender wasn't mad at them.

"I'll tell you what, Joey," Decker said. "How about if we just get on down the road. No need to make a big fuss over a jealous drunk, if it's okay with you."

Long took out his wad of bills.

"Here's a few bucks to cover the mess," he said.

Joey waved off the money. A warm smile spread across his face.

"I've been hoping somebody would kick this guy's ass," Joey said. "This loaded weapon will get him banned from Cowgirls. Y'all just head on out. I'll take care of this sack of shit."

"Thanks, man. It's been good to meet you," Decker said. He handed Joey his business card.

"My pleasure, Kyle. See you around."

Decker and Long walked straight through the club, oblivious to the naked women dancing all around them. The crone at the entrance glanced up when the pair hurried through the front door but she didn't say anything.

They hardly spoke until they entered Central Texas Expressway heading east. Then Decker started teasing Long about the strippers. Long started teasing Decker about Joey.

By the time they turned south on I-35, they were both laughing so much that Decker could hardly drive.

# CHAPTER TWENTY-SEVEN

Decker and Long got back to Asher a little after midnight. Before Decker went to bed, he scanned the photo into his computer and enlarged the image until the license plate was legible. He was anxious to give Zepeda the picture so Asher PD could issue a warrant for Ronnie Evans' arrest.

Decker was pacing the sidewalk when Gus Janek opened the cafe the next morning.

"What are you doing up so early, Decker?" Janek said jovially. "I thought you private investigators got to sleep late."

"Not today, Gus," Decker said, "Gotta catch a murderer."

"You better have a good breakfast then. I'll get you some coffee."

Decker was sitting alone in the corner booth sipping that first steaming cup of coffee when Zepeda arrived. It was only ten after six on Monday morning and Zepeda already looked stressed.

"I was finishing a decent night's sleep when you called at five," Zepeda said. "What's so damned important? I missed breakfast with the kids and pissed off my wife."

Decker put the enlarged photo on the table where Zepeda could see it.

"That's Ronnie Evans. He's the truck driver we're looking for. You can read the plate number."

"You're shitting me. You sure it's the right guy?"

"Nanci Evans found Chris' credit card in her husband's shirt pocket Saturday night. She gave me this picture of him standing in front of his red truck. He also fits the hooker's description of the man who gave her the camera."

Zepeda was studying the photo when Gus came over to take their order.

"Ready to order or you just want more coffee?"

Decker smiled up at him.

"I'll have some huevos rancheros and a glass of milk," he said.

"Make mine biscuits and gravy, Gus, and keep the coffee coming," Zepeda said. "I'm still half asleep."

Janek laughed. "Hell, I've been up at five every day for thirty years. It's not so bad at all, once you get used to it."

"What does your wife think about that?" Zepeda asked.

"She's just as glad I get up before her. She never liked sex or conversation before noon anyway."

Janek flipped his towel over one shoulder and returned to his grill.

More customers came in, joking with each other while taking their usual places around the room. The early cool front required jackets and sweaters for the first time since spring. Soon, the aroma of bacon blended with the smells of fresh coffee and aftershave.

Zepeda listened carefully as Decker explained how Nanci Evans had implicated her husband in the credit card theft. Decker omitted some of the details, like interviewing her in a strip club and the altercation in the restroom.

"This is the truck driver we're after, Ernie. He killed Todd Watson and left Chris out there to die."

Zepeda looked at Decker, then at the man in the photo. He nodded.

"I do believe you're right, partner. It shouldn't be too hard to find him unless the bastard's gone into hiding."

"I'd bet he's too damn dumb to hide."

Janek brought their breakfast, served up with good-natured insults. Decker spooned salsa on his eggs and dug in.

Between bites of biscuits, Zepeda said, "I went to see Chris last night and taped his statement. He remembered someone unloading a truck over at that warehouse Saturday morning. It must be the same truck. This should be enough to justify a search warrant for the trailer and Smith's warehouse."

"Chris may be going home from the hospital this morning. I'm taking him to my house."

"Sounds like he might be planning on moving in. You sure you're ready for that?"

Decker smiled.

"Absolutely."

After breakfast, Zepeda and Decker left in different directions. While Zepeda went to the office to start the paperwork, Decker drove out to the hospital.

Hospitals are busy places at seven-thirty in the morning. There's no rest for the infirm at that time of day. Blood has to be drawn. Charts get updated with the latest vital signs. Breakfast carts crowd the hallways.

Decker checked in with the guard and then looked in the open door. Chris was sitting up in bed, sipping his tea. When he saw Decker, his smile was radiant. Even with the swelling and the dark bruises under his eyes, Chris had a beautiful smile.

"Come over here and give me a hug," Chris said. "I was hoping you'd come by here first thing."

"You're looking good. How are you feeling?"

"A lot better. I don't know if it's the drugs or just knowing I can go home this morning. Dr. Murphy should be here soon to sign my release form."

"I better kiss you quick before he shows up," Decker said with a grin. "I brought you that UW sweatsuit and clean undies you asked for."

Decker sat on the side of the bed and they held each other for a while. Then they enjoyed a slow kiss, oblivious to hallway traffic slowing up to gawk at two men embracing.

"I really needed a weekend in Austin with you." Chris sighed. "I'm sorry I messed it all up."

"I hope we can spend every weekend together, from now on. I never want to lose you, Chris."

Decker hugged Chris again. Then he sat up and held Chris' hand.

"I found that woman in Harker Heights, the one with your credit card. She gave me a photo of her husband with his truck. Want to see the picture?"

"Really? Is it the truck that hit us?"

Decker nodded. He handed a copy of the photo to Chris and sat back proudly.

"I think we've identified the hit-and-run driver. We can nail the bastard from this photo."

Silently staring at the picture, Chris ignored the license plate Decker was pointing to and focused on the grill decorations. The photo showed two large chrome figures of naked women facing each other, standing on tiptoes, bent at the waist, their hands meeting at the center of the huge truck grill. Script lettering between them read *The Twins*.

"This is the truck that hit us. I'm certain of it."

"I think so too. It all adds up with the stolen credit card and the camera. The truck's even red like the paint residue left on the city car."

"I'm positive that's the truck!" Chris stated emphatically. "The chrome ornament ... the naked woman on the right ... that's the angel I saw. I thought I was going nuts but it was just a tasteless ornament on this asshole's truck."

Chris was indignant.

"That proves it. You're a witness. This is the truck that ran into you and left the scene," Decker pointed at the man in the photo. "Since it's his truck, Evans was probably the driver."

"That's his name, Evans?"

"Ronnie Evans," Decker said.

"I can positively identify the truck. I'm glad I can finally contribute something. I'll testify that this truck with *The Twins* on its radiator grill is the truck that hit us."

"I better call Ernie and tell him."

"Then you have to tell me all about your trip to Harker Heights."

"Oh, God, Chris," Decker said. "You're going to love this story but you can't say anything to Kenny's wife about it."

A few minutes later, a nurse looked in and asked them to hold it down. Their laughing was disturbing the other patients.

# CHAPTER TWENTY-EIGHT

It was almost nine o'clock on Monday morning when Zepeda secured a search warrant for Ted Smith's warehouse and the transport trailer parked at the loading dock. It took another hour to get everyone out there.

In the judge's chambers, Zepeda theorized that Chris Jensson and Todd Watson had witnessed illegal activity on the warehouse dock. The truck driver then attempted to kill both witnesses. The warehouse's owner of record, Ted Smith, was killed later the same day. There must be a connection. The search might uncover a meth lab or other illegal drug activity. Judge Claude Faber was skeptical but he was willing to allow the search if it might shed light on the two deaths.

Zepeda met the crime scene unit, comprised of Lieutenant Gene Stratton and one forensic technician, and two of the drug task force tactical officers at the warehouse. Stratton videotaped as one officer checked for trip wires or other booby traps. The other officer carefully cut a lock and opened the trailer doors. The interior was empty.

"Let's close her back up until we're through in the warehouse," Stratton said. "Since there aren't any license plates, we'll have to run the serial number."

Zepeda moved over to the warehouse door. Stratton videotaped one officer working on the door with a pry bar. The other prepared his assault weapon and pulled down the visor on his helmet.

"Okay, guys, let's go in." Zepeda said. "Be careful."

The door flew open and the two officers rushed inside. Zepeda and Stratton followed closely behind them. The lead team moved quickly to check the small office area. The building was declared clear and Zepeda flipped on the overhead lights. Stratton's technician was the last in.

The warehouse only contained a dozen fifty-five gallon barrels. Stratton checked the label on one of the barrels.

"Looks like agricultural pesticides and herbicides. It seems to be stored properly and nothing is spilled or leaking. This stuff isn't even very dangerous."

Zepeda asked the two tactical officers to stay until Stratton was finished.

"I'll call you if we come across anything useful, Ernie, but I doubt if that'll happen," Stratton said.

"Any luck with the fingerprints on the real estate sign?"

"There were two sets of prints on it. One was Smith's but we haven't matched the others yet."

"What about those tire tracks in the barn?"

"There was too much hay on the ground in the barn to get anything clear enough but we did find a tire print in the soft dirt just outside the barn door. It's from a truck tire with some miles on it. We got one good tread impression about 18 inches long."

Zepeda was making notes.

"Since it rained Friday evening," Stratton said, "the truck had to be there sometime between late Friday night and early Sunday morning when Smith's body was discovered. I'd bet it's the same truck from the Watson homicide."

"Too bad we couldn't get any tread marks from Old Bridge Road," Zepeda said.

"The surface was too uneven. Besides, the fire department tromped all over what little was there. At least we have the tire track from outside the barn and we have the debris and paint residue from the wreck."

"Now we just need a truck to match it with," Zepeda said.

"You going to the Smith autopsy this morning, Ernie?"

"Yeah, I better get on over there. The pathologist is waiting on me." He patted Stratton on the shoulder. "Thanks for taking time to do this, Gene. I know you had a busy weekend."

Zepeda drove over to the morgue. It was in a nondescript one-story building next to the hospital. DeLeon County contracted with a local pathologist named Davenport to do the two or three autopsies required each month. He had examined Todd Watson's body earlier in the morning and determined that the cause of death was blunt force trauma to the sternum and a crushed rib cage. Todd had died on impact.

As soon as Zepeda was ready, Davenport started dissecting Smith's body. Smith was healthy, aside from early stages of coronary artery blockage. The only other finding was a bullet lodged in the left ventricle. It was near the end of the puncture wound caused by the yard sign stake. According to Dr. Davenport, the fatal gunshot wound preceded the stabbing by only a few minutes.

Someone shot Smith in the back. Then, after he fell, someone jabbed the yard sign stake into the entry wound just for emphasis.

Since he was already at the hospital, Zepeda decided to check on Chris Jensson. The reserve officer was no longer at Chris' door. Decker was packing Chris' things while Chris supervised from a wheelchair.

"I can carry the flowers in my lap if you'll carry my new potted plant and that little bag," Chris said. "I think we're ready to roll."

"Can I help with anything," Zepeda asked.

"Hey, Ernie, you're just in time," Decker said. He handed Zepeda the plant and the bag. "I'll drive."

As they passed the nurse's station, Eloise was talking with the morning shift supervisor. She held up her hands to stop them.

"Wait just a minute there," she said. "Where do you think you're going with my favorite patient?"

"I'm out of here, Eloise," Chris said.

"You're not leaving until I get a hug, young man. I came in early just so I could roll you to the door and say goodbye."

While Chris thanked the staff and Eloise gave him instructions about caring for his injuries, Zepeda pulled Decker aside and brought him up to date.

# CHAPTER TWENTY-NINE

"**Y**ou treat that bird dog better than your wife," the gate attendant said. "You wouldn't go home at lunch if Janie was sick."

"That's because she can get her own medicine," Kelly said. "Janie's gone into town for groceries and a hairdo and that pup can't take care of herself."

"Take your time, Kelly," the attendant said. "So far we only have those same two carloads. It's a slow day for Texas tourism. I'll radio if we need you."

Matthew Kelly's brand new gray Chevy Tahoe pulled away from the park gate and started down the winding entrance road. A crimson male cardinal flew across his hood and Kelly could hear a mockingbird singing in the midday sun. It was the first day of fall weather and he was outdoors. What a great day to be a park ranger.

Kelly rarely regretted his decision to work for the Texas Parks and Wildlife Department instead of the Texas Department of Public Safety. When he was in the highway patrol academy, struggling through the boot camp he had worked toward for years, he realized that he just wasn't cut out for the DPS after all.

At age twenty-five, Kelly was strong, athletic, and good with a firearm; but he really hated grabbing people with his hands. Highway patrol officers have to wrestle with bad guys all the time. After having to repeat his hand-to-hand self-defense qualifications, Kelly concluded that he should pursue a law enforcement career with the park service. He decided he would fare better with wild animals than with wild criminals.

As a park ranger, he rarely had to use force except to subdue drunken fishermen or handcuff vandals. Since he'd washed out of DPS academy, he wasn't sent to the Rio Grande border like most of the park rangers in his class. He was glad he got assigned to a quiet little park in central Texas.

The area's state troopers, sheriff's deputies, and local police all knew Matthew Kelly. They often met over coffee to swap fishing stories. He was part of the region's law enforcement fraternity and happy with his chosen career.

This particular Monday noon, Kelly was returning to his house because his year-old bird dog had been barfing her chow all weekend. The vet was afraid she'd get dehydrated, so Kelly had to go check on her at lunch. He rented a tiny house on private land near the Fort Parker State Park recreation area only a couple of miles from his post at the old restored fort.

Kelly routinely flipped his radio to the trooper's channel as he left the main gate of the Fort Parker Restoration. He listened to it whenever he had the chance so he could keep up with whatever was going on in Limestone County. Rather than the usual banter about where various units were stopping for lunch, Kelly heard a state trooper report that he'd arrived at a roadblock. The dispatcher confirmed their location.

Kelly pulled to the side of the narrow road and listened intently. Something very unusual was going on, something requiring a highway patrol roadblock.

To Kelly's amazement, he heard the report of a trooper in high-speed pursuit southbound on State Highway 14 south of Mexia. The trooper and a Mexia police unit were chasing a trucker at over sixty miles per hour. As Kelly listened, the Mexia unit stopped to assist a motorist who struck a highway sign after being forced off the highway by the trucker. Limestone County Sheriff units were responding and the Groesbeck Police were advised the chase was heading south toward their community. Speeds increased to seventy-five.

Sheriff's units arrived at the growing roadblock near the old Navasota River. The plan was to stop the trucker before he could reach the vicinity of the Groesbeck high school on Highway 14. A speeding semi could cause a catastrophe. The driver had to be stopped.

Kelly scattered gravel as he sped off toward the river. The rural road he was on would lead him to the roadblock location from the west, across an old steel truss bridge leading to the main highway.

Kelly flipped on his emergency lights and turned up the police radio. The trucker was passing cars and forcing others off the highway. He narrowly missed another truck when he swerved through the traffic. Soon there was no oncoming traffic so the trucker drove mostly on the wrong side of the road to pass slow cars in his lane. The chase was approaching the Fort Parker

State Park entrance, closing fast on the roadblock, only a minute away at those speeds.

North of Groesbeck, State Highway 14 makes a fairly sharp curve to the right and drops down to cross perpendicular to the river. The trucker wouldn't be able to see the roadblock until he was bottled up by the river bridge. Then the chasing units could close the trap and they'd have him. Maybe nobody would get hurt.

Kelly could see the roadblock through the trees when he reached the west end of the old bridge. He'd have a great view of the action from his vantage on the old bridge so he stopped and waited with his lights flashing. Over to his right, on Highway 14, there were three cars at angles and another four cars a hundred feet further on. The officers all had their weapons ready. He could hear approach-ing sirens and the scratching of nine police radios all tuned to the same dispatcher.

Things happen entirely too fast sometimes. Kelly would later recall the odd, dismal sound of the truck driver locking all his brakes in panic. It was the scream of a great beast, straining with all its might to create enough friction to reverse the forces of momentum. The groan of tires on pavement vibrated in the little valley like the death throes of a dinosaur.

Then Kelly saw the truck arching around the curve, descending toward the river bridge. The trailer was engulfed in a cloud of white smoke boiling from the first set of dual axles. Air brakes brought the big rig into a slow skid, the red cab twisting to the right as the trailer jack-knifed to the left. The cab slid sideways like it was turning its face from the impending trap.

The red cab lifted a little, then the rig slowed and the driver expertly stopped the skid. Two police cars skidded past attempting to avoid hitting the truck.

Suddenly, black smoke blasted out of the twin stacks and the cab lurched forward, again taking charge of the trailer. Kelly heard it roar, heard the gears grinding and straining.

At precisely that moment, everyone, especially Matthew Kelly, realized there was still an escape route available to the trucker. He could take the old highway bridge on which Kelly was parked. No one thought the trucker would stop in time to make the cutoff. But he had.

Second gear, third, the semi gained speed as it approached the old steel truss bridge. Kelly was startled out of his daze by the vibration of the bridge under him. He knew then that he was the only impediment to escape. He turned his gray Tahoe sideways between the concrete bridge abutments. The truck roared directly at him.

Kelly leaped from the Tahoe and pulled his sidearm from the holster. The trucker was rolling faster. Less than a hundred feet separated them. Kelly ran to the front of his vehicle, gripped his weapon with both hands, and fired. Four rounds hit the windshield in a tight pattern before the rig smashed into Kelly's vehicle.

From the roadblock, officers could see Matthew Kelly's uniformed body launched over the far side of the bridge and saw the splash where he hit the muddy surface of the Navasota River twenty feet below. They prayed the Tahoe would not follow him.

The red truck came to a shearing, screaming halt between the Tahoe and the rusting trusses. Troopers and deputies raced on foot along the riverbank.

Cruisers drove up behind the truck and officers ran from their cars with weapons drawn. Voices yelled angrily and, in moments, the driver was face down on the pavement, arms wrenched behind him and cuffed. He was bleeding.

A group formed around Kelly as his body was dragged up the bank in the tall Johnson grass. When he sat up, and threw up, a cheer went around the scene from the river to the bridge to the roadblock. Matthew Kelly became a Limestone County legend in that lunch hour and Ronnie Evans became a prisoner.

# CHAPTER THIRTY

When Decker and Chris pulled into the parking lot, they saw that Chris' front door was open. There was a man just inside the apartment.

"I'll check it out," Decker said. He handed Chris his cell phone. "You're my backup. Bring the pepper spray."

Decker ran to the apartment, grabbed the startled man, and took him straight to the ground outside. The man was yelling in Spanish and English while Decker pinned him down and frisked him.

By the time Chris limped up to them, Decker was helping the man to his feet.

"Should I call 911?" Chris asked.

"This is Mr. Sanchez," Decker said. "He's from maintenance."

"The police called the office on Saturday," Sanchez said. "The manager sent me to change your lock today."

"I am so sorry, Mr. Sanchez. I'm Chris Jensson. Someone stole my keys. We thought you were breaking in."

Decker shook the man's hand. "Sorry I got a little rough with you."

"De nada," Sanchez said. "I'm okay. I get knocked down a lot playing soccer." He looked at Chris' cast and bruises. "They said you got hit by a truck and someone was killed."

"Yeah, two days ago," Chris said. "It was really awful."

Sanchez looked uncomfortable. He didn't know how to respond.

"I shut your cat up in the bedroom so it wouldn't get out," Sanchez said. "I'll be done here in a few minutes."

Chris thanked him and then went inside to see about Sas. Decker carried in Chris' plants and things while Sanchez quickly installed a new lock set on the door.

A few minutes later, Chris was getting produce from the refrigerator when Decker came into the kitchen. Sas was weaving between their feet, hoping for some lunch of his own.

"I was thinking we'd have a salad for lunch but I don't think I can cut it up with my left hand. Would you mind doing it while I brew some tea?"

"Sure," Decker said. "I guess you'll have to learn to do things with your left hand until you get that cast off."

"No kidding," Chris said. "Watching porn will be a new challenge."

"I'll take you to get a new iPad and cell phone as soon as you're up to it. You don't need a mouse with them."

"Carol cancelled my wireless account so nobody could use it. You don't think I'll get my electronics back, do you?"

"Nope. They're long gone by now."

After lunch, they settled into the couch together. Decker stretched out his legs and Chris leaned up against him. His cast rested on Decker's leg. Decker wrapped his arms around Chris and nuzzled his hair.

"Phew, you smell like hospital soap."

"Sorry about that. I need a long shower and some fresh clothes."

Decker slid a hand up under Chris's sweatshirt and stroked his warm furry body.

"You feel so good," Decker whispered. "I've missed touching you, baby."

After enjoying a few minutes of being petted, Chris moved the hand down under his waistband so Decker could feel that he was aroused.

"We've got to get you out of these clothes, horny boy."

"Sounds good to me. Let's both get naked."

Decker pulled off Chris's pants and carefully slipped the sweatshirt over his head. While Chris struggled to get the cast out of his sleeve, Decker quickly undressed. He stood fully erect in front of the couch.

"Mmm. You did miss me," Chris said. "Come here, big guy."

As the activity on the couch began to heat up, Decker accidentally leaned against Chris' bruised ribs. Chris jumped from the pain and thumped Decker's elbow with the cast. He apologized for being clumsy and Decker apologized for hurting his ribs. When Decker changed position with his face in Chris' lap, he gripped

Chris' swollen knee. Chris flinched and bumped Decker in the chin with his other knee. They swapped apologies until both of them were snickering.

Soon, the laughing stopped and Decker adjusted the pillows and cushions until Chris was comfortable. Their explorations were slow and deliberate, mindful to ensure maximum pleasure while avoiding pain. Chris' new vulnerability required him to tell Decker what he needed and wanted. His instructions excited Decker, whose caring attention heightened Chris' sensations all the more. They eased into cautious but hungry lovemaking.

Forty minutes later, Decker led Chris to the bathroom and joined him in the shower. He bathed Chris very thoroughly while Chris held his cast in the air. Decker's cell phone was ringing repeatedly but neither of them heard it. They were toweling off when it rang again. Decker hurried naked into the living room to find the phone among his clothes.

"Hey, Kyle," Zepeda said, "I've got some great news."

"Can I call you back in few minutes?"

"The truck driver's in custody. DPS caught him up in Limestone County."

"No shit? That really is great news, Ernie."

"He was wounded but they patched him up in Mexia and DPS is transporting him to Asher as we speak."

"Is he talking?"

"Not yet," Zepeda said. "Listen, you need to come on down to the station. I can fill you in here. Also, Chief Dixon wants to see you in his office. Says it's urgent."

Chris came out of the bedroom, still trying to dry himself off. He looked at Decker quizzically.

"I've got to get Chris squared away here," Decker said. "I'll be there in half an hour."

Decker told Chris what Zepeda had said and Chris had a dozen questions Decker couldn't answer. While they were dressing, the doorbell rang.

Decker answered the door. A petite woman stood on the porch holding a suitcase. She had curly blonde hair, blue eyes, and a familiar smile.

"You must be Kyle," she said. "I'm Susan Jensson, Chris' mother."

# CHAPTER THIRTY-ONE

Decker watched the emotional reunion between mother and son. The son, traumatized by the recent tragedy, needed his mother. The mother, who had very nearly lost her son forever, needed to hold him close and help him heal.

Decker had witnessed many scenes like this as a cop. He knew how to remain silent and be supportive. But this was different. This was the man he adored and the woman who had nurtured Chris into manhood.

Decker was amazed by how much Chris and Susan looked alike. She could easily pass for his older sister. Decker was a little turned on by the blending of male and female when he saw them holding each other. The moment was growing awkward. Decker was glad he had an urgent excuse to leave.

After they were formally introduced, Susan gave Decker a hug and a kiss on the cheek. Decker loved Susan immediately.

"My goodness," she said. "You are even more handsome than I expected. My son certainly has good taste in men."

"Thank you, Mrs. Jensson. That was kind of you to say."

"Kyle, please don't call me *Mrs. Jensson*." She winked. "I'm Susan to you."

"Kyle was just leaving, Mom," Chris said. "He has a meeting in twenty minutes."

"Can you join us for dinner?" Susan asked.

"That would be great," Decker said. "I'll bring some wine and we can get acquainted this evening."

Susan gave Decker her cell phone number and Decker promised to call as soon as he had a chance. When Decker was gone, Susan went to put her things away in the spare bedroom and freshen up from her journey. When she returned to the living room, she found Chris sound asleep on the couch with Sas between his feet.

Susan quietly finished the leftover salad and had some yogurt. She was looking around the apartment when the doorbell rang. Susan rushed to answer it before it rang again. Chris was already stirring on the couch. She opened the door and went out on the porch to see what the slovenly man at the door wanted. Chris heard them raise their voices. Then Susan came back inside and firmly shut the door.

"Chris, honey, I'm sorry to disturb your nap. There's a newspaper reporter at the door name Charlie Hawkins. He says he knows you and insists on talking with you."

"Please ask him to call me tomorrow. I don't feel like seeing anyone right now."

"I tried that. He said he'll just sit on the porch until you're willing to speak with him."

"He's a nice guy," Chris said, "but a pain in the ass sometimes."

Chris was getting to his feet when a gruff voice reached him from just outside the door.

"Chris, it's Charlie," Hawkins said. "The truck driver's been caught. I talked to one of the arresting officers. I thought you'd want to know all the details. If we could just talk face-to-face, it'd be a lot easier."

Chris opened the door and glared at Hawkins.

"Your persistence has paid off again, Charlie. Come on in."

Hawkins moved slowly across the living room, taking in every detail of Chris' apartment. He circled the couch and lowered himself onto it like an big dog finding a shady spot.

"You've met my mother," Chris said as he took the chair across from Hawkins. "She's just arrived from Seattle."

Hawkins nodded. "Yes, I've had the pleasure."

"Would you like some iced tea, Mr. Hawkins?" Susan asked.

"If it's already made, ma'am, that would be refreshing. But, don't let me put you out."

"You've already accomplished that, Mr. Hawkins."

Susan went into the kitchen, closely followed by the cat.

"Okay, Charlie, tell me about this truck driver," Chris said.

"I'd really like to get some background on the accident so we can kind of put it all in chronological order."

"If you want to hear another word out of me, Charlie, you'll tell me about the truck driver first."

Susan returned with a tray with three glasses of iced tea and the usual condiments. She pulled the chair over from the library table to avoid sitting on the couch with Hawkins. They each took a glass of tea.

"All right then," Hawkins said. "They caught the trucker between Mexia and Groesbeck, that's up near Lake Limestone on the way to Dallas. Seems the suspect in your hit-and-run case was spotted leaving the Pump Jack Cafe at lunchtime by a Mexia police officer. Damned fool tried to outrun the police in a semi."

Hawkins noisily sipped his tea. Sas studied him from under Susan's chair.

"As I was saying, the troopers chased the truck until he crashed into a roadblock they set up on state Highway 14. The trucker, a man named Ronald Evans, was wounded but they're bringing him back to Asher for questioning."

"That's good news," Chris said. "That he's been caught, I mean, not that he was shot. Not that I really mind him being shot."

"Well, I hope he's in a lot of pain," Susan said.

Hawkins smiled.

"Now, Chris, can you tell me why you were out there in the first place on Saturday morning in a City car?"

"When will they have Evans here in Asher?" Chris asked.

"I honestly told you all I know about the truck driver." Hawkins sipped his tea. "Can we talk about the accident?"

"Chris isn't up to discussing that right now," Susan said. She stood up. "I think you'd better leave, Mr. Hawkins."

Hawkins didn't budge. He flipped open his tattered notepad and pulled a ballpoint covered with lint from his coat pocket. Hawkins wiped the lint off with his fingers and scribbled on the pad to make certain the pen still worked. Hoping to avoid an ink stain on the upholstery, Chris handed him a tissue to wipe his fingers on.

"It's okay, Mom," Chris said. "This way I can tell you both about the wreck at the same time instead of having to repeat myself."

"You don't have to do this, sweetie," Susan said.

"Yes, I really do, Mom. Charlie needs to hear the whole story and so do you."

Susan sat back down.

Chris described the events on Saturday morning up to the point of the impact. He spent a lot of time on the devastation of Tract B and his dismay about losing the rare stand of Aggie Sage. He emphasized the need for a clearing and grading ordinance to prevent such environ-mental destruction in Asher. Chris told them that he and Todd had taken some photos of Tract B.

Hawkins was careful not to interrupt the flow of Chris' monologue. He took notes quickly and expertly using a strange kind of shorthand notation. He turned pages with the hand holding the pad while hardly missing a stroke of his pen with the other.

Susan sat forward on the edge of her chair.

It was more difficult for Chris when he described being thrown against the dashboard and windshield and landing, helpless, in the front seat. He omitted the angelic vision part of his experience. Chris choked up when he said that Todd died on impact. He explained that someone opened the car door but didn't help him.

Chris ended the story with paramedics helping him on the roadside.

Susan wept and had to excuse herself to go blow her nose.

"Chris, was there a truck parked at the warehouse when you were taking the photos for the zoning hearing?"

"Actually, there was. It was backed up near the dock. Some men were unloading the trailer. I used it in the background to give some scale to the photos of Tract B so the City Council could see how totally barren the property is now."

"Were there any other vehicles at the warehouse?"

"Maybe, but I really don't remember. I was concentrating on the pictures," Chris paused for a sip of tea. "I'm wondering if all this has something to do with the City Council zoning hearing tomorrow night."

"Why would you think that?" Hawkins asked.

"The hearing was suddenly rescheduled ahead of time and the property was cleared before there were any permits. When we went out to do field work on the case, Todd was killed and I was left for dead. Then Ted Smith, the applicant in the rezoning, turned up murdered. It's all too much of a coincidence."

Susan came back and quietly took her seat. Hawkins never looked up from his notebook.

"Chris, why was the zoning hearing rescheduled so early?"

"I couldn't say. You'll have to ask Tommy Nelson about that. He made the decision to move it ahead on the calendar."

"Do you know an attorney from Houston named Nick Lucas?" Hawkins asked.

"I met him once at a Planning Commission hearing on Tract B. Remember when we delayed the Tract B rezoning before, based on the rare wildflowers? Lucas was the lawyer who told the commissioners he would sue the City. Why are you asking about him?"

"I understand he will be presenting the case for the applicants at the zoning hearing tomorrow night since Ted Smith is out of the picture. By the way, do you happen to know what they use that existing warehouse for?"

"I wouldn't know. It's up to the building inspectors to make sure it's used in compliance with the zoning. The warehouse is zoned industrial. Nearly anything can be stored or fabricated in there."

"Is there anything that they couldn't put in there?"

"I'm not positive but I think even some hazardous materials are allowed if they are handled according to EPA and OSHA standards."

Hawkins flipped back through his notes. The notebook and pen disappeared in a coat pocket. Chris waited silently while Hawkins slurped the remainder of his tea and wiped his mouth with the ink-stained tissue.

"Well, thanks for the iced tea, Mrs. Jensson," he said. "You've been very helpful, Chris. I appreciate you talking with me about what happened. I'm really sorry about Todd Watson."

Hawkins began the laborious process of extracting himself from the couch cushions. Several grunts and puffs of breath were necessary before he reached the door.

"Thanks for telling me about the truck driver, Charlie."

Hawkins nodded.

"Glad to see you're feeling better. It's always a pleasure talking with you."

Watching Hawkins amble out to his beat-up old station wagon, Chris knew his aspect was deceptive. He knew from his writing that Hawkins was like a great spider, patient but certain.

Chris had checked him out online the previous spring after Hawkins interviewed him on the Aggie Sage story. Charlie Hawkins earned a master's degree in journalism from Missouri. He won two Pulitzers as a young reporter writing for the Chicago Tribune in the sixties. He dropped out of sight after the '68 convention riots, disappearing without a trace and reappeared in Asher twenty years later.

His persona was a contradiction. Even though he seemed like such a slothful man, Hawkins was an active environmentalist, a supporter of the Sierra Club, Nature Conservancy, Environmental Defense Fund, The Audubon Society, and Greenpeace. He had recently written a nationally circulated piece against the development of LNG terminals along American coastlines. He had also been associated with the ACLU, the Human Rights Campaign, and other groups whose work exposes racism and bigotry.

Chris borrowed Susan's cell phone and called Decker.

"This is Kyle Decker," he answered. "Is everything all right, Susan?"

"It's me," Chris said. "What the hell is going on? You promised to call me."

"Sorry, Chris. I have been talking with Stratton while I'm waiting to see Chief Dixon. Dr. Davenport found a bullet in Smith's body during the autopsy this morning. Evidently the killer stuck the yard sign in Smith after he was shot in the back. We're waiting on ballistics to see if the pistol is in the system. There were some prints on the sign that Stratton's been trying to match."

"I really don't give a shit about Smith," Chris said. "Charlie Hawkins just left here. He knew all about the truck driver getting caught."

"The state troopers chased him down south of Mexia and wounded him. His ear was half shot off but he's okay. Zepeda and a uniformed officer are at Asher Hospital to take him from DPS and lock him to a bed. Ernie wouldn't let me go because he was afraid I might strangle the sorry bastard. He was right."

"Don't hurt him, Kyle. I want that man to rot in prison."

"We can definitely nail him on vehicular homicide and he's in deep shit with the DPS and the Limestone County Sheriff," Decker said. "There's something else. When Evans was at the hospital in Mexia, he tried to call Ted Smith instead of calling a lawyer first. Someone at the real estate office told him Smith was dead and Evans freaked out. Zepeda thinks he knows something about the Smith homicide."

"Did Evans have my bag, Kyle?"

"Ernie didn't mention your bag but I'm sure DPS is processing the truck. If it's in the truck, DPS will find it. We may have to go back to Harker Heights and search his mobile home."

"When Hawkins was here, he was asking me about the warehouse and transport trailer next to Tract B. Did Ernie search the warehouse yet?"

"He did it this morning but there was nothing useful. The trailer was empty and the warehouse only contained some barrels of agricultural chemicals. "

"Well, we saw some men unloading barrels over there when we were taking pictures."

"Why would they run into your car and steal your things?"

"It might be totally unrelated. Has the truck driver said anything yet?"

"No, but I plan to be there when Ernie questions him in the morning."

"Dinner's at six. Mom's really looking forward to it. She's in there messing up my kitchen right now. It smells great though."

"I'm going in to see the Chief now," Decker said. "His assistant just waved to me. See you later."

"Have a good meeting. See you later, stud muffin."

# CHAPTER THIRTY-TWO

Chief Dixon greeted Decker at his office door. Carol Bailey was seated in Dixon's office when Decker entered.

"Have a seat, Kyle," Dixon said. "I was hoping to meet with you and Carol earlier but I've been on the phone with this damned prisoner transfer. We had to get Evans admitted to the hospital and checked out by a doctor before DPS would sign him over to us. Then the hospital had to find a secure room we could put him in."

"Is that what you wanted to see me about, Chief?" Decker asked.

"Damn fine work you did on this Decker," Dixon said. "You identified the suspect in less than forty-eight hours and we've got him locked up already."

"We just got lucky with the photo," Decker said. "Zepeda thinks the guy knows something about the Smith murder too."

"Ernie briefed me on that," Dixon said. "I don't want the prisoner interrogated until he's formally charged and his legal counsel is appointed."

Decker looked at Carol, who has been sitting quietly. She smiled but still didn't say anything.

"So, what exactly can I do for you, Chief?" Decker said.

Dixon shifted in his chair and leaned forward.

"You know I want you to come back to work for the department, Decker. I've told you that before. But Carol tells me there are some unresolved issues. I want them resolved, dammit. Right now!"

Carol held a hand up to interrupt the Chief. He leaned back in his big leather chair.

"I've never understood why you left the department, Kyle," Dixon said. "I've heard some rumors but nothing adds up. Ernie Zepeda, and Carol here, won't tell me what happened. They both say its got to come from you."

"What difference could it make now?" Decker said.

"It could make a lot of difference to all of us," Carol said. "Please, just tell the Chief why you resigned. It's time for you to lay those cards on the table."

Decker studied his hands while he decided what to do. He looked at Carol again. She nodded. They both looked at Dixon.

"When I was with the department," Decker said, " I was gradually coming out as a gay man. Zepeda was fine with it. A few people knew and others found out as they got to know me. It wasn't easy. It never is for gay police officers."

"Your being gay has never been a problem for me," Dixon said. "You're a role model for the other gay and lesbian members of the department and you're a damned good cop."

"I appreciate that, Chief," Decker said. "Zepeda and I usually dealt with homophobic or awkward situations pretty effectively. Then there was an incident where things really got out of hand."

Dixon looked surprised. He started to say something but Carol gestured for him to wait.

Decker stood up and walked over to the window to collect his thoughts.

"A former boyfriend of mine owns that gay bar over across the river. A City health inspector showed up one day and found a couple of minor violations. He threatened to shut down the bar unless Gareth had sex with him. My friend was afraid of losing his business, so he gave the inspector a blow job in the storeroom. The inspector told him that he'd be back the next day for more. Gareth called me to see if I could do something about it."

Decker walked back over and stood behind his chair.

"Zepeda and I were waiting in a booth when the inspector came into the bar the next afternoon. He saw us sitting there so he took Gareth back into the storeroom. The inspector had his pants down when we busted him. Things got ugly so we cuffed him and put him in the car."

"Did you actually hear the inspector extort the bar owner?" Dixon asked.

"No, the music was too loud. It was Gareth's word against his," Decker said. "Anyway, we were going to bring the inspector in when he started yelling about how the bar owner was trying to bribe him with sex to get out of the violations and how we were ruining his career and his marriage. He said he'd swear that Zepeda and I hung out together at the gay bar and provided protection for the owner."

Dixon shook his head.

"Zepeda and I decided we needed to build a better case against the inspector. We told him to stay away from the bar and we cut him loose."

"You made the right decision," Dixon said. "At the minimum, his accusations would have set off an internal affairs investigation."

"It gets worse," Decker said as he sat down again. "That evening, Charlie Hawkins called me. The inspector had been to see him with this ridiculous story of how Zepeda and I had conspired with Gareth to entrap him, an honest, hard-working health inspector, because he wouldn't accept a bribe. If we arrested him for any reason, he wanted Hawkins to publish the story immediately. Charlie wasn't about to print it, of course, but somebody in the media would have had a field day with it. I'm sure my relationship with Gareth would have come out eventually and then it would have been all over the Internet."

"That's when Kyle came to see me," Carol said. "He resigned to protect Ernie's family and career, Chief. He also saved the City from an especially nasty scandal."

"That would have caused a major shit storm," Dixon said. "So, what happened to the damned inspector?"

"He retired two weeks later and moved to Phoenix," Carol said. "The problem went away."

"After we'd already lost one of our best detectives," Dixon said. He shook his head. "Sometimes I'm glad nobody ever tells me anything."

"Shit happens, Chief," Decker said. "It cost me my shield. I can't complain, though. Investigating insurance and worker's comp claims is working out okay for me now."

Carol opened a folder she had been holding in her lap.

"Chief Dixon and I have structured a proposal we think you'll like much better," she said.

"I want you to come back in a new position we've created for you, Decker," Dixon said. "You'll be a senior detective assigned under cover as our homeland security liaison."

"That includes a substantial raise and the full benefits package," Carol said. "The City Manager has even signed off on reinstating your retirement benefits with no gap in service."

Dixon opened a desk drawer and took out Decker's badge and new Glock. He laid them on the desk and slid them toward Decker.

"You'll also get these back," he said, "but don't use either of them unless lives are at risk."

Decker leaned forward, looking at the badge that had meant so much to him.

"What do you mean by under cover?" he asked.

"I need someone who can operate covertly, you know, go some places and do some things without attracting attention. Your insurance investigation business is a perfect cover."

"This sounds like a great opportunity," Decker said. "Where do I sign up?."

"I'll handle the paperwork for you," Carol said. "No one else will know you're working for Chief Dixon again."

"This is ironic," he said. "I can live as an openly gay man but I'm deep in the closet as a police detective."

"Zepeda will be your primary contact," Dixon said. "I've already discussed it with him. You'll sort of be partners again."

Decker smiled and picked up his badge and the weapon. He dropped the badge in his breast pocket and slipped the Glock under his waistband. It felt reassuringly familiar under his sports coat.

Zepeda was waiting in the hall when he came out of the Chief's office.

"Did you accept their offer?" he asked.

"Hell, yes," Decker said. "I'd be crazy not to. What the fuck is a homeland security liaison anyway?"

"It's just a bullshit job title. Dixon has this special account they set up to funnel DHS and FEMA grants funds through. There's enough money sitting there to pay half the department. Dixon just has to label everything *homeland security* something or other."

"That's just fine with me."

"It's not like you're having new business cards printed up."

"Well, Ernie, you're my primary contact. What do I do first?"

"Same thing we've been doing, partner. We figure out who killed Smith and we put Evans away for the rest of his life."

Decker looked at his phone. It was after five.

"Right now I have to get over to Chris's apartment. I'm having dinner with him and his mother."

"I'm taking Maria out tonight," Zepeda said. "I called a babysitter and made reservations at that steakhouse she likes."

"Maybe you'll get lucky."

"I'll be lucky if she's even talking to me again. She was really pissed when I left this morning."

"Sorry I called you out so early but it really paid off. We have the shit head in custody."

"We've got to get Evans to talk. He's our main mission tomorrow. You need to stop by Stratton's office before you leave. He has something for you."

"Can I do it in the morning?"

"It's Chris' bag. DPS recovered it from Evans' truck and gave it to us when they delivered the prisoner."

# CHAPTER THIRTY-THREE

Decker got to Chris' apartment in time to have a glass of wine before dinner. Susan had prepared a pasta dish and the apartment smelled like garlic bread.

"I'm really glad you're here, Kyle," Susan said. "Chris told me so much about you while we were fixing dinner that I feel like I already know you a little."

"I just told her the good stuff," Chris said. "She'll have to find out the rest for herself."

"I understand that you guys are considering moving in together," she said. "I hope you like cats and obsessive compulsive behavior."

"Mother!"

"I meant the cat's behavior, dear."

They all laughed.

"I think we'll get along just fine," Decker said. "The cat will have more room and Chris will have a great time organizing the house."

"I've been thinking about how we can arrange the furniture," Chris said.

"I can't wait to see what you'll do with the kitchen cabinets and the pantry," Decker said. "I am concerned about the closets though."

"You might just have to get rid of all your clothes," Chris said. "I'm going to need all the closet space."

Susan laughed and stood up.

"While you boys negotiate space," she said, "I'll get dinner on the table."

During the bruschetta, Susan talked about Chris' childhood in Seattle. Kyle already knew that Susan had been a single mother. Chris was only three when his father died in the first Gulf War. Susan needed to talk about it and Chris didn't seem to mind.

"Chris was such a sweet little kid," Susan said. "He took everything in stride. He helped me around the house and I never had to worry about the laundry. Chris kept the place cleaner than I did."

"Mom always worked so hard, Kyle. She gave me everything I wanted. Well, except for the racing skis."

"I wasn't going to have my child flying off the side of a mountain," Susan said. "I got you that little sailboat instead."

"I loved sailing on Lake Union," Chris said.

"Did you grow up here in Asher, Kyle?" Susan asked.

"No, I was raised near Abilene. It's 160 miles west of Fort Worth. My family was in the ranching business so I grew up working cattle whenever I wasn't in school. My folks sent me to Texas A&M to become a large animal vet but I hated it. I switched to the prelaw program my sophomore year."

"How did that go over with your family?" Susan asked.

"Not well. They don't have much use for lawyers. When I told them I wanted to be a defense attorney, it really hit the fan. I was on my own after that. I had to get a job to support myself."

"Is that when you became a police officer?" Chris asked.

"Not right away. I worked part-time as a paralegal for an attorney in Bryan while I finished my degree. I spent a lot of time bailing out his clients and helping guilty lowlifes avoid jail. I agreed with the prosecutors most of the time. When I graduated, I passed the police officer exam in Bryan and went through the academy."

"It's interesting how people end up in their professions," Susan said. "Chris wanted to be a ballet dancer when he was little."

"No kidding!" Decker said. "That explains so much."

"Mom," Chris said, "you don't have to tell him everything you know."

"He pretended he was Barishnikov. The other boys in the neighborhood picked on him unmercifully."

"Until I beat up Freddie Johnson behind the gym in junior high," Chris said. "Then they elected me captain of the swimming team."

"Wait a minute," Susan said. "Wasn't Freddie the boy you were sneaking around with your senior year?"

Chris grinned.

"We made up," he said.

"I caught them diddling with each other in the basement," Susan said. "That's when Chris told me he was gay. Like I didn't already know by then."

"It took me a little longer to realize I was gay," Decker said. "I was nearly twenty before I stopped trying to be straight. I'd dated girls but were a lot more interested in my body than I was in theirs. Then I had an experience with a wonderful older man."

"When did you tell your family?" Susan asked. "You have come out to them, haven't you?"

"Christmas, 2008," Kyle said. "I was home for a visit. My father was going on and on about Proposition 8 passing in California and stopping the queers from ruining the American family. When he said that all the faggots should be lined up and shot, I told him to be careful. Some of us are well armed."

"Damn, Kyle," Chris said. "Nothing like dropping the old Q-bomb at Christmas dinner."

"I could have been more subtle. Anyway, we almost came to blows and my mother was crying. I left an hour later. I haven't been back since."

"That's too bad," Susan said. "So many families get torn apart by senseless homo-phobia."

"Abilene's a very conservative place," Decker said, "and my family is big in the Church of Christ out there. I doubt if they'll ever accept me for who I am."

He took a bite of pasta.

"Anyway, I've moved on with my life," he said.

They all sat quietly while Decker finished eating. Chris looked at Susan and nodded toward the kitchen. She stood up.

"I hear that Blue Bell ice cream is really good," she said. "I'll get you guys some dessert."

When she went into the kitchen, Chris squeezed Decker's hand. The conversation had clearly upset Decker.

"She didn't mean to pry," Chris said. "Are you okay?"

"I'm fine, really," Decker said. "It's been too good a day to end it on a sour note."

"How'd your meeting with Chief Dixon go?"

"I have something to tell you later."

Decker fished his badge out of his pocket and showed it to Chris.

"Holy shit, Kyle."

"You can't tell your mother or anyone else. I'm back on the job but I'm under cover."

"That's great ... I think."

Just then Susan brought in dessert. When they were finishing their coffee, Decker excused himself and retrieved a large manilla envelope he'd left by the door. He handed it to Chris.

"I have a surprise for you," he said.

Chris opened the clasp and peered inside.

"Oh, my god! It's my stuff."

Chris poured his phone, keys, wallet, and iPad out on the couch cushion. Sas jumped up on the couch to see what the excitement was all about. He sniffed each item then climbed to the back of the couch to watch Chris.

"DPS found your bag in Evans' truck," Decker said. "Your cash, credit cards, and driver's license are missing but your City ID card was still in your wallet."

"Where's my messenger bag?"

"Sorry, your bag will have to stay in evidence. It was ruined anyway. We'll get you a new one."

Chris looked back in the envelope, then held it up and shook it.

"What about the memory card from the camera? I put it in my bag just before the impact."

"It was in the bag too but Stratton still has it. We're going to look at your photos in the morning."

Chris powered up the iPad.

"I'm so glad to have this again," he said. "What a relief."

"Stratton charged it for you and said it seems to be working fine. Your phone's charged too. He tried to get all of the fingerprint powder off of everything."

"Did he find any prints besides mine?"

"Just the truck driver's and yours on these things. Somebody else's prints were in the bloodstains on the bag. Stratton will run them first thing in the morning."

After they cleaned up the kitchen, Chris suggested a walk so he could exercise his sore knee. Susan said she'd rather relax on the couch with the book she started reading on the plane. As soon as they were alone outside, Chris asked Decker about the detective badge. Decker swore Chris to secrecy and told him about the meeting with Chief Dixon and Carol Bailey.

"So, basically, you're Ernie's partner again but undercover as a private insurance investigator," Chris said. "Are you okay with that arrangement?"

"It's great, Chris," Decker said. "I'll have a good salary and paid health insurance again. I can be a detective without all the bureaucratic bullshit of working inside the department."

"But isn't undercover work more dangerous?"

"Nobody will even know I'm a cop. I'll just be doing what I've been doing, as far as they can tell. Besides, I'll be armed if anything does come up."

Decker pulled up the leg of his jeans so Chris could see the ankle holster and the small S&W pistol tucked into his boot.

"I'll usually have my department issued firearm with me, under my coat or jacket. Otherwise, I'll be wearing this one. My service weapon is locked under the seat in my vehicle right now."

"Damn, Kyle. This will take some getting used to. I've never been around guns."

"You have a few times, babe. You just didn't know it was in my boot."

Chris stopped and stared up at Decker. Decker was looking away. Decker had a very serious expression on his face.

"Anything else I don't know about?" Chris asked.

"Did you know that there's a patrol car in front of your apartment?"

Chris turned around to look just as Zepeda pulled up behind the patrol unit. Zepeda spoke briefly with the officer in the car. Decker whistled to get his attention and Zepeda met them on the sidewalk.

"Sorry to intrude on your evening, guys, but we have a problem. Can we talk inside?"

They went into the apartment. Chris introduced Zepeda to Susan. Then they all sat down in the living room.

"I got a call from the hospital a couple of hours ago," Zepeda said. "The drugs they gave Evans earlier today had worn off and he was raising hell with the officer we have guarding him. Evans was demanding to be taken over to the jail. He's afraid that the man who killed Smith will come after him in the hospital."

"Why would Evans think that?" Decker asked.

"I told him I'd need to hear the whole story before we'd even consider transferring him to the jail," Zepeda said. "Evans was ready to talk, so I set up the video camera and advised him of his rights again. He waived his right to have an attorney present during questioning."

"I wish I'd been there," Decker said. "Why is the uniform parked outside?"

"Because of what Evans told me, I thought it would be best to have an officer guarding Chris for a while."

"This Evans person, the truck driver," Susan said, "isn't he the man you were after?"

"It's more complicated than we thought, ma'am," Zepeda said. "When Chris and Todd Watson were taking photos Saturday morning, there was some activity at a nearby warehouse. Ronnie Evans and Ted Smith, the murder victim we found Sunday, were unloading barrels from a trailer. There was a third man with them."

Zepeda looked at Decker, then at Chris.

"The trailer was almost empty when you showed up in the City car and walked in the direction of the warehouse. The three men thought you were taking pictures of them."

"The warehouse was just in the background to help give scale to our photos of the cleared land," Chris said. "We weren't paying any attention to the warehouse. I didn't even recognize Smith over there."

"Well, the third man, the one in charge according to Evans, got very anxious when they saw you two shooting photos. He told Evans to start the truck and he got into the cab with Evans. They drove around to Old Bridge Road. By then, you and Todd were back in the car. Evans said that, just as they were about to pass you, the other man grabbed the wheel and caused the crash. Then the man jumped out of the truck, took the camera and your bag from the City car, and got back into the truck. He pulled out a pistol and forced Evans to drive away without helping you."

Decker and Chris were stunned, silently imagining the horror as Zepeda described it to them. Susan looked furious.

"Who is the son-of-a bitch?" Decker asked.

Zepeda leaned forward, his elbows on his knees, fingers clasped in front of him.

"He's convinced the same man killed Ted Smith. Evans swears he doesn't know the man's name or anything else about him."

"Did you move Evans to the jail?" Decker asked.

"Hell, no," Zepeda said. "The doctor hasn't released him yet. Besides, as long as Evans is desperate, he's talking."

"Do you believe Evans' story?" Decker asked.

"Yes, I do," Zepeda said. "I think he was genuinely remorseful about the wreck."

"And this other bastard might think that Chris can identify him since he was the one who reached into the car to get the camera," Decker said.

"That's right," Zepeda said.

"I was barely conscious," Chris said. "I couldn't see anything by then. There was blood in my eyes."

Decker rubbed his forehead.

"What the hell was in those barrels?" he asked. "It must be something illegal for him to react so violently."

"All we found in the warehouse were some barrels of agricultural chemicals," Zepeda said. "Stratton is checking the contents to be sure they match the labels.

Evans wouldn't tell me where he picked up the load or who was paying him to haul it."

"I'm sorry, Detective," Susan said. "I'm confused. How does all this relate to the Smith murder?"

"Evans said that, after the wreck, the man forced him to drive to a vacant farmhouse west of the Interstate. Smith met them there and Evans parked his damaged truck in a barn."

"That must be the barn where we found the tire tracks and the fresh oil," Decker said.

"The man wanted to stash the truck until after dark," Zepeda said. "He erased all the photos from the camera and told Evans to get rid of it and the bag. Then Smith dropped Evans off at the motel to hide for the afternoon."

"And Evans gave the camera to the hooker," Chris said.

"After dark, the other man and Smith came back for Evans in the man's pickup. They returned to the farm. The other man was highly agitated that you had survived the wreck. He told Smith to go to the hospital and finish you off before you could come to and talk. Smith refused. Smith even threatened to go to the police."

"I never imagined that Smith had a conscience," Chris said. "Now, I'm sorry he was killed."

"While Smith and the other man were arguing, Evans started up his truck to leave. The man climbed up to the driver's window waving his pistol around and told Evans he would shoot him if he said a word to anyone. Evans drove away, leaving Smith and the other man yelling at each other in the yard outside the barn."

"Which is exactly where Smith's body was found on Sunday morning," Decker said.

"Did Evans give you a description of the man?" Susan asked.

"He gave us a good description," Zepeda said. "He's white, late fifties or early sixties, short gray hair, six foot three, and two hundred pounds. He drives a new, black, crew cab pick-up. According to Evans, he's already committed two murders and he intended to kill Chris."

Zepeda looked at Chris.

"I want you protected around the clock until the suspect is identified and arrested," he said.

"Thanks, Ernie," Chris said.

Zepeda stood up and straightened his suit.

"I doubt if he'll try anything with a patrol car out front," he said. "It was nice to meet you, Ms. Jensson. I need to get home now."

Decker locked the door after Zepeda left. The apartment was silent except for Sas crunching some cat food in the kitchen. Decker put his arm around Chris.

"Maybe I should sleep here with you tonight," he said. "I can take your mom over to my house."

Chris looked at Susan, then at Decker. It was an awkward moment.

"There's no way I'm leaving Chris to-night," Susan said. "If that man shows up, he'll have to deal with me and I'm pissed."

"Do you want my pistol, Chris?" Decker said. "I can show you how to use it."

"No thanks," Chris said. "I have my pepper spray and Mom swings a mean baseball bat."

"We'll be fine, Kyle," Susan said. "You should probably go home now. We all need to get some rest."

Reluctantly, Decker let them see him to the door. He stopped at the curb to swap cell phone numbers with the officer in the patrol car. Then he pulled his Expedition out of the parking spot, turned it around, and backed into the same space. From there, he could see Chris's apartment and watch the whole parking area.

Decker took the Glock out of the gun safe under the seat and tucked it between the console and his leg. Then he leaned his seat back and settled in for the night.

# CHAPTER THIRTY-FOUR

Officer Luedecke tapped on Decker's window a few minutes after six. Decker startled and went for his weapon. Luedecke jumped back. Decker quickly realized who it was and lowered the window.

"Damn, Tom," he said, "don't sneak up on me like that. You here for the day watch?"

Luedecke handed Decker a cup of coffee from a paper bag he was holding.

"Serve and protect," Luedecke said. "I'm your boyfriend's bodyguard today."

"I appreciate it. Keep an eye out for a black crew cab pickup. We think that's what the suspect may be driving."

"I'll call you if I see anything."

Decker drove home to shower. Zepeda called while Decker was having breakfast. They decided to meet at the station to watch the Evans video and prepare follow-up questions. Decker was waiting in the reception area when Zepeda arrived at seven-thirty and they went back to Zepeda's office.

"We need to find that black pickup," Decker said. "There can't be very many late-model black crew cabs registered in DeLeon County, assuming it's local."

"We can check the DPS database," Zepeda said. "I was thinking about the timeline on Saturday. If we can figure out where Smith was between the time he dropped Evans off at the motel and that night when Smith and the suspect took Evans back out to the farm, we might find a witness who saw Smith with the suspect."

"Good point," Decker said. "We don't know where Smith was all afternoon."

"Well, since I found his car at his office, the suspect must have picked Smith up there sometime before they went to the motel to get Evans."

Zepeda was connecting the little video camera to the computer when Stratton came in.

"Good morning," Stratton said. "I thought y'all would want to know that the latents from the leather bag matched the prints from the real estate sign. Too bad they aren't in AFIS."

"They will be when we arrest him," Zepeda said.

"Chris really appreciated getting his things back, Gene," Decker said. "Thanks for expediting that."

"No problem," Stratton said. He spread out three enlarged photos on the desk. "I printed up these from the memory disk last night."

The first two photos showed Ronnie Evans and Ted Smith moving barrels into the warehouse. They showed Evans' rig parked in front of the trailer. The trailer was already disconnected from the cab. Smith's red Cadillac was parked on the other side of the trailer.

In the last photo, three men were standing on the dock behind the trailer looking toward the camera. Smith and Evans were in the sun and easily identifiable. The other man was in the shade of the trailer, shown only in silhouette. He was almost as tall as Evans but heavier. Zepeda and Decker both strained to see the face.

"Sorry guys," Stratton said. "I tried to enhance the image, but the resolution is bad. The face is just a dark blur."

"At least this confirms Evans' story," Zepeda said. "There was a third man with them Saturday morning."

"Any analysis on the chemicals from the warehouse yet?" Decker asked.

"We should get the lab report back this morning. I'm pretty sure we found nine barrels of common pesticides."

"Only nine?" Decker said. "I thought it was a trailer full of barrels."

"If that's the case," Zepeda said, "someone moved the rest of them out of the warehouse between Saturday morning and Monday morning."

"We need to figure out where those barrels are now," Decker said.

"Good luck with that," Stratton said. "I'll call you when I get the lab results."

Stratton left the detectives to watch the Evans interview. They viewed it twice, pausing several times to discuss possible lines of inquiry. They planned to press Evans about his cargo and who hired him to haul it. Maybe he knew where it went after it left the warehouse.

Decker called a friend at the courthouse to find out if a public defender had been appointed yet for Evans. There had been a delay in appointing an attorney for Evans. Evidently, none of the local defense attorneys wanted the Evans case. Everyone was finding excuses or calling in favors to avoid representing Evans in a certain conviction. Decker's friend said that someone would get the short straw by the end of the day.

Zepeda called the assistant district attorney who prosecuted major criminal cases. He promised to send the video over so the ADA could watch it. The ADA advised Zepeda not to question Evans again until he had legal counsel in the room.

Decker could tell that Zepeda was not please when he put the phone down.

"Well, shit, Kyle," Zepeda said. "We can't question Evans again until he has a lawyer. It might not be until late this afternoon before they appoint one."

"We have plenty to do until then. Maybe we can identify the killer before we interview Evans."

"I'll tell you what," Zepeda said. "I'll call the local farm supply stores and arial spraying companies about recent pesticide deliveries. You try to look up that black pickup truck in the database. Then we'll head out and try to find a witness or two. We might get lucky."

"Speaking of getting lucky, how was your dinner with Maria?"

"Everything was going fine until they called me from the hospital. When I got home from Chris' place, my pillow was waiting for me on the couch. Breakfast was tense this morning, to say the least."

"We need to close this fucking case before it ruins your marriage, Ernie."

# CHAPTER THIRTY-FIVE

The sun reflected off the patrol car parked directly in front of the apartment when Chris and Susan stepped out about nine. Luedecke was filling out a report on the computer mounted in the car. He got out to greet them.

"Good morning, officer," Chris said. "I'm Chris Jensson and this is my mother, Susan Jensson."

"Morning, I'm Tom Luedecke. I've been assigned to your protection detail."

"I appreciate you looking out for me, Tom," Chris said. "I need to go to City Hall to take care of a couple of things. Should I ride with you or should my mother take me downtown?"

"I can drive you. I'm your personal chauffeur and bodyguard today."

Susan was reassured that Chris would be going with the officer and by the big pistol on Luedecke's hip. While Chris told Susan goodbye, Luedecke moved some paperwork out of the front seat.

Between the cast, bruised ribs, and stiff knee, getting into the cramped passenger seat was painful for Chris. He'd never ridden in a police car before and he was surprised by the electronics at the officer's disposal. He was a little disconcerted by the shotgun clipped to the dashboard between them. Luedecke reported to the dispatcher that they were leaving and their destination.

Another uniformed officer met them at the curb in front of City Hall and took up a position near the front door before they even got out of the car. Chris was a little embarrassed about the security but it reminded him how close he'd come to death on Saturday. Someone had tried to murder him with a truck and then tried to coerce Ted Smith into killing him in his hospital bed. He walked very close to Luedecke until they were inside the building.

Chris spent half an hour letting co-workers sign his cast and offer wishes for a speedy recovery. Todd Watson's death was heavy on their minds. Finally, Chris and Luedecke reached the Planning and Transportation Department.

Tommy Nelson's bitchy secretary, Barbara, raised her eyebrows in disapproval when Luedecke checked the office suite. He took a seat in the reception area where he could see anyone who came in the door.

Barbara immediately confronted Chris.

"I'll tell the Mr. Nelson you're here to clean out your desk. He may want to speak with you."

"Excuse me, what did you say?" Chris asked.

"I thought the Director called you already," Barbara said. "Mr. Nelson has suspended you for using the City car without authorization."

Chris was astonished.

"What the hell are you talking about?" he asked.

"Your termination hearing will be held later this week."

Chris stormed into the Director's office. Nelson was on the phone but hung up quickly when Chris thumped his cast on the desk.

"I'm very busy now," Nelson said. "You'll have to wait outside."

"No, Mr. Nelson, I won't wait," Chris said. "Todd Watson and I were on City business. We were taking photos for the Tract B hearing."

"As your immediate supervisor, I can say you were driving that City car this weekend without my approval. I can suspended you and schedule a termination hearing."

"This is total bullshit! I can't believe Carol Bailey or the city manager will let you get away with this."

"We'll see about that. The fieldwork you claim you were doing could have waited until Monday. As far as I'm concerned, you and your subordinate were out there without authorization."

"You're being ridiculous! No one will believe that Todd and I were out joyriding at dawn on Saturday morning."

"Maybe you were sneaking around on your boyfriend," Nelson said. "Poor Todd. As his supervisor, it was your fault."

"If you hadn't screwed up the hearing schedule, this wouldn't have happened. Why did you move the tract B hearing forward?"

Nelson stood up and stepped around his desk.

"There were circumstances that required setting an earlier date," he said. "I don't have to justify my decisions to you."

"What kind of circumstances?"

"The Asher Economic Development Commission is supporting the rezoning. They requested an early hearing in order to obtain state incentive funds for the new industry to be built on Tract B."

"Did Ted Smith pressure you to move up the hearing?"

"It's a shame about Ted too," Nelson said, shaking his head.

Chris restated the question Nelson was avoiding.

"I'm asking you who wanted the hearing moved up. Was it Smith?"

Nelson stepped close to Chris. His foul breath made Chris turn away.

"I don't take orders from developers. Now, get out of my office."

"I won't let you blame this on me."

"I've got you cold for violating City policy, but you might change my mind."

Nelson unzipped his pants. He put his hands on Chris' shoulders and tried to force Chris down on his knees.

"Suck my dick, you little faggot," Nelson said.

Chris pushed him away and pointed a small canister at Nelson's face.

Nelson gasped when the pepper spray filled his eyes and mouth. He frantically wiped at his face with his shirtsleeves. His yellow eyes turned blood red, filled with rage. Spitting and grunting, he lunged forward. His hands grabbed Chris' throat.

Chris' arms flew up, breaking Nelson's grip. Then Chris' slammed his cast into Nelson's solar plexus. Nelson was moaning, trying to catch his breath.

"Don't ever touch me again, you piece of shit," Chris growled.

He picked up the pepper spray, slipped out of the office, and quickly closed the door behind him.

Luedecke and Barbara were both on their feet.

"You okay, Chris?" Luedecke asked.

"I'm fine," Chris said, wiping tears from his own eyes.

"What's going on in there?" Barbara said.

"Mr. Nelson was overcome by recent events," Chris said. "He'd rather be alone for a while."

Luedecke followed Chris to the restroom, where Chris carefully washed his face and hands. Then they went to Carol Bailey's office. Luedecke waited outside the door.

Chris told Carol what had just happened in Nelson's office.

"That bastard!" Carol said. "What a moron."

"Can he really get me fired, Carol?"

"Of course not. Roberts had him on the carpet first thing yesterday. We're already working with the insurance company to pay your hospital bill and get the life insurance to Todd's parents."

"What about the car?"

"The adjuster totaled it out. The City will replace it just like we do with wrecked police cars. No big deal."

"Why would Nelson act that way?"

"Because he's an idiot. When Mr. Roberts hears about this, Nelson's history. You need to document everything in a memo to me immediately."

"What about the pepper spray?"

"That was clearly self defense," Carol said. "In addition to the sexual harassment, he physically attacked you."

"I'll go back to my office and send you a memo right away."

"Stay close to Officer Luedecke, Chris. If Nelson tries anything else, tell Tom to arrest him for assaulting you."

Chris went straight to his office in the Planning and Transportation Department. Using the keyboard and mouse was awkward. His arm was throbbing in the cast and he had a headache but at least Nelson was in pain too.

Luedecke again took a seat in the waiting area. Tommy Nelson came out and looked to Barbara for an explanation. She shrugged.

"Can I help you with something, Officer?" he asked.

"No, thank you," Leudecke said. "I'm here with Mr. Jensson. We just want to make sure no further harm comes to him."

Nelson stiffened and his face flushed.

"I'm sure Mr. Jensson can take care of himself," Nelson said. Then he hurried out the department door.

Luedecke asked Barbara, "What was that all about?"

Barbara gave him one of those glares that nonverbally told him that hell would freeze over before he got any information from her. She picked up the phone and ignored him.

Chris wrote the memo to document Nelson's violations of city policies regarding sexual harassment and threatening city employees, including the earlier threats against him and his mother. He mentioned the zoning irregularities and the notification problem. When he finished, he emailed it to Carol Bailey with a copy to his own private email address. He thought about sending it to Decker but didn't. Decker had two murders to solve, not one to commit.

Chris knew that going on the record with such serious complaints would make it difficult if he ever applied for a position somewhere else. But he was pissed off and it was time to put a stop to Nelson.

As long as he was being bold, Chris decided he would do whatever he could to stop the Tract B rezoning and prevent Tracts A and C from being bulldozed. He needed some political leverage, some controversy. The City Council's default reaction whenever there was a crowded zoning hearing was to deny the rezoning or table the matter for further study. They never voted against a vocal opposition. They waited until later, when no one was watching.

The first call Chris made was to Dr. Lloyd, the horticulturist at Texas A&M who had named the Aggie Sage and who was working on the endangered species designation. Dr. Lloyd was outraged to hear what had happened to Todd and Chris and that Tract B had been cleared. He promised to drive to Asher and testify at the hearing.

Chris knew the president of the Asher Garden Club from volunteering on their city beautification committee. Their members often hosted receptions for local politicians and made large campaign contributions to city council candidates. A call to the president would guarantee ten or twelve influential members in attendance at the hearing. Chris made the call and described the destruction of the native wildflowers on Tract B. He also suggested that the garden club members might arrive early to get seats near the front of the council chambers.

The third call Chris made was to a friend at Crockett State University who coordinated the student environmental groups on the Asher campus. He was also a recruiter for Greenpeace. The activist was glad to help. He said they were looking for a local issue to get things rolling for the fall term. The loss of native habitat would be perfect. A protest would get the new leadership of all the groups together and launch their fall membership push.

When he got off the phone, Chris used a graphics app on his iPad to draw a small diagram of the area outside City Hall. He estimated where the late afternoon light would be best and where the plants would provide a lush green background for video of the protest. Chris came up with a few slogans for the protest signs and emailed it all to the activist along with the hearing information.

Chris checked his office voicemail and discovered several messages of condolences and concern about his injuries. There were a couple of calls he had to return. It was very difficult for Chris to talk about Todd's death. Regardless of Tommy Nelson's role in the tragedy, Chris felt responsible for Todd being with him on Saturday morning.

# CHAPTER THIRTY-SIX

There wasn't much for Luedecke to read in the waiting room, mostly city planning journals and magazines about highway engineering. He finally got interested in an article about gated communities in Boca Raton. His reading was interrupted by the arrival of a Channel Five news crew.

Lori Latimer wanted to tape an interview with Mr. Jensson. They showed him their press credentials and the picture identification cards issued by the television station. He told them to wait while he checked with Chris.

Chris was feeling unusually talkative with the public hearing only hours away. Chris said he would grant an interview but he wouldn't allow any videotape because he didn't want to be on television with his face so bruised. Ed, Lori's videographer, dumped his heavy equipment unceremoniously on the floor in the small waiting area and slouched in a chair.

Lori sat in the side chair in Chris' office, pad and pen in hand, nervous about taking notes during an interview. She always relied on videotape to capture quotes and on the station's writer to prepare stories for her. Lori usually only asked questions and summed up. She carried a notebook for effect, as a prop. The hit-and-run was such a big story for Lori, however, she decided to risk taking notes this time.

"Mr. Jensson," Lori began, "Mr. Tommy Nelson, your supervisor told us yesterday that you were using the City vehicle without proper authorization. What exactly was so important for you and Mr. Watson to drive out on that country road on Saturday morning?"

"If you're asking me why we took the City car out there," Chris replied, "it was because we had some work to do for the department. We certainly wouldn't be riding around in a city car on Saturday morning just for fun."

"So you deny it was unauthorized?"

"Of course! Mr. Nelson was mistaken, Lori. We were out there taking pictures of a piece of property scheduled for a rezoning hearing tonight. It was a last minute effort because Mr. Nelson mysteriously moved the case ahead on the City Council agenda."

Chris was delighted to see Lori's eye-brows raised at the word *mysterious.*

"Why do you say it's mysterious, Mr. Jensson?" Lori obliged.

Chris lowered his voice and looked at the door nervously.

"Well, this is just between us, on background. Okay?"

Lori leaned over, pen poised for a quote, "Sure. Tell me what's going on, Chris. Can I call you Chris?"

"Of course. We're on the same side here, aren't we?"

Chris nodded his head. Lori nodded too, as expected. The pact was sealed.

"For some strange reason, Mr. Nelson moved the Tract B rezoning way ahead on the schedule. He won't tell me why. I wonder if Ted Smith pressured him into it. Smith was the rezoning applicant before he was murdered. The legal notification doesn't even meet the state requirements. It could get Mr. Nelson in trouble to be out of compliance with the state statute."

Lori was unable to keep up in her notebook. Her writing was large and loopy, full of false starts and scratched-out words. Lori held up her hand to stop Chris. She asked Chris to explain about notification noncompliance. Chris handed her a printed copy of the notification requirements, complete with the referenced Texas statute, from the department's procedure manual.

"I just don't know why Mr. Nelson so blatantly violated the state law on this case, Lori. I can't help but wonder about Ted Smith's murder and Tommy Nelson's strange behavior lately."

Lori finally caught on to the significance of this development in the story, but she had no idea how to tie it together with the hit and run.

"It's the strangest thing, Lori. Todd Watson and I were out there taking pictures while some men were unloading a truckload of barrels into Smith's warehouse." Chris explained slowly, guiding the reporter to the news value of the story. "The truck driver and another man crashed into the city car to steal the camera we were using."

"So you, like, witnessed a crime or something. And then they drive around and smash into you with a truck? Oh, my god, it's like a movie!"

"The other strange thing is that this is the same piece of property where we found the rare wildflowers. Remember, Lori, the rare Aggie Sage that was discovered? It might be an endangered species. It's as though someone was hurrying to wipe out the plants before they could be protected."

"So, they tried to kill you over wildflowers before the zoning?" Lori looked totally bewildered. "You've lost me now. What is the connection with the endangered species thing?"

She struggled to spell species correctly in her notes but soon gave up.

"I'm not sure, Lori, but I'm afraid Mr. Nelson may be involved."

Lori was flustered.

"Chris, you're going too fast for me," she said.

"The main thing to write down, Lori," Chris said carefully, "is that Todd Watson and I were on City business Saturday. We had to take some pictures for the zoning hearing because Mr. Nelson scheduled it ahead of time." He waited for Lori to catch up in her notes. "While we were working, some men connected to Ted Smith crashed into us on purpose to prevent us from showing the photos. Todd Watson was killed and I was left for dead."

Lori read from her scratchy notes.

"So, you guys go out there Saturday to take pictures about this zoning thing because of Mr. Nelson's schedule with the city council and you get pictures of something maybe illegal. It's the same property where the rare Aggie flowers were. The next thing you know, this truck smashes into you and Mr. Watson. Then they snatch the camera and drive off?"

Lori looked to Chris for approval like a kid in a classroom.

"That's very concise, Lori. You may want to note that part about the notification too. And don't forget to look up the Aggie Sage stories in your archives."

Lori made more notes in the margins of the full page.

"The news writer may need to check some facts with you later this afternoon. Can he call your cell number?"

"I'd be happy to talk with him. Say, Lori, you will be at the hearing tonight, won't you?"

"You mean this zoning meeting is tonight?"

"Yes, and they allow news coverage of all council meetings."

Chris smiled and nodded. Lori mirrored Chris' nonverbal actions.

"You'll want to get live video of the Tract B public hearing," Chris said. "It will be very controversial."

Chris stood and leaned close to the reporter. He lowered his voice.

"Ted Smith's murder may even have something to do with this, Lori. This is growing into a major news story."

The reporter could hardly contain herself. She began gathering up her bag and notebook and trying to shake hands with Chris, all at once. Chris stood calmly and waited until Lori was ready to leave.

"I need to phone this in and get them working on it," Lori said breathlessly as she fumbled with her cell phone. "Thanks, Chris, you've been very helpful. I'm really glad you weren't hurt too much in that wreck."

"I'll see you tonight," Chris said.

"For sure," Lori said.

A satisfied grin spread across Chris' still puffy mouth.

*The bastards deserve this and worse,* he thought.

Chris gathered his things and collected Luedecke as he left the department. When they got in the car, he turned to Luedecke.

"Thanks for hanging in there with me this morning, Tom."

"No problem," he said. "That secretary and your boss were sure acting peculiar. Are they always so nervous?"

"It's been a stressful morning for us all."

"Kind of boring for me," Luedecke said, "but that's good. I didn't have to stop a bullet for you or anything."

"Tom, I think there might be a few college kids protesting outside the City Council chambers this evening. It's mostly for news coverage. If they are well organized and just walk in a line for the television crew, would that cause any problems from the Police Department's perspective?"

"I don't think so," Luedecke said. "I'll give the patrol sergeant a heads up, just to make sure."

"Should I assume you plan to attend the city council meeting?"

"I wouldn't miss it for the world. I need to get some rest this afternoon but I'll be ready to come back to City Hall before six."

# CHAPTER THIRTY-SEVEN

After spending the remainder of the morning unsuccessfully trying to track down the chemicals and the black pickup, Decker and Zepeda treated themselves to the enchilada special at Rosa's Cafe. While Zepeda waited in line to settle the bill, Decker stood by the car and called Chris.

"We're at Rosa's Cafe," he said. "Nothing like TexMex and draft beer after a frustrating morning of detecting. How are you doing, hot stuff?"

"Fine," Chris said. "My arm's a little sore."

"How's your Mom holding up?"

"She just took Tom Luedecke a ham sandwich. They're becoming great pals. Tom drove me to City Hall this morning so I could take care of a few things."

"How did that go?"

"I'll tell you all about it later. The Tract B hearing is shaping up to be quite a show. I need to be there."

"I'm not sure that's a good idea," Decker said. "Tom might not be able to protect you in a crowd."

"Nobody would try anything in a televised city council meeting. Especially not with you and Tom right there with me. Can you pick me up at 5:30?"

"As much as I would *love* to go to a zoning meeting with you, Ernie and I are planning to question Evans late this afternoon. I'll have to catch the council meeting on reruns."

"I hope you guys use your rubber hoses on that Evans shithead. Sometimes a little torture is in order."

"You'd be a lot safer if you stayed home. Maybe you should watch the hearing on TV."

"No way, Kyle. Besides, there will be extra police officers at City Hall to monitor the protestors."

"Protestors?" Decker said. "What have you been up to, Chris?"

"I just made some strategic phone calls and wound Lori Latimer up like an alarm clock. It'll be great watching the council members shit themselves when they see the turnout."

"Chris, we confirmed Evans' story that there's a third man who could be the killer. He was in one of your photos but we couldn't see his face and we haven't identified him yet. You really need to be careful until we have this guy in custody."

"Well, I'm going to take a long nap this afternoon while you catch the bastard and throw him in jail."

"We're doing our best," Decker said. "It's just a matter of time."

"I'll see you in my dreams, big guy."

"Mmmm. I hope they're wet dreams."

Zepeda winced when he overheard that last comment. Decker laughed and promised to meet up with Chris after the Evans interview.

Zepeda and Decker decided that their best bet would be to look for witnesses at the businesses near Smith's office since they knew Smith was there sometime Saturday afternoon. Someone might have seen who picked up Smith there.

Ted Smith's real estate office was in one of those commercial areas that was well past its prime. Three other businesses occupied the small strip center. A convenience store was on the north end of the building, then a pet grooming place, Smith's office, and a dry cleaners at the other end. There was a funeral home just south of the strip center. A resale clothing shop occupied an old house adjacent to the strip center on the north. Across the street was an empty parking lot for a former building supply and hardware store defaced by graffiti.

The detectives started with the convenience store since Zepeda needed the restroom. The clerk knew Ted Smith and remembered that Smith bought a packaged sandwich, chips, and a six pack of beer about two on Saturday afternoon. He didn't see any black pickup truck and there was no surveillance camera outside.

The owner of the pet grooming business, a slim woman in her thirties, said she was closed Saturday afternoon. She said she honestly wouldn't miss Smith as a neighbor because he complained about the dogs barking and made lewd comments to her female customers. The Hispanic man in the dry cleaners didn't speak much English and seemed very nervous to be around police. Zepeda talked with him just long enough to learn that he either hadn't seen anything on Saturday afternoon or that he wouldn't tell them even if he had.

The funeral director was more helpful. He's been parking the hearse when Smith pulled up and they had talked about football for a few minutes. He said Smith was friendly, as usual, but that he seemed troubled about something. He said Smith went into the convenience store after they spoke. The funeral director had been working in the embalming room the rest of the day and had not seen any black pickup trucks at Smith's office.

Decker and Zepeda walked back north to the resale shop. It was a modest brick house built in the early forties when the neighborhood was all residential. There was a Ted Smith yard sign leaning against the side of the porch. It had been pulled up out of the yard recently. The shop owner, Mary Johnson, was hanging some clothes on a rack when the little bell over the door signaled their entrance. She was a tiny, stooped woman in her seventies with thinning white hair and a hearing aid in one ear. Reading glasses hung from her neck and rested on her flat chest when she looked up to see Decker's face.

"Good afternoon," she said. "Can I help you find something?"

Zepeda handed her his business card and introduced Decker as a consulting private investigator. She studied the card carefully. It was hot and musty inside the shop.

"We'd like to ask you about Ted Smith, Mrs. Johnson," Zepeda said. "We noticed the real estate sign outside."

"Yes, so sad, isn't it? He was such a nice young man. Ted was helping me sell the store. I don't know what I'll do now that he's gone."

"Were you here on Saturday afternoon, ma'am?" Decker asked.

"All day, every day, except Sunday. Business was real slow. I was pricing my stock that I bought at the garage sales last week."

"Did you happen to see Mr. Smith or anyone else at his office during the afternoon?" Zepeda asked.

"Well, yes, you know. I saw his car over there," she said. "I was planning to go over and visit with Ted after closing, at five, but he got busy just as I was locking up."

"Was someone else at his office?" Decker asked.

"As I said, I was locking up the shop when a big black pickup truck came just tearing into the parking lot. It pulled up next to Ted's car. I was afraid it might scratch Ted's pretty red Cadillac, you know. He hurried into Ted's office so I just headed on to the grocery store. I figured I'd just go see Ted on Monday. I can't believe he passed, you know. It's just awful."

"Did you recognize the man driving the black truck, Mrs. Johnson?" Zepeda asked.

"No, no, I don't know him," she said. "But I have seen that truck over at Ted's office before. I don't miss much that goes on in this neighborhood, you know, because of the vandalism problem. I've been in business here for over eighteen years. I started out selling vintage wedding dresses and used prom gowns. My late husband, George, set me up in business years ago. He passed last year. Prostate cancer took him from me, you know. Now I just want to sell the shop and travel with my sister. She lives in the Valley, you know, and ..."

"Excuse me, Mrs. Johnson," Zepeda said. "Sorry to interrupt but we need to focus on Ted Smith and his visitor. Did you see them leave together?"

"As I was saying, Detective, this man drove up and went directly into Ted's office. I went on to do my grocery shopping so I couldn't say when they left."

"Could you describe him for us, ma'am?" Decker asked.

"Well now, let me think," she said. "He was a large man, not fat, but quite large. He had on blue jeans and boots and a very nice white western shirt, you know, kind of fancy with dark buttons and stitching."

"Did you see his face?" Zepeda asked.

"I couldn't really see his face because he was kind of looking down, you know, not looking around at all. He had grayish hair, worn fairly short. He must have had some serious business with Ted."

"Anything else? " Decker asked. "Do you recall if he had any distinguishing features, maybe like a limp or anything?"

Mary thought about it for a minute. She stared out the window, trying to remember the man going into Smith's office.

"No," she said. "He was just regular looking, I guess. A large man, well dressed, you know, but all business. He just charged right into the office. I didn't want to go over there and interrupt them."

"What about the pickup truck? Ford, Chevy, Dodge?" Zepeda asked.

"I don't know what make it was, but it was one of those with four doors, you know," Mary said. "I remember because George, my late husband, used to have one for his plumbing business. He called it a crew cab because his laborers could ride in the back seat sometimes. Usually it was full of tools and fittings, you know, but two men could sit back there if need be."

"You didn't happen to notice the license number, did you?" Zepeda asked.

"Why on earth would I do that?" she said. "It wasn't any of my business. It was just a man in a truck. I didn't think any more of it until you asked me just now."

"So, you saw a large man with gray hair arrive in a black crew cab pickup truck about five o'clock on Saturday and he went directly into Ted Smith's office," Zepeda said.

"Yes, sir. That's what I saw," she said. "Did he have something to do with Ted's murder, you think?"

"That's a possibility, ma'am," Decker said. "We don't know for sure but we do need to talk to him."

"If you think of anything else or if you see him again, please call me immediately," Zepeda said. "It's very important that we find the man you saw."

"I'll certainly do that, Detective," Mary said. "While you're here, would you like to buy something for Mrs. Zepeda? I have some lovely fall dresses and sweaters priced very reason-ably."

"No thanks, ma'am," Zepeda said, "but I'll tell her about your shop. Maybe she'll come by sometime."

Decker and Zepeda thanked Mrs. Johnson and left before she could launch into any other stories. It wasn't an easy getaway.

In the parking lot, Zepeda called the district attorney's office. A public defender had been appointed. Zepeda called the attorney next and set up an interview with Evans at the hospital at six.

# CHAPTER THIRTY-EIGHT

Decker and Zepeda got to the hospital a few minutes early. Decker stopped near the entrance to call Chris. Zepeda carried the camera and tripod to Evans' room. Evans' attorney had not arrived yet.

Ronnie was in much more trouble that he knew. He was incarcerated in a private room directly across the hall from the room Chris Jensson had occupied. The irony was not wasted on the hospital staff, especially Nurse Eloise.

"You've got to get me out of here," Evans said. "That damned nurse is torturing me. This is cruel and unusual punishment or some legal shit like that."

"What's the problem?" Zepeda asked.

"Since you got me handcuffed to this bed, they put a tube in me to pee through. That nurse came in twice today and said it wasn't working. She yanked the tube out of my dick and then fucking stuck it back again. She also ripped the bandage off my head and scrubbed the glue off with alcohol. Felt like my head was on fire. Getting my fucking ear shot off didn't hurt as bad as that!"

"Quiet down," Zepeda said. "There are actual sick people in here."

"Just take me to jail, Detective. I'm begging you."

Zepeda set up the tripod and video camera.

"If you cooperate with us tonight, we'll probably transfer you to the County jail in the morning."

"Well, shit," Evans said. "Could you at least give me the TV remote? They put it over there where I can't reach it."

Zepeda handed him the remote. Evans was flipping channels when Decker came into the room.

"So, this is Ronnie Evans," Decker said, "the ass wipe that rammed his truck into two innocent people and then left them for dead."

Decker moved menacingly toward the bed. Zepeda stepped between them. They had worked out the good cop, bad cop routine years before but Decker's genuine anger was surfacing.

"This is Kyle Decker," Zepeda said to Evans, "the City's insurance investigator. He's been looking forward to meeting you ever since you damned near killed his best friend on Saturday."

Zepeda stayed between Decker and Evans while they eyed each other.

"I'm really sorry, man," he said. "It wasn't my fault. I feel real bad about what happened."

Zepeda motioned for Decker to step over by the door with him.

"Sorry piece of shit," Decker said under his breath.

"How's Chris doing over at City Hall?" Zepeda asked.

"He's okay. There's a little protest growing over there. Three car loads of college students are marching around with signs outside the council chamber."

"Are they causing any trouble?"

"Not yet. They formed a line outside the building but they aren't in the way of people showing up for the meeting."

"Is the media there covering it?"

"Oh, yeah. They raised up the dish and they're setting up inside the council chambers. Channel Five will be broadcasting it live."

Zepeda's phone rang. It was Evans' attorney saying he'd be a half-hour late due to a problem with his car. Zepeda told him they would wait.

Zepeda took the remote from Evans and changed the channel. On the television mounted high on the wall, a commercial ended and the screen showed Debra Olsen, the Channel Five anchor.

"For our lead story tonight, we're taking you live to Asher City Hall where Lori Latimer is standing by at a highly charged city council meeting. Lori, can you tell our viewers what's stirring up Asher citizens tonight?"

The screen was suddenly filled with Lori's smiling face in front of a room crowded with well-dressed senior citizens and college students in jeans and Greenpeace sweatshirts. City staffers huddled near the front looked surprised and self-conscious.

"Thanks, Deb," Lori said. "The City Council meeting is being delayed a few minutes while City officials make their way through the crowd of protestors here at City Hall. A major zoning controversy brings out the environmentalists tonight. Behind me are members of the Asher Garden Club, angry about the destruction of native wildflowers."

As Lori's voice continued, the control room played video recorded earlier outside City Hall.

"As you can see," Lori narrated, "environmentalists from Crockett State University are staging a real protest. They've been threatening to take over the Council chambers and hold a sit-in to show solidarity with the Garden Club."

The scene flashed to Debra, looking very concerned.

"In just a moment," Debra said, "Lori will tell us why this zoning dispute smells like something other than wildflowers."

Zepeda grimaced and switched to the local access channel that always broadcast the Council meetings.

"Hey," Evans said, "can you put on NASCAR or something? This is boring as shit."

Decker leaned over Evans' bed and looked him square in the face.

"Don't push your luck," Decker said.

"Let's just watch the television while we wait for Mr. Evans' attorney to arrive," Zepeda said.

The television camera panned the Council chamber. The front third of the room was filled with the built-in curved council table. A small rail on the front of the table held the name plates of the members. Microphones curved upward to record the wisdom of the local politicians. A wooden podium with a microphone was centered in front of the Council table.

Two large glass-topped tables flanked the council table. The one to the council's left was for City staff members. Tommy Nelson was seated there studying the contents of a three-ring notebook. The City Secretary sat next to him concentrating on her laptop computer. The table to the council's right was reserved for the print media. Charlie Hawkins sat there alone. The Channel Five videographer was set up near the news media table.

Seating for the audience filled the remainder of the room. The garden club members occupied the first three rows. Citizens and college students were rapidly filling all of the available seats. The camera showed students entering in an orderly manner with their protest signs. They stood, lining the back and side walls.

While the camera continued to pan the room, it showed Chris and Susan entering the chambers with Luedecke close behind them. Chris greeted several people as they made their way to the center aisle. He introduced Susan to a man dressed in khakis and a sport coat. Luedecke looked around apprehensively, like he needed rear-view mirrors or eyes in the back of his head. He wanted Chris in the back corner of the room but Chris insisted on sitting where he could see and hear everything.

Mayor Harris and the City Council took their places. City Manager Roberts and the City Attorney sat down at the staff table. The meeting was called to order. They approved the minutes and the Mayor opened the public hearing to rezone Tract B. The Mayor called Tommy Nelson to the podium to present the case.

Ronnie Evans shifted in the bed, his eyes riveted to the television screen. Decker glared at him but Evans didn't even notice.

Tommy Nelson approached the podium and a colored map of the Tract B area was shown on a screen above the press table.

"As you can see," Nelson said mechanically, "the subject property is located on Old Bridge Road near the Asher Industrial Park. Surrounding land uses are industrial and agriculture. Old Bridge Road is shown in the thoroughfare plan as a future four-lane divided arterial. The airport is to the south. There are no dwellings within a thousand feet of the subject property. We notified eight adjacent property owners and received no objections. The adjacent tracts are either industrial or undeveloped. The property is flat. There are no drainage problems and the subject property has been cleared for development."

There was a general shuffling and some loud grumbling from the audience. Someone in the rear shouted, "Destruction for dollars." Someone else yelled, "Wildflowers not warehouses."

The mayor admonished the audience, promising everyone a chance to speak during the hearing. He smiled anxiously at the ladies from the garden club.

In his hospital bed, Evans looked anxiously at Zepeda but said nothing. His attention returned to the television.

"See someone you know?" Zepeda asked.

Evans just shook his head but he was clearly lying.

On the television, Nelson said, "That's all I have Mayor Harris, unless the council has any questions."

Mayor Harris looked surprised.

"Don't you have any photographs of the site to show us, Mr. Nelson?" he asked.

"Not at this time, Mr. Mayor," Nelson said.

No one else asked a question so Nelson returned to the staff table. The Mayor thanked Nelson and called for the representative of the applicant to come forward.

The man who took the podium wore a tailored Italian suit and had the manicured features of someone wealthy. He cleared his throat, looked at each council member, then addressed the Mayor.

"Mayor Harris, honorable members of the City Council, my name is Nick Lucas. I am an attorney with offices in Houston and I represent the owners of Tract B."

Evans stiffened in his bed. Decker and Zepeda looked at him. Evans shook his head again but he obviously recognized someone on the screen.

Lucas explained to the council that the rezoning was in compliance with the Asher comprehensive plan and endorsed by the economic development commission. He said that the new business would employ ten local people, guaranteed as a condition of state economic development funds they were seeking. A colored site plan appeared on the screen behind the press table. The plan showed an industrial building surrounded by green landscaping and lots of trees. With a laser pointer, Lucas identified Tracts A, B, and C on the plan.

Throughout the room, a soft humming began as Lucas spoke. The volume slowly increased to the point where the television audio picked up the sixties folk tune, *Where Have All the Flowers Gone*. The melody grew louder and louder, eventually drowning out Lucas' presentation.

The Mayor banged his gavel repeatedly as the other council members looked on astonished.

It seemed everyone was humming. Even the garden club members were smiling, some giggling, as Mayor Harris smacked his gavel over and over and yelled into the microphone for order.

In frustration, the Mayor threatened to empty the chamber. Then he called a brief recess to consult with the City Attorney. He jumped to his feet and dragged the city attorney over to the front corner of the room. Roberts remained seated, trying to look expressionless.

Councilman Ben Kemble pointed at Nelson and motioned for him to come around behind the council table. Kemble started chewing Nelson out. His words were inaudible but his actions spoke clearly.

Ronnie Evans sat straight up in the bed, staring intently at the television. Zepeda and Decker watched him, on the alert.

"Son-of-a-bitch, son of a fucking bitch!" Evans' voice began as a whisper, then grew louder.

"Who is it?" Zepeda asked, leaning near to Evans. "Who do you mean?"

"That's him! That's the bastard who did it," Evans yelled. He pointed at the screen. "He's the one who wrecked my truck and got me into this fucking mess."

"Do you mean this man?" Decker asked, indicating Tommy Nelson.

"No, the other guy, that big bastard. He's the asshole who made me hit that car. I'll never forget him sticking that fucking gun in my face."

"Do you mean Councilman Kemble?" Zepeda asked. "Was he in the truck with you? Did he grab the steering wheel causing your truck to hit the car?"

"I'd know that bastard anywhere. He's the one that was arguing with Ted that night. I shouldn't have left him there with that crazy son-of-a-bitch."

Zepeda reached over and turned on the video camera. It started recording.

"For the record," Zepeda said, "state your name and that you know you are being video recorded without an attorney here representing you."

"Sure, what the hell," Evans said, "if I'm going to prison, so is that bastard. My name is Ronald Evans and I know you're recording me."

Zepeda pointed at the television again.

"Was Ben Kemble, this man on television, the man who caused your truck to collide with a car on Old Bridge Road? Did he take the camera and bag from the wrecked car and force you at gun point to leave the scene of the accident?"

Evans looked at Zepeda, then Decker, then the television.

"Yes, sir, that's the guy," Evans said. "You've got to arrest him. He must have killed Ted Smith at that farmhouse."

Zepeda turned to Decker.

"We better get over there," Decker said.

Zepeda grabbed the camera and tripod. As they turned to leave the room, Zepeda saw the rage in Decker's face. In the hospital hallway he stopped Decker.

"Kyle, let's just do our jobs and be careful."

# CHAPTER THIRTY-NINE

The City Attorney was trying to calm down Mayor Harris. They were still standing behind the council table and the audience was humming even louder than before.

"You can't clear the room," the City Attorney explained. "It's a public hearing. The public has to be allowed to attend."

"What about the noise?" Harris said. "These people can't just sing during a council meeting. We can't hear the testimony."

The City Attorney was getting nervous. He hated being in the spotlight. He always took the line of least resistance, particularly if he could pass the problem on to someone else.

"Maybe Nick Lucas would agree to reserve his remaining time for the rebuttal. Then we can go ahead and let the opposition get it out of their system."

Harris stormed back to his seat and summoned Lucas to come forward to the council table. The Mayor held his hand over the microphone to prevent anyone but Lucas from hearing him. Lucas leaned over the table toward the Mayor. After brief whispering, Lucas nodded several times and quickly returned to his seat.

The Mayor called the meeting back to order and opened the opposition portion of the hearing. The man seated next to Susan, the one in the maroon sport coat and khakis, calmly walked to the podium. He was a tall, thin, middle-aged man with bifocals and a pleasant manner.

He introduced himself as Dr. Frank Terry, from Texas A&M University, and explained that he was an expert in native plant horticulture with impressive credentials. Dr. Terry handed the council members several color photos of various types of native sage blooms, ending with the new variety called Aggie Sage. Then Dr. Terry announced that, in his expert opinion, the new variety would qualify as an endangered species of native wildflower.

When Dr. Terry finished his testimony, Councilman Kemble leaned over toward his microphone and did a fair impression of Bill O'Reilly being condescending.

"Dr. Terry," Kemble said, "it's all well and good if you want to have pretty little flowers around but I don't see how it could be relevant to this rezoning hearing on Tract B."

"Well, Councilman Kemble," Dr. Terry replied respectfully, "so far, the Aggie Sage has been found only on Tracts A, B, and C in this location."

"You obviously haven't done your homework, professor," Kemble said, pointing a pencil at the map on the screen, "There aren't any little flowers on Tract B. It has been cleared off. Tract B is the only property we're discussing tonight."

The audience reaction was spontaneous and immediate. Humming began anew, louder and more forcefully, filling the room in seconds. Kemble thumped his finger on the microphone. Dr. Terry shook his head and returned to his seat.

Mayor Harris threw his hands up in disgust and turned to Kemble.

"Did you really have to say that? We have enough trouble without you egging them on."

Harris banged away with his gavel until the humming subsided.

"Ladies and gentlemen," the Mayor said, "please refrain from humming so we can get through this hearing. We have a long agenda to cover this evening and it's not getting any shorter. Is there anyone else to speak for the opposition?"

A petite woman in a blue business suit approached the podium. She placed her notes on the podium, adjusted the microphone for her height, and smiled at the council members and Mayor.

"Mayor Harris, members of the Asher City Council, Asher citizens, my name is Joan Carter and I represent an organization called Texas Against Toxic Waste. We are an Austin-based nonprofit organization formed to protect Texans from the improper disposal of hazardous materials. I'm here tonight to expose a criminal conspiracy being perpetrated by highly placed Asher officials to bring large quantities of dangerous medical waste into Asher."

The Mayor looked confused, as usual. Other council members, especially Kemble, grew more attentive to the woman's presentation. Nelson glanced quickly in

Lucas's direction before studying his own fingernails as though they'd suddenly grown longer.

Lucas' expression changed from concern to consternation. This was a turn of events he hadn't anticipated. Someone was going to have to answer her charge and it was his responsibility to present the public rebuttal. He looked toward Kemble and discovered that Kemble was looking directly at him. Lucas silently mouthed, *stop her now.*

Kemble sat forward in his chair, preparing to destroy Ms. Carter's testimony at the first opportunity. His sudden aggressive move often intimidated presenters but not Joan Carter.

She reached into the pocket of her coat and held a red tag up in the air.

"I am holding a numbered tag which was used to identify a transport trailer full of contaminated medical waste. It was trucked into Asher from Houston during the predawn hours of Saturday morning."

Unable to hold back, Kemble interrupted the speaker.

"Mayor Harris, I don't know where Ms. Carter is going with this but we're hearing a zoning case. This testimony has nothing to do with Tract B."

The Mayor nodded in agreement with Kemble.

"Ms. Carter, could you get to the point, please?" Harris asked. "Like I said, we have a long agenda ahead of us tonight."

"Certainly, Mayor Harris," she said. "The point is that this truckload of biohazardous materials was gathered from numerous medical offices, nursing homes, and clinics in Harris County. One of our members attached this red tag to a 48-foot trailer at a warehouse in

Houston owned by Mr. Nick Lucas. This same tag was found on Saturday by another one of our members affixed to that same trailer parked at a warehouse right next to Tract B. That warehouse was owned by the late Ted Smith, the applicant in this rezoning case, and a group of Houston investors including Mr. Nick Lucas."

Several members of the City Council looked at Lucas. There was murmuring and talking in the audience.

Kemble motioned to the Mayor to do something. The Mayor was totally perplexed.

Kemble's face grew darker as he looked from the speechless Mayor, to Lucas, and finally to Ms. Carter. Kemble leaned forward, his face nearly touching the microphone.

"Mr. Mayor, this woman is obviously trying to incite more trouble here tonight. If these people aren't going to testify specifically about rezoning Tract B, I move we close the hearing and get on with the vote."

Joan Carter responded just as assertively.

"Councilman Kemble," she said, "if you will stop interrupting my testimony, I'll explain how this is very relevant to the rezoning of Tract B."

She paused, allowing the silence in the chambers to intensify.

"Now, it seems," Ms. Carter continued, "Mr. Lucas and the other investors behind Ted Smith's development want to build another warehouse. Asher citizens should ask why. What will be stored in the new warehouse? Contaminated medical waste?"

She scanned the City Council to make sure they were all listening to her. She noticed that Kemble was looking at Lucas. When she turned to look at Lucas, he was staring hatefully at her. She turned back to address the council.

"Mayor Harris, members of the council," she said, "the medical waste from Houston was not in the trailer or the warehouse when the Asher Police searched them yesterday morning. It had been removed. A team of our members quietly did a grid search of the entire airport industrial district yesterday afternoon and found two old bunkers on the airport property where there were fresh tire tracks and a lot of recent digging. Forty-one barrels containing surgical waste, used needles, and deteriorating human tissue, were found buried in the old bunkers less than an hour ago. EPA and State investigators are, at this moment, securing the area."

The citizens in the council chamber, young and old, were appalled. The garden club members were voicing their disgust openly. One woman in the front row, bent with osteoporosis and hard of hearing said loudly, "Well, my word, who would do such a thing? Shameful."

Lucas was squirming in his seat and tugging on his silk tie. He glared at Nelson, who would not return his look. Nelson was now concentrating on his own belt buckle.

Kemble knew he needed to do something quickly. He tried to get Nelson's attention but Nelson's eyes were now darting around the room like a trapped animal looking for a way out.

Chris smiled. He knew it was all over for Nelson and Lucas. Although this latest turn in the Tract B saga was far more serious than Chris had anticipated, someone would now have to answer for clearing Tract B.

"Given their blatant disregard for the law so far," Ms. Carter continued, "we can only expect the worst from Mr. Lucas and his associates. I implore you to deny this industrial rezoning pending a federal criminal investigation."

The City Manager was at the staff table asking Nelson questions. Nelson looked terrified. Lucas shook his head, warning Nelson not to say anything.

At that point, Zepeda and Decker came into the council chamber with two uniformed officers. As they pushed through the protesters in the back of the room most people assumed that they had been called to calm the meeting. Lucas feared, as always, that the police were there for him; but the officers seemed to be focusing on someone else.

Decker motioned to Luedecke to get Chris out of the room. The detectives continued to move toward the front of the council chambers. When Kemble realized that Zepeda and Decker were looking straight at him instead of Lucas, he panicked.

Kemble jumped to his feet, knocking over his big chair and the Texas flag behind him. For a large man, Kemble was quick. The detectives were startled but they had Kemble trapped in the front of the room. There was no way he could get past them.

As Kemble lunged behind the Mayor. He threw his arm around Harris' neck and pointed a small pistol under the Mayor's right ear. Zepeda and Decker both drew their weapons and aimed them at Kemble.

Luedecke pushed Chris and Susan down behind a row of seats.

City officials scattered. Joan Carter ducked behind the podium. The room was in chaos as people hid behind chairs or searched for escape routes. Lori Latimer dropped her microphone and started for the exit.

Zepeda and Decker moved around in front of the podium, closing the distance. Zepeda motioned for Joan Carter to leave while she had their protection. She scurried to the far aisle.

Ed, the Channel Five videographer, quickly reestablished a live feed and hurried over by the podium behind the detectives. Channel Five viewers were getting another live special that might quickly become a gunfight in a crowded room.

Zepeda yelled out, "Kemble, don't do anything stupid. Put the gun down. Let Harris go, now!"

Kemble yelled back, "I'll kill him!"

His arm clamped around the Mayor's chest, Kemble started inching along behind the curved council table using Harris as a shield. The other council members were cowering in the far corner. The City Attorney and City Manager hid behind the staff table. Nelson started sneaking down the side aisle toward the exit.

Zepeda and Decker inched closer to the Council table.

"Everybody freeze or I'll kill the Mayor," Kemble shouted. "I swear, I'll shoot him right now and empty this gun into the crowd."

Kemble was dragging the Mayor moving slowly toward the press table occupied by Charlie Hawkins. Hawkins sat calmly making notes in his pad as though nothing was happening.

Seeing the police fixed on Kemble, Lucas grabbed Nelson's arm and pulled him down the side aisle. Soon they were in the crush of frightened people shoving toward the exit.

Chris saw Lucas and Nelson going down the side aisle. He told his mother to stay where she was and climbed out from behind the seats. Luedecke followed Chris, struggling to keep up with him. Chris headed toward the same exit as Lucas and Nelson, reaching the door into the foyer just as they moved through it with the river of panicked citizens. Luedecke pushed his way through the door right behind Chris.

As the mass of humanity thinned in the foyer, Chris reached over Lori Latimer's shoulder and grabbed Nelson's collar. Lori screamed when Nelson jerked to a halt.

Lucas was still pulling Nelson forward but Nelson stopped. Lucas turned toward Nelson and grabbed his shirtfront.

"Keep your mouth shut," Lucas hissed in Nelson's face, "or you're a fucking dead man."

Between Lucas twisting his shirt and Chris clutching his collar, Nelson could do nothing. He gasped and gagged, turning pale. As Chris tugged Nelson backward, Lucas let go of his shirtfront and rushed toward the City Hall door.

Nelson spun around and made one of the worst mistakes of his life. He took a swing at Chris but punched Tom Luedecke right in the face.

Luedecke's first blow was to Nelson' torso, knocking the air out of his lungs. Nelson's breathing, like his other internal functions, momentarily failed to sustain him. He folded over in agony. Luedecke lifted Nelson up from his doubled-over position. When Nelson flailed weakly at him again, Luedecke's right hook caught him square in the mouth, breaking Nelson's jaw.

Chris hurried to the door and saw Lucas heading for the parking lot. He shouted to a police officer, the same one who had been guarding the door earlier in the day, to stop Lucas.

Lucas jumped in his Mercedes and backed out of the parking space. The arriving backup units had inadvertently blocked the parking lot exit so Lucas tried to drive over the curb. Both front wheels sunk in a muddy flowerbed. When the officer approached the car, Lucas reached for a gun he kept in his glove box. Before he could retrieve the handgun, the alert officer dragged Lucas out of the car, threw him face down in the parking lot, and cuffed him.

The young officer single-handedly apprehended one of the most powerful organized crime figures in the southern United States, without a shot being fired.

Inside the council chamber, the standoff continued.

"Hold it!" Kemble bellowed. "Stay where you are. I swear to God, somebody's going to die. Don't move!"

Everyone in the council room, even those crowding toward the exits, froze like statues. The force of Kemble's voice stunned them all.

As Kemble moved past the press table, Hawkins silently stood up and stepped in behind him. Hawkins raised his left hand to Kemble's left ear. Surprised, Kemble stopped moving. With fluid grace, Hawkins slid his cheap ballpoint directly into Kemble's right ear.

Kemble screamed in pain.

"Put down the gun or I'll shove this filthy pen through your demented brain," Hawkins said calmly. "Don't even breathe or you'll be a vegetable."

"I'll shoot," Kemble said. "I'll kill Harris."

"Go ahead, do the community a service," Hawkins said.

Hawkins slowly lifted Kemble by his ears. Kemble stretched up onto his tiptoes as Hawkins raised the pen. A stream of blood trickled down Kemble's neck and stained his white shirt collar. Kemble's hands began to tremble. He moaned.

Kemble's gun hand dropped to his side. He released his hold on the Mayor. Zepeda moved in fast, grabbing the weapon from Kemble's shaking hand. Decker pointed his Glock directly at Kemble's face, inches from his nose.

Mayor Harris whimpered, crawling away on his hands and knees.

Hawkins still held Kemble, suspended between life and brain damage. Kemble was balanced in agony on his tiptoes. Sweat beaded on his face and dripped from his nose and chin. He was trying not to move but he shivered involuntarily.

Hawkins stood silently behind Kemble holding the deadly ballpoint like a surgeon's knife. Zepeda observed a peculiar glow in Hawkins' eyes. The pen twisted.

"Don't do it, Charlie," Zepeda said quietly. "We've got him now. Let him down. Easy, now, Easy."

Zepeda motioned with both hands for Hawkins to lower Kemble.

Ed's camera captured Kemble's terror and his bleeding ear. He also captured the extraordinary look on Hawkins' face as he slowly lowered Kemble.

A moment passed. Zepeda reached for Hawkins' hand. Hawkins slowly pulled the bloody ballpoint from Kemble's ear.

Decker and Zepeda took Kemble to the floor. Decker jumped on top of Kemble with his knee in Kemble's back while Zepeda cuffed him. Zepeda read Kemble his rights.

Ed continued filming his prize winning news video as Hawkins wiped the ballpoint pen on his handkerchief and returned it to his baggy coat pocket. Lori Latimer started blurting out incomprehensible questions but Hawkins held up his hand to silence her.

Hawkins looked directly into the camera lens.

"You see, the pen is mightier than the sword," Hawkins said. He paused as a faint smile softened his features. "I've always wanted to say that."

Out in the foyer, Tommy Nelson was propped up against a wall. A trail of blood dribbled from his mouth. Luedecke knocked Nelson to the floor and snapped the cuffs on his wrists.

Within minutes, Kemble and Nelson were treated by emergency medical technicians and handcuffed to their stretchers. They were then transported to the Asher hospital in separate ambulances with police escorts. Lucas rode to jail in the back seat of a police cruiser driven by the young officer who had arrested him.

# CHAPTER FORTY

City Hall was in turmoil following Kemble's arrest for murder and news of the charges pend-ing against Tommy Nelson. City productivity almost ceased entire-ly for days. There was more gossiping than working go-ing on. The Transportation and Planning Department was closed for a week while internal auditors and the police investigated Nelson.

Carol Bailey and the City Manger were tasked with sorting out the appropriate actions to take regarding City liability. Todd Watson's parents had the potential for a multi-million dollar wrongful death jury award. Even though his death was the result of a criminal act, he was killed by an elected City official while perform-ing his duty as a City employee. An out-of-court settle-ment was negotiated exceeding two million dollars.

The City's liability for Chris Jensson was also sig-nificant. Chris had been injured in a collision caused intentionally by an elected City official. His immediate supervisor had threaten-ed to have him killed if he blew the whistle on the zoning irregularities. Chris had also experienced sexual harassment so severe that he was required to defend himself physically. Juries had awarded plaintiffs millions of dollars for lesser grievances.

On the other hand, Chris Jensson had violated City policy when he arranged a protest at a public hearing and granted a media interview without notifying the public information office.

After lengthy negotiations between Chris' new attorney, the City Attorney, City Manager Roberts, Carol Bailey, and the City's insurers, the City of Asher was ready with a settlement offer. Chris was prepared to accept the settlement and move ahead with his life.

Chris was sitting in the conference room with Carol and Roberts. Decker and Susan were waiting outside.

"Well, Chris," Roberts said, "we have several issues to resolve this morning. I'd like to come out of this meeting with a mutually beneficial arrangement. I believe we can protect the City's interests and provide a suitable settlement for you as well."

"That sounds reasonable to me, Mr. Roberts," Chris replied. "I've been discussing the situation with Carol, and I think we have an agreement."

Roberts sipped his coffee and studied the papers in front of him.

"Fine, well then," he said. "Chris, do you agree that you violated City policy when you arranged that demonstration and allowed the interview with Lori Latimer?"

"Yes, sir. I acted unethically."

"And you are willing to accept an immediate two-week suspension coinciding with two weeks of paid vacation leave."

"That's correct, Mr. Roberts. I've already signed a memorandum to that effect. The memo also states that no other City employees were involved in arranging the protest."

"All right then," Robertson said, turning the page, "I guess we should review the settlement agreement now. Carol, would you read the list of conditions stipulated by Mr. Jensson and agreed to by the City Attorney and City Council?"

"There are several conditions under which Mr. Jensson agrees to release the City and its insurer from future liability resulting from the assault on his life by former Councilman Kemble and the threats and sexual harassment by former Director Nelson. Chris agrees that, once these conditions are met, the City will be held harmless regarding their willful criminal acts. Chris still reserves the right to sue each of them individually."

Carol read through several paragraphs of legal jargon saying the insurers and the City Council wanted the matter resolved immediately. Then she reached the actual conditions of the settlement.

Roberts stood up and refilled his coffee mug while Carol continued to read whereas and hereinafter clauses in the agreement. Chris glanced up at him standing by the conference room drapes. The month since Kemble terrorized the council chambers had been tough on Roberts. His youthful face was tense. His hair had been combed by running his fingers through it frequently. The discovery of two old concrete bunkers filled with contaminated medical waste at the old airbase had created a public relations nightmare for him. He returned to his chair and listened to Carol reading the contract as he sipped his steaming coffee.

"The first condition is that the City will purchase Tracts A, B, and C. If the Houston investment group refuses to sell, the City will use eminent domain to acquire the property for parkland. The property will then become the Todd Watson Memorial Wildflower Center.

Secondly, the city's insurance carrier will pay Chris a cash settlement of $500,000 and will honor any claims resulting from future health problems caused by Chris' injuries in the car wreck.

Third, after his administrative leave, Chris Jensson will return to work with the title Director of Planning. He will be responsible for hiring two new city planners and a secretary.

The final condition is complicated because it involves a third party. The agreement stipulates that undercover Detective Kyle Decker will be allowed to claim unused vacation time from previous years and will immediately take two weeks off coinciding with Chris Jensson's administrative leave."

"Have you had an opportunity to discuss this stipulation with Chief Dixon yet, Mr. Roberts?" Chris asked.

"We talked by phone just before this meeting."

"So, are both of you ready to sign the settlement?" Carol asked cautiously.

"I'm ready to sign it," Chris said.

"Let's do this while I still have time to make it to the noon Rotary club," Roberts said.

The City Manager and the new Director of Planning each signed two long pages. Carol signed as witness. They all stood and Roberts shook hands with Chris before hurrying out of the conference room.

Carol waited until the door quietly closed before she hugged Chris. Decker and Susan hurried in from the hallway. He kissed Chris and held him warmly until Susan started hugging them both. Then Decker hugged Carol while Susan hugged her son. Soon, they were all laughing.

Decker handed Chris a note.

"The florist called while you were inside. She has a problem getting something you ordered for the party tonight."

"I'll call her this afternoon. Mom and I are going to have lunch with the caterer."

"I guess I'll just have to eat with Kenny today," Decker laughed. "It's my turn to buy the barbecue."

They all moved out into the hallway outside the conference room.

"Oh, by the way," Decker said, "the travel agent confirmed our hotel in Paris and sent me our rail passes."

"I can't believe we're going to Paris and Amsterdam," Chris said. "I've always wanted to see Europe."

"Me too," Susan said. "I think you should take me along."

"Not this time, Mom. We'll send pictures," Chris said.

"Well, some of us have to get back to work now," Carol said. "Did you do it yet, Chris?"

"Do what? I just got the job half an hour ago." Chris said. "Am I already behind on something?"

"I want to know if you canned Barbara yet." Carol said.

"Not yet, I knew you'd want to be there."

"Maybe we should call Charlie Hawkins," Decker said, "in case things get ugly and you need someone to quiet her down."

# CHAPTER FORTY-ONE

Federal arrest warrants flew through the state in the weeks following the incident at City Hall. Indictments came down quickly for Nick Lucas for racketeering and transporting illegal wastes. Hundreds of barrels of contaminated medical waste were discovered in five towns where Lucas owned property, including Mexia.

The DeLeon County jail held former City Councilman Ben Kemble, who was facing murder trials in the deaths of Todd Watson and Ted Smith, attempted murder charges for injuring Chris Jensson, and a long list of charges from the hostage taking in City Hall. Since the gun he used in the Council chamber matched the slug taken from Smith's body, the DeLeon County prosecutor was seeking the death penalty. Kemble was also indicted on racketeering, conspiracy, and environmental charges.

Ronald Evans agreed to testify against Kemble and Lucas in exchange for a reduced federal charge of transporting illegal materials. State charges were pending from the high-speed chase involving multiple counts of attempted murder and vehicular assaults on police officers. Evans faced decades in prison.

Tommy Nelson spent time in the hospital having his jaw reconstructed after the altercation with Luedecke. Several citizens testified that Tommy Nelson had punched Officer Luedecke before the policeman struck Nelson. Nelson was quickly convicted in municipal court of assault on a police officer. He was also facing trial for bribery and criminal conspiracy.

Following what locals referred to as "all the excitement," the community returned to a more normal existence. Talk around the tables at the Commerce Street Cafe centered again on football and fishing.

The new City Council member named to fill out Kemble's unexpired term was a former Planning Commissioner who vowed to pass a new landscaping ordinance complete with a clearing and grading permit. Mayor Harris made the appointment. Enjoying the press coverage, the Mayor was positioning himself to ride the wave of sympathetic publicity into a state legislature race.

Decker and Chris filed domestic partnership forms in DeLeon County, the closest thing to marriage for gay men in Texas. Susan was there to witness it. She returned to Seattle with a promise that Chris and Decker would come for a visit when the rains cleared for the summer.

After their vacation together in Europe, the couple settled into Decker's little bungalow and made it their home together. Sas was apprehensive at first but soon enjoyed his larger territory and the addition of another human to attend to his needs.

**James Gaston**

It was wetter and cooler than usual in Asher that fall. The first frost hit early in October. As sometimes happens, the changing foliage was stripped from trees in a gusty downpour. A layer of colorful leaves carpeted Tract B, providing a nutrient-rich shelter for shoots of winter grasses and tiny oak trees sprouting from the underground remnants of the native flora. Unseen and unnoticed, roots of Aggie Sage pushed outward through the damp soil to provide an anchorage for spring growth.

# ABOUT THE AUTHOR

***Bad Planning*** is James Gaston's first venture into the mystery genre. As a young man, Jim was a city planner for eleven years in Texas and Washington State before doing his graduate work. He has taught management and public administration courses at the university level for twenty years.

Jim has written dozens of articles for association publications over the span of three careers. He also coauthored a personnel development book for the fire service. *Fire Officer Coaching*, 2nd Edition, is available from Amazon.

Jim lives with his partner, David Elias, in Austin, Texas. He is currently working on two more novels in the Asher Mystery series and is writing an historical fiction.

Made in the USA
Charleston, SC
12 May 2014